Lo

Somerset Maugham

Short Stories

Longman Study Texts **General editor: Richard Adams**

Titles in the series:

Jane Austen
Emma
Pride and Prejudice
Charlotte Brontë
Jane Eyre
Emily Brontë
Wuthering Heights
Charles Dickens
Great Expectations
Oliver Twist
George Eliot
Silas Marner
The Mill on the Floss
Thomas Hardy
The Mayor of Casterbridge
Aldous Huxley
Brave New World
D H Lawrence
Sons and Lovers
George Orwell
Animal Farm
Nineteen Eighty-Four
Paul Scott
Staying On
Virginia Woolf
To the Lighthouse
Oliver Goldsmith
She Stoops to Conquer
Nadine Gordimer
July's People
Ben Jonson
Volpone
Christopher Marlowe
Doctor Faustus
Somerset Maugham
Short Stories
Alan Paton
Cry, The Beloved Country
Terence Rattingan
The Winslow Boy
Willy Russell
Educating Rita
Peter Shaffer
Amadeus
Equus
The Royal Hunt of the Sun
William Shakespeare
Macbeth
The Merchant of Venice
Romeo and Juliet
Bernard Shaw
Androcles and the Lion
Arms and the Man
Caesar and Cleopatra
The Devil's Disciple
Major Barbara
Pygmalion
Saint Joan
Richard Brinsley Sheridan
The Rivals
The School for Scandal
John Webster
The White Devil
H G Wells
The History of Mr Polly
Oscar Wilde
The Importance of being Earnest

Editor: George MacBeth
Poetry for Today
Editor: Michael Marland
Short Stories for Today

Somerset Maugham

Short Stories

edited by
Roy Blatchford

Longman

LONGMAN GROUP LIMITED
Longman House
Burnt Mill, Harlow, Essex CM20 2JE, England

This edition first published by Longman Group Limited in association with William Heinemann Ltd 1986.

ISBN 0 582 33187 0

Set in 10/12pt Baskerville, Linotron 202

Produced by Longman Group (F.E.) Limited
Printed in Hong Kong

For my father

Contents

Introduction

Somerset Maugham: 1874–1965

Duality

There was about William Somerset Maugham's life an extraordinary and telling duality. An Englishman raised in France with French as his first language, he was never able to identify completely with England; he was passionately fond of his mother, but his own actions and writings testify to his low opinion of women; he married and had a child, and was primarily homosexual; he kept his own life private but relentlessly pursued the personal lives of others in search of literary material; he was disdainful of critics but deeply affected by their comments; and, perhaps most intriguing in relation to his short story writing, he had a low opinion of the human species but a great understanding of and sympathy with human frailty.

Writing of Maugham in the definitive biography of the author, Ted Morgan observes poignantly:

> He made a pact with himself to live out his allotted span as fully and productively as he could. If he was a great man, it was because of this: believing life had no meaning, he determined to make it matter. He always wanted to take things, including his own life, 'to the end of the chapter'.

Maugham was born on 25 January 1874 (four years after the death of Charles Dickens) in the British Embassy in Paris; thus born on British soil even though in a foreign country. His father Robert, reputedly a very ugly man, was solicitor to the Embassy and seventeen years older than his beautiful wife Edith. For much of his early childhood Maugham was on his own with his mother, his older brothers having been sent to school in England by the time he was four. Tragically, Edith suffered from the then virtually incurable disease tuberculosis, and early in 1882 she died. Maugham himself died when he was ninety-one (in the midst of the 'swinging sixties' and the Vietnam War), but even towards the end of a long life he was to say that he had never recovered from his mother's death. Undoubtedly her death was intensified by that of his father only two years later, in 1884.

Money

Maugham then, at the age of ten, able to speak little English, was torn from his protected, sheltered environment and entrusted to his uncle, the Reverend Henry MacDonald Maugham and his German-born wife Barbara, a childless couple. The years that he spent with them in Whitstable, Kent, were to be the most miserable of his life. He had not only lost the love and affection of his parents but also the easy living he enjoyed in Paris. His uncle and aunt had to live carefully within their means. Maugham's father had left each of his sons one hundred and fifty pounds a year income: a not inconsiderable sum in those days but relatively small in the young Maugham's eyes, and for the whole of his life he was to make the acquisition of money and the achieving of financial security a major preoccupation.

> I have never had the bohemian trait of being unconcerned for the morrow. I have never liked to borrow money. I have hated to be in debt. Nor has the squalid life had any attraction for me . . . I was glad to earn a great deal of money as a dramatist. It gave me liberty. I was careful with it because I did not want ever again to be in a position when for want of it I could not do anything I had really a mind to.
>
> (Maugham writing in *The Summing Up*)

Maugham was sent to one of the country's leading public schools – King's Canterbury – where he was to encounter the merciless response of schoolboys to the physical disability of one of their number. Maugham suffered from a stammer which plagued him all his life; he was fair game for his companions and, sadly, some of the masters too. He tells the story of waiting in a long queue for a ticket at a railway station; when his turn came he was unable to say 'Whitstable' and was impatiently pushed away to rejoin the back of the queue. He never forgot the humiliation, and always looked upon his stammer as a symbol of his separateness from other people.

From an early age Maugham wished, above all else, to become a writer but on leaving school was urged by his uncle to enter the Church. The decision was delayed for a few years by his going to live in Heidelberg in Germany where he attended lectures at the University. On returning to England it was decided that he should become a doctor. In 1892, at the age of eighteen, Maugham registered at medical school; the medical profession did not interest him but gave him the opportunity to live in London and gain the experience of life that he hankered after and the freedom for which he yearned.

The Summing Up

At this time Maugham began to keep a notebook and although he passed his medical examinations regularly, all spare time was devoted to his own reading and writing. His notebooks were filled with ideas for stories and plays, scraps of dialogue and descriptions of his work as a trainee doctor in the slums of Lambeth and

> foul courts that the police hesitated to enter, but in which my black bag amply protected me . . . . Even now that forty years have passed I can remember certain people so exactly that I could draw a picture of them. Phrases that I heard then still linger in my ears. I saw how men died. I saw how

> they bore pain. I saw what hope looked like, fear, and relief; I saw the dark lines that despair drew on a face; I saw courage and steadfastness.
>
> (*The Summing Up*)

Maugham makes a further telling point in *The Summing Up* about these formative and memorable experiences, a point which must serve as a constant reminder to any writer: 'But of course human nature may be displayed before you and if you have not the eyes to see you will learn nothing.' Perhaps he was paraphrasing the great Greek philosopher Heraclitus: 'Eyes and ears are bad witnesses to men if they have souls that understand not their language.'

It is worth drawing the attention of students of Maugham to *The Summing Up*, a volume he wrote at the age of sixty-four which offers a fascinating record of the various stages in his apprenticeship as a writer, though he was at pains to highlight that the book was not an autobiography nor a compendium of recollections.

One further extract from *The Summing Up* gives a valuable insight into Maugham the writer and focuses his disdainful view of the world and those who people it:

> But when we come to judge others it is not by ourselves as we really are that we judge them, but by an image that we have found of ourselves from which we have left out everything that offends our vanity or would discredit us in the eyes of the world. To take a trivial instance: how scornful we are when we catch someone out telling a lie; but who can say that he has never told not one, but a hundred? We are shocked when we discover that great men were weak and petty, dishonest or selfish, sexually vicious, vain or intemperate; and many people think it disgraceful to disclose to the public its heroes' failings. There is not much to choose between men. They are all a hotchpotch of greatness and littleness, of virtue and vice, of nobility and baseness.

The writer

Maugham possessed an acute power of observation and in his wide travels through Europe and the Far East he accepted every experience that came his way. He put his ideas and impressions on paper and wrote and rewrote, building up his picture into a plausible harmony stemming from his own understanding of life and knowledge of human nature.

> You cannot write well or much (and I venture the opinion that you cannot write well unless you write much) unless you form a habit; but habits in writing as in life are only useful if they are broken as soon as they cease to be advantageous.
>
> (*The Summing Up*)

Maugham admitted that although at the outset of his career he had read a great deal and without discrimination he knew nothing about writing: thus his stress on the importance of daily writing practice and the development of the ability to write engaging English through unremitting application.

Maugham's first novel, published in 1897, was *Liza of Lambeth* in which he described without addition or exaggeration the people he had met in his hospital work both as an obstetrics clerk in the out-patients' department of a London hospital and in his house to house calls. A few weeks after the publication he qualified as a doctor and was offered an assistantship by one of the consultants at St Thomas's Hospital in South London. He refused, wishing to devote himself to literature, although he was later to say that it was a decision he regretted.

No doubt he began to regret it in the first decade of the new century for although Maugham, always industrious, had written seven novels and a volume of short stories after the success of *Liza of Lambeth*, they had been coolly received and it was not until 1907 that *Lady Frederick* (based on a short story titled 'Lady Habart') became his first play to be acclaimed on the London stage. Indeed such was its success that by the following year Maugham had four of his plays running in the West End, it has to be said much to the wonderment and chagrin of more than one theatre critic.

Maugham was never to be poor again. He could now live the easy life for which he craved and indeed had striven; as he later observed in characteristic vein – 'Money was like a sixth sense without which you could not make the most of the other five.'

The traveller

Maugham began to travel the world at will: an occupation, almost vocation, he was to pursue for the rest of his life. Indeed, he is perhaps the most widely travelled writer in history. On one of these voyages to the Far East he met Bertram Alanson, an American stockbroker with whom he developed a firm friendship. Alanson invested the thousands of pounds that Maugham periodically entrusted to him so wisely that in time Maugham became a millionaire.

Maugham married Syrie Barnado – daughter of Dr Barnado, the founder of the orphanages called Barnado Homes – in Jersey City, USA, in 1917. She had been the wife of a wealthy American, Henry Wellcome, but was divorced in 1915 when Maugham was cited as correspondent, and they had had a daughter Liza some two years before the divorce. For Maugham their marriage provided a form of respectability in the eyes of society and enabled him, much against Syrie's will, to travel throughout the world with his secretary and lover Gerald Haxton. He developed a dislike for the society in which he had moved in London, but this was as nothing compared to his inner hatred of his wife whom he considered had duped him into marriage. Much of this was mirrored in his successful plays – *The Constant Wife* and *For Services Rendered* – which centred upon the seamy side of contemporary society, the collapsing class structure, and how to avoid the bondage of a respectable marriage.

In the late nineteen-twenties the French Riviera was a haven for English and American writers and artists; leaving Syrie behind him, Maugham moved to the luxurious Villa Mauresque, a fortress he occupied until his death. It may well be that Maugham would have liked to break away from the society in which he had been reared; nevertheless, he lived the next forty years with the conventional society of the wealthy and the sheltered. The titled and the renowned – which included Winston Churchill and Edward VIII after his abdication – as well as attractive young males were always welcome at the villa, but were never allowed to disrupt Maugham's unchanging routine. After breakfast at 8 a.m. and discussion on the day's menus with his cook, he worked in his study, writing in longhand, until 12.45 p.m. In the afternoon he liked to play golf and tennis.

Why Maugham never returned to England he never revealed. One reason may well have been that Gerald Haxton was deported as an undesirable alien in 1919 following suspicions about his homosexuality; Maugham, as his companion, had little alternative but to remain abroad. More positively, the South of France was an ideal 'stepping off' point for their travels – voyages and visits around the world which provided Maugham with so many of the characters and settings of the short stories.

Last years

The last years of Maugham's life were sad ones. He delighted in being rude to people, guests or not, and although he remained physically fit he gravitated into senile dementia and a sorry state of behaviour. He fell out with his family and wrote wickedly of Syrie, whom he had divorced in 1929.

Maugham's biographer sums up the writer's long and varied life with these well chosen words:

> Maugham was all of these: an alienated child, a medical student, an avant-garde novelist and playwright, a bohemian in Paris, a successful West End dramatist, a London social lion, an ambulance driver on the Flanders front, a spy in Russia, a promiscuous homosexual who paid for the favours of boys in remote lands, a cuckolded husband, a host to the famous persons of his time, a World War II propagandist, the most widely read novelist since Dickens, a living legend kept alive by cellular therapy, and a senile old man who tried to disinherit his daughter and adopt his secretary.
> (Ted Morgan)

And all of these shaped the storyteller.

The short story

The telling and recording of short stories have been with us from the earliest times. Those in the Old Testament are narratives that have come through from the ancient cultures of Greece, India and the Near East. 'The Prodigal Son', for example, is a short story of extraordinary conciseness and power; the opening six words introduce the three main characters – 'A certain man had two sons.'

From the early Middle Ages we have the tales of the Arabian Nights, told by Scheherazade through the nights to save her neck, Boccaccio's *Decameron* and Chaucer's *Canterbury Tales*. The compelling need to tell stories has continued through succeeding centuries, through the eighteenth-century essay with its brevity and wit, as well as through the traditional ballad, folk-lore and even contemporary popular music.

It is generally agreed however that as a special kind of literary work – a *genre* – the short story did not appear until the beginning of the nineteenth century. It revealed itself at that time particularly in America in the writings of Washington Irving, Nathaniel Hawthorne and Edgar Allan Poe, to be followed by a stream of other American and European writers, each one of whom advanced the frontiers of the genre.

In Europe Nicolai Gogol enjoys the reputation of being the 'father of the short story', an accolade he shares with Poe in America (by a strange quirk both Gogol and Poe were born in 1809). But two European writers stand out in the later decades of the century: Anton Chekhov and Guy de Maupassant, each very different in style from the other. It was in fact the novels and short stories of the French writer Maupassant that had the most influence on Maugham when he set himself to write. He had read most of Maupassant's work by the time he was twenty and admired him for his lucidity and directness, his ability to capture quintessentially the atmosphere of a relationship or event, and his unerring knack of getting the utmost dramatic value out of the story he had to tell.

But what exactly *is* a short story? Is it a story which is short? And how long is 'short'? Is it to be read at a sitting, and how long should that 'sitting' be? Does it tell a tale from a beginning through a middle to an end? Is the story a tale? Has it to have a captivating beginning or a surprise ending? Is it easier, because of its length, to write than a novel? Has a story to have an exotic setting or recognisable style? Are there specific subjects and situations which lend themselves to the telling of a story? Has every person, as it is often claimed, a story to tell? What makes a good story? Does everyone enjoy the same story – if not, what are we to make of what the critics say?

Some questions raised; you can no doubt think of others.

Short stories may in fact vary greatly in length from a few hundred words to several thousand. A popular form of story is one that tells a tale recounting a series of events with a definite beginning, middle and end. But others may have very little plot and may never move to a completed action; things may be left in the air, nothing seemingly changed, but something – no matter how imperceptibly – has caused us to see a situation slightly differently. *Then* the author will have made his or her mark.

Dubliners, a collection of short stories by the Irish writer James Joyce, was published at the beginning of the First World War and had a marked influence on later writers. The stories had very little action, did not move to a dramatic climax and did not have surprise endings, but they were acknowledged to be outstanding examples of the genre, rich in pathos, irony and comedy. They offered 'a little slice of life' and caught characters in – as Joyce described it – 'moments of epiphany'.

Maugham wrote that a short story 'is a piece of fiction dealing with a single incident that can be read at a sitting; it is original, it must sparkle, excite and impress. It should move in an even line from its exposition to its close'. Such a definition befits the Maupassant and Poe approach but not that of Chekhov or Joyce who rejected this linear development in favour of allowing their characters to reveal traits of the human condition and their inner consciousness. Edgar Allan Poe wrote of the short story: 'In the whole composition there should be no word written of which the tendency direct or indirect is not to the pre-established design', a view endorsed by Roald Dahl's words, that what characterises the short story is 'that there is no time for the sun shining through the pine trees'.

Maugham and the short story

It is possible then to see Maugham in the tradition of Poe and other American writers. Equally, he recognised Chekhov as a great master of the short story genre; Maugham saw his characters as 'shadowy',

> less as persons than as human beings. Each one is, as it were, a part of everyone else and the hurt that one does

another is bearable because in a way it is a hurt that he does to himself. And because they are shadowy they remain secret. We understand them as little as we understand ourselves. And so Chekhov gets the effect which is perhaps the most impressive that the writer of fiction can achieve: he fills you with an overpowering sense of the mystery of life.

It is interesting to compare the phrase 'as little as we understand ourselves' with Maugham's own words in *The Summing Up*: 'Long habit has made it more comfortable for me to speak through the creatures of my invention. I can decide what they would think more readily than I can decide what I think myself.' This suggests the child who reluctant to speak and lacking confidence will nevertheless, when given a puppet, play her part in developing the make-believe. Indeed, Maugham's much publicised difficulties in his personal life may well be reflected here.

Starting up as a writer Maugham acknowledged – at least in later years! – that 'my language was commonplace, my vocabulary limited, my grammar shaky, and my phrases hackneyed. I would struggle for a couple of hours over two or three sentences that I could in no way manage to straighten out'. But he had no ambition to be stylish. He wanted to write without any frills of language in as bare and unaffected a manner as he could. He wanted merely to set down the facts; he thus aimed at lucidity, simplicity and euphony.

Initially Maugham wrote short stories for magazines without startling success, and he maintained that his inability to write humorously did not endear him to the editors, though by the early 1920s he was being commissioned to write for the American magazine *Cosmopolitan* at 2,500 dollars a tale! In collected book form the stories proved a more instant success. Maugham moreover enjoyed short story writing – living with the characters of his fancy for two or three weeks and then able to leave them alone. He had no time to grow sick of them as an author could during the writing of a novel, and they gave him considerable scope to develop a theme concisely, as he had done in the writing of his plays.

In the twenties Maugham enjoyed a huge public readership but had little appeal to most of the professional critics of his day. This may have been influenced by his waspish tongue, and biting criticisms of many of his contemporaries, in whom he aroused great animosity. But he always regretted that although the masses liked him he was regarded as a second-class writer by many of those whose good opinion he would have valued.

The stories in this collection

The ten stories collected in this volume have been chosen first and foremost as fine examples of the short story genre and because they offer a representative selection from amongst the hundred or so tales that Maugham penned during his lifetime: a life, we might remind ourselves, that began just after the death of Charles Dickens and ended as humans were about to land on the moon.

The volume reveals Maugham's great craft as a writer; his gift for compression; his strong characterisation within tales of humour and tragedy; his skills as a 'portrait' painter, both in terms of people and of places; his shrewd eye for the quizzical; his sense of romance and morality. The stories should also go some way towards reflecting the author's personal interests and those issues which he felt were important for the writer to broach: personal quests for happiness and adventure; marital betrayal and infidelity; lost love; human vanity; family passions; the facts of life with all their accompanying comedy and tragedy. And, of course, the tales reveal Maugham *in* and *of* his period, with all his preoccupations and prejudices.

The stories are set in France (the Riviera he knew so well, Paris, and the wartime occupied zone), Samoa, Capri, French Guiana, Spain, England, and aboard ship where Maugham spent a not inconsiderable period of his life. Maugham was a relentless 'globe-trotter', making notes of characters, settings and incidents wherever he went. But this did not always endear him to those who had entrusted their stories to him. Malaya, for example – in which many of his tales are set – was almost 'Maugham Country', but it is doubtful whether he would have been well received there later by those who had welcomed him on his first visits in the 1920s. He depicted the worst elements of their colonial society – drink, adultery, murder, cowardice and seduction. In his stories he divulged much that had been told to him confidentially, and he drew heavily on facts, adding what was necessary to suit his ends; 'and many people think it disgraceful to disclose to the public its heroes' failings' – quoted earlier – has a certain ring as a disclaimer.

> I journeyed over a dozen seas, in liners, in tramps, in schooners; I went by train, by car, by chair, on foot, or on horseback. I kept my eyes open for character, oddness, and personality. I learnt very quickly when a place promised me something and then I waited till I had got it. I accepted every experience that came my way . . . Looking back on that long procession I cannot think of anyone who had not something to tell me that I was glad to know.

These words from *The Summing Up* remind us how seriously Maugham viewed his professionalism as a writer. He possessed a marvellously observant eye for places, able to inject a ring of authenticity into every setting he wrote about; his eye for appearances and material possessions was equally acute, and combined with a great gift for narrative, capturing the reader's attention at the beginning of a story and retaining it to the end.

Maugham wanted to write stories that proceeded tightly knit in an unbroken line from the exposition to the conclusion. He saw the short story 'as a narrative of a single event, material or spiritual, to which by the elimination of everything that was not essential to its elucidation a dramatic unity could be given'.

Finally, for Maugham, people *are* what they are – but the author loads the dice.

'The Facts of Life'

Maugham is ever concerned in his work with the themes of freedom, independence and bondage. One of his greatest novels, a deeply-felt work in which Maugham comes close to laying bare his soul, is *Of Human Bondage.* It is an autobiographical novel, the title deriving from an affair between Philip, an orphaned cripple, and Mildred, dishonest, mocking and unfaithful, who are involved in the degrading bondage of one human being to another.

'The Facts of Life' draws on a related subject – a young student's first taste of unsupervised freedom. Maugham was himself sent to the French Riviera when he was fifteen to recuperate from a lung infection, and when he was sixteen, to Heidelberg. He would recall that latter period vividly since that was the time when he probably experienced his first full homosexual relationship with a man who was later to feature as the character Wilson in 'The Lotus Eater'.

Maugham describes the central figure Nicky in some detail; it may be that this is necessary for developing the right kind of balance within the story, but certainly to be popular, athletic, tall with a graceful figure, attractive to women, good at games, admired by everyone was all that Maugham himself would like to have been. Perhaps too he remembered his 'Lotus Eater'? At the end of the day, maybe Maugham simply wrote in his characteristic style: 'I have taken living people and put them into the situation, tragic or comic, that their characters suggested. I might say that they invented their own stories.'

'The Facts of Life' is an admirable title with certain

nuances. Is it to be construed as the Father counselling the avoidance of involvement in the three areas – gambling, lending money and consorting with women – or is it the completed action of the story which gives it its title? And may one further wonder whether the father was as genuinely annoyed as he makes out, or does he feign annoyance to allow the tale to be told and thus indulge in extolling the excellence of his son? Would *you* say: the moral of the story is, 'It's better to be born lucky than to be born rich'?

'The Unconquered'

This was Maugham's only short story with a Second World War setting and first appeared in a collection called *Creatures of Circumstances* published in 1947. 'The Colonel's Lady' and 'The Mother' were also included in that publication.

The title plays on the fact that although France and many of its people had surrendered and indeed collaborated with the Germans, Annette had certainly not. She displays a true spirit of resistance. Indeed there is within the story a microcosm of that general picture of France at the mercy of Hitler's invading armies; the parents gradually come to terms with the invader but Annette stands fast. Similarly, there is the understanding that resistance incurred rape, destruction of heritage, home and cherished care, and her resistance meant too the destruction of part of herself.

Maugham tells the story here almost as a reflection of how it must have been for many French people living in the occupied zone. The disturbing climax is in harmony with the tale's backcloth, a harmony that Maugham also sought for his characters. Maugham possessed outstanding gifts of narrative, but joy and compassion are seldom to be found in his writings. There is certainly little in this story, and a reading of 'The Mother', 'The Colonel's Lady', 'Red' and others in this volume would tend to support this view.

'Mr Know-All'

'Mr Know-All' is one of the three stories from this collection in which Maugham is the first-person narrator (the other two are 'The Luncheon' and 'The Lotus Eater'). The story shows Maugham at his best in conforming to his own stated parameters about the short story form: it is concise and direct, an unbroken line to the completion of his pre-established design. The narrator is in the story but remains uninvolved, merely keeping the story moving, a technique much admired by other writers, and one which releases light onto the quirk of character within us all.

In *The Summing Up* Maugham writes: 'I have no natural trust in others. I am more inclined to expect them to do ill than to do good.' Such a sentiment certainly runs through this tale; perhaps the storyline might remind us of the Biblical phrase, 'O Lord, help me to tell the truth unless it is unkind', or indeed of the saying:

> There is so much good in the worst of us
> And so much bad in the best of us
> That it behoves none of us
> To talk about the rest of us.

Although Maugham was an inveterate traveller, as he reveals in *The Summing Up* he was not a naturally gregarious man:

> I have many disabilities. I was small; I had endurance but little physical strength; I stammered; I was shy; I had poor health . . . I had, whether for any of these reasons or from nature I do not know, an instinctive shrinking from my fellow men that has made it difficult for me to enter into any familiarity with them . . . I do not think I have ever addressed someone I did not know in a railway carriage or spoken to a fellow passenger on board ship unless he first spoke to me.

One can thus imagine Maugham's genuine fears expressed in the opening paragraphs of this story, anxiety which in real life was frequently dispelled by Maugham's travelling companion and lover Gerald Haxton, 'a companion who had an inestimable social gift . . . that enabled him in a very short time to make friends'.

And it is this undercurrent of Maugham's suspicion of a fellow human being which makes 'Mr Know-All' such compelling reading. Indeed, it is the very clever repeated use of 'I did not like Mr Kelada' – or slight variations on this wording throughout the tale – which gives the qualification of that statement in the final paragraph such an impact. It is also worth noting how much more telling the use of 'I' is in that statement – 'At that moment I did not entirely dislike Mr Kelada'; to have had an observer, a third-person narrator, make that remark would have significantly lessened the effect.

There is one further sentence in the story worth dwelling on for what it tells us of Somerset Maugham's own attitudes and prejudices. The narrator says of Mr Kelada: 'The Union Jack is an impressive piece of drapery, but when it is flourished by a gentleman from Alexandria or Beirut, I cannot but feel that it loses somewhat in dignity.' (page 57) Before the Second World War the British Empire still had great meaning, at least for the inhabitants of the British Isles; no doubt for Maugham, educated in a public school ('Waterloo was won on the playing fields of Eton'), the rest of the world was indeed inferior and occupied by second-class members of the human race. To have one of these 'foreign gentlemen' with a British passport, a man 'born under a bluer sky than is generally seen in England' (page 57), was altogether too much for Maugham's deep-set prejudices. So too was Mr Kelada's familiarity in the use of Maugham rather than *Mr* Maugham.

But people are not always what they seem and the 'vulgar' Levantine turns out to be a gentleman saving a lady's reputation at the expense of his own. It is perhaps worth noting here that many critics have roundly attacked Maugham for the misogyny evident in his work; certainly his lack of trust in women – intensified by his own personal life – surfaces in Mr Kelada' final remark:' '"If I had a pretty little wife I shouldn't let her spend a year in New York while I stayed at Kobe"' (page 62).

'Lord Mountdrago'

'Lord Mountdrago' was a story that Maugham had put off writing for several years since he thought that it was terribly difficult to make convincing. It was eventually published in 1940 in a collection of short stories titled *The Mixture as Before*. *The Times* newspaper had used this same expression in its review of Maugham's earlier collection, *Cosmopolitans* (1936); Maugham was keen to make some kind of riposte at his critics and thus adopted their rather disparaging phrase for his own uses.

The story is one of Maugham's rare departures from the everyday, naturalistic world he is usually most happy writing about, and in both style and content, its creation of tension and the bloody, dramatic ending, it is a tale reminiscent of Edgar Allan Poe. Yet there are other details worth dwelling on. Examine carefully this description of Dr Audlin's work:

> He had saved men from suicide, others from the lunatic asylum, he had assuaged griefs that embittered useful lives, he had turned unhappy marriages into happy ones, he had eradicated abnormal instincts and thus delivered not a few from a hateful bondage.
>
> (page 65)

Maugham had strong homosexual feelings and spent much of his life with homosexuals; yet in all his writings he did little or nothing which might have helped change the public's viewpoint on this subject. No doubt he, in common with other writers and artists, had the memory of Oscar Wilde's imprisonment for homosexuality to contend with, and, more vitally, he probably feared a fickle reading public. Certainly it is fair to say that the 'abnormal instincts' and 'hateful bondage' received no assistance towards liberation from Maugham.

Though an intensely private man, Maugham was not averse to echoing his own thoughts in the attitudes of his fictional characters. Look for a moment at these words about Dr Audlin:

> Nothing could shock him any longer. He knew by now that men were liars, he knew how extravagant was their vanity; he knew far worse than that about them; but he knew that it was not for him to judge or to condemn.
>
> (page 66)

Maugham is stating here exactly the principles which formed a corner-stone of his life and writings. He preferred to stand outside and aloof, letting the characters speak and act out life for themselves. You will recall – see page 10 – that he maintained that we judge others not by ourselves as we really are, but by an imagined image we have found of ourselves. Yet many of Maugham's critics have made this very detachment an object of scorn, describing much of his writing as being 'superficial' as a result. In the end, of course, it is the individual reader who must decide.

'The Colonel's Lady'

It was the American Brander Matthews who helped popularise the modern concept of the short story at the end of the nineteenth century. For him 'A true Short-story is something other and something more than a mere story which is short . . . A Short-story deals with a single character, a single event, a single situation emotion, or the series of emotions called forth by a single situation'. In many ways 'The Colonel's Lady' exemplifies such a definition and provides fine examples of much that is best in Somerset Maugham.

The dialogue is effortless, fluent and recognisable – look, for example, at the conversation which opens the story. But it is the writer's handling of character description which is the most notable feature. Study carefully pages 93 and 94. We begin with a rounded but potted account of George Peregrine's background from an observer's viewpoint; then there is a subtle change to Peregrine's description of his own inner feelings, a shift which admirably displays Maugham's skills as a story-teller. The paragraph beginning 'He had been putting on weight lately' is told from the third-person narrator standpoint; the following paragraph imperceptibly moves to Peregrine talking about himself, with phrases like 'you know', 'not a chip off the old block', 'his fool of a mother', and 'she hadn't any vitality, that's what was the matter with her' offering clues to the reader that the voice of the story has changed.

Happy marriages do not figure prominently in Maugham's writings; indeed they occur rarely. The frailty of marital fidelity is commonplace in his novels and plays; as Harry Blane advises George, the past is best forgotten, accept things as they are and Evie as she is. More unusual in Maugham's fiction is that in this tale it is the woman who has the upper hand, a fact which generates the splendid dramatic irony that underpins the whole plot, and which reaches a memorable climax in Peregrine's closing words.

'Red'

In writing the short story it is essentials that matter. As in a great drawing, so in a great short story: it is the lines that are left out that are of paramount importance. Not that this is all; it is knowing what lines to leave out that is of the

> greatest importance . . . The short story must depict more by implication than by statement, more by what is left out than left in. It ought, in fact, to resemble lace: strong but delicate, deviously woven yet full of light and air.
>
> (H. E. Bates)

'Red' is a story which displays an intricate balance between what is made explicit and what is left implicit for the reader; it repays repeated readings with the words of H. E. Bates held firmly in mind. Moreover, it is a piece which reveals Maugham's unerring eye and ear for a sense of place; his evocation of setting and creation of atmosphere are probably nowhere better seen in all his writings than in this Samoan tale. Pages 126–8 are certainly worth close study in this respect.

But 'Red' is also a further example of the writer's cynicism concerning the unlikelihood of a complete and loving relationship between two people over a protracted period. He paints a colourful and engaging picture of the good within Red and Sally, but almost arbitrarily sows a seed of doubt before Red's unexpected departure:

> Do we not know that the essential element of love is a belief in its own eternity? And yet perhaps in Red there was already a very little seed, unknown to himself and unsuspected by the girl which would in time have grown to weariness.
>
> (page 128)

It is almost as though Maugham cannot bring himself to admit of a human relationship which will not only endure but flourish.

The story finally leaves the reader in doubt as to whether Red is the original Red, or whether Neilson, the doctor of philosophy, has talked and thought himself into a disturbed state of mind:

'I am of sober habit,' smiled the Swede. 'I intoxicate myself in ways which I fancy are more subtle. But perhaps that is only vanity.'

(page 121)

The writer's achievement lies in the crafting of a tale within which one of the central character's doubts communicate themselves to the reader who, on successive readings, can vacillate between acceptance and rejection of the likelihood of Red being who he says he is. In common with many of his stories, the writer here seems intent on some kind of literary balancing act.

'The Lotus Eater'

This story raises some intriguing questions about character motive. After an initial read-through we might be tempted to ask the following questions:

Is Maugham telling the tale of a weak man and accepting him as a weak 'fallen' individual – he certainly hints at this in the suicide attempt?

Is the writer portraying the leading protagonist as having strength, particularly strength of purpose?

Does Maugham actually believe Wilson to be of strong character?

This last assumption would certainly accord with the author's own concern for living an unrestricted life, an existence free from bondage. Indeed, in many ways Wilson epitomises an image of liberty, freedom from ties, freedom from the imprisonment of body and spirit, that Maugham quested for all his life.

On the other hand, Wilson's near withdrawal from human relationships and the inability to see himself as others saw him may well have contributed to the immaturity in his character; it succeeded anyway in providing ammunition to those critics who claimed that Maugham, as a writer, singularly fails to get inside his characters and develop them to the full. Whatever the merits of that criticism, it must have been deeply depressing for Maugham to see Ellingham Brooks, his first lover, upon whom he based the character of Wilson, dying in poverty and humiliation.

The circumstances in which Wilson leaves his banking job in London are interesting to compare with Maugham's own feelings towards England, voiced in the *The Summing Up*:

> I am attached to England but I have never felt myself very much at home there. I have always been shy with English people. To me England has been a country where I had obligations that I did not want to fulfil and responsibilities that irked me. I have never felt entirely myself till I had put at least the Channel between my native country and me.

Perhaps Maugham, in creating 'The Lotus Eater', was attempting to come to terms with his own inability to find freedom and peace except through travel and exile.

Maugham wrote in one of his short stories – 'The Book Bag' – that human beings are incalculable and 'he is a fool who tells himself that he knows what a man is capable of'. It is a feature of many of the writer's stories that characters embark on courses of action which lead them to unpredictable ends and acts which they would not have guessed themselves capable of. Wilson's Faustus-like pact, Mr Know-All's change of heart, Annette's murdering of her child in 'The Unconquered', La Cachirra's vendettas in 'The Mother' – each is prompted into behaviour, seemingly out of character, but which the writer manages to make both convincing and compelling reading.

'An Official Position'

In 1935 Maugham, with his constant companion Gerald Haxton, visited the penal colony of St Laurent de Maroni in

French Guiana where the guillotine was still in use. The executioner, recruited from among the convicts, received a hundred francs per severed head. One of the previous executioners had been found knifed to death. These basic facts served as the trigger for a story in which Maugham's mastery of setting is once more in evidence. An atmosphere of high tension is established and sustained throughout the tale, even though we might guess from quite an early point that what happened to the previous executioner – 'They found a man hanging by the neck from one of the branches' (page 164) – will happen again.

In reading the story we might also be prompted into questioning what Maugham's own thoughts on imprisonment were. The experience of other homosexuals – imprisoned for their 'crime' – he had doubtless shared in conversation; are the writer's own horrors and fears then invested in Remire? Remire is clearly happy within the prison and in some senses is actually free within it. Some readers might suggest that he is released from his imprisonment by death itself; others may feel that Remire gets his just deserts for being on the side of the Establishment as their executioner. The echoing irony in Remire's remark: 'He only got what he deserved' when speaking of his predecessor will not be lost on any reader, and is worth comparing with one verdict on Wilson in 'The Lotus Eater' – 'After all, he's only got what he deserved.'

The idea of characters 'getting what they deserve' is recurrent in this collection: Lord Mountdrago, George Peregrine, Hans in 'The Unconquered', the prostitute in 'The Facts of Life'. But what is worth reflecting on is the extent to which we may feel that Maugham – in so shaping his tales – is consciously moralising and taking sides. It is probably fair to conclude that the author – in common with most writers – does not take sides once the story starts, but that he has already done so in creating the character in the first place.

'The Luncheon'

There is a deeply satisfying roundness and sense of completeness to several of Somerset Maugham's shorter short stories: 'The Verger', 'The Poet', 'The Man with the Scar', and 'Mr Know-All' and 'The Luncheon' in this collection number among them. Humour is not a hallmark of Maugham's stories, but these five engaging vignettes evince a wry comedy that demonstrates his great range as a writer.

'The Luncheon' is first and foremost a tale of stunning simplicity, one in which there is neither a word out of place nor a word more than the author needs. Indeed, there is real art in its brevity. The prolific short-story writer H. E. Bates once commented:

> Writing a short story may be compared with building a house with matchsticks. There comes a point in its construction when the addition of another stick may well bring down the whole affair in ruins. Thus balance is one of the supreme essentials to its creation and nowhere is this more true than in the very short story, say of one thousand words or less.

It is worth reading 'The Luncheon' with these observations in mind, in order to appreciate its carefully crafted prose and the skilful balance of spare narrative and lively dialogue which advances the plot to its telling denouement.

There is humour of a high order apparent throughout the tale's six pages, probably more on reflection once we know the narrator is delivered of his immediate fear, that of being unable to pay the bill; the opening paragraph's 'I hardly think I would have recognised her' assumes a splendid irony in the closing, boldly stated words – 'Today she weighs twenty-one stone'; and, in common with 'Mr Know-All', there is a most effective use of repetition – 'I never eat more than one thing' lives on in the reader's mind as a kind of gourmand's catch-phrase.

Another vital part of the story's success is the way in which Maugham involves his reader: from the understated irony of 'Did I remember?' (page 182) to the satisfying final paragraph's 'But I have had my revenge at last' (page 186). We can all empathise with the writer/narrator in his predicament and fears, both for the possible outcome of this lavishly expensive meal and also with the inward thought of short-sightedness, not to say stupidity, that had brought him to the position in which he found himself. Many could say with Maugham, 'Did I remember?'

'The Mother'

> I have been called cynical. I have been accused of making men out worse than they are. I do not think I have done this. All I have done is to bring into prominence certain traits that many writers shut their eyes to. I think what has chiefly struck me in human beings is their lack of consistency . . . There is nothing more beautiful than goodness, and it has pleased me very often to show how much of it there is in persons who by common standards would be relentlessly condemned. It has seemed to me sometimes to shine more brightly in them because it was surrounded by the darkness of sin . . . I am touched when I see the goodness of the wicked and I am willing to shrug a tolerant shoulder at their wickedness. I am not my brother's keeper. I cannot bring myself to judge my fellows; I am content to observe them.
>
> (*The Summing Up*)

These words amount to nothing short of a statement of Maugham's creed as a writer of fiction; 'The Mother' clearly stands as testimony to such a creed. Maugham portrays unambiguously how brightly La Cachirra's love for her son shines through the squalid environment and the personal degradation which she has experienced in her life. On the one hand we learn that she is very poor with wretched clothes, worn down by years of imprisonment; yet when she greets her son goodness shines unequivocally: 'She fondled him and with a loving gesture stroked his face with both her hands. The girl and her mother who watched would never have thought her capable of such tenderness' (page 192). It is in this last sentence that Maugham conveys one of his strongly held opinions: namely, that people cannot and do not readily accept the many facets of character embodied within one person.

'The Mother' also returns us to one of the writer's recurrent themes: La Cachirra is in *bondage* to her own extreme jealousy and passion; her freedom of action is completely circumscribed by her utter inability to share her son. (He too, in consequence, has his independence compromised because he cannot meet her impossible demands.) Indeed, such is the overwhelming, all-consuming nature of her love that she kills not once but *twice* for her son – 'Do you think I loved Pepe Santi? I endured his blows so that I could give you bread; and I killed him when he beat you'. (page 200) Not for nothing is she called La Cachirra, the vixen!

Reference was made earlier to the influence the French writer Guy de Maupassant had on Somerset Maugham, and there are certainly distinct echoes in this tale of Maupassant's 'The Vendetta', in which a woman avenges her husband's death with premeditated cunning. Above all, 'The Mother' impresses as a story of great force and passion; it contains Maugham's characteristic attention to detail of character (see page 189); the direct and beautifully controlled narrative unfolds towards an inevitable climax without ever becoming predictable; the closing lines offer the same sense of satisfying roundness encountered in 'The Luncheon'; and, extraordinarily, we can find ourselves as readers sympathising with a murderess who *is* what her emotions dictate – impossible to control.

The Facts of Life

IT WAS HENRY Garnet's habit on leaving the city of an afternoon to drop in at his club and play bridge before going home to dinner. He was a pleasant man to play with. He knew the game well and you could be sure that he would make the best of his cards. He was a good loser; and when he won was more inclined to ascribe his success to his luck than to his skill. He was indulgent, and if his partner made a mistake could be trusted to find an excuse for him. It was surprising then on this occasion to hear him telling his partner with unnecessary sharpness that he had never seen a hand worse played; and it was more surprising still to see him not only make a grave error himself, an error of which you would never have thought him capable, but when his partner, not unwilling to get a little of his own back, pointed it out, insist against all reason and with considerable heat that he was perfectly right. But they were all old friends, the men he was playing with, and none of them took his ill-humour very seriously. Henry Garnet was a broker, a partner in a firm of repute, and it occurred to one of them that something had gone wrong with some stock he was interested in.

'How's the market today?' he asked.

'Booming. Even the suckers are making money.'

It was evident that stocks and shares had nothing to do with Henry Garnet's vexation; but something was the matter; that was evident too. He was a hearty fellow, who enjoyed excellent health; he had plenty of money; he was fond of his wife, and devoted to his children. As a rule he had high spirits, and he laughed easily at the nonsense they were apt to talk while they played; but today he sat glum and silent. His brows were crossly puckered and there was a sulky look about his mouth. Presently, to ease the tension, one of the others mentioned a subject upon which they all knew Henry Garnet was glad to speak.

'How's your boy, Henry? I see he's done pretty well in the tournament.'

Henry Garnet's frown grew darker.

'He's done no better than I expected him to.'

'When does he come back from Monte?'

'He got back last night.'

'Did he enjoy himself?'

'I suppose so; all I know is that he made a damned fool of himself.'

'Oh. How?'

'I'd rather not talk about it if you don't mind.'

The three men looked at him with curiosity. Henry Garnet scowled at the green baize.

'Sorry, old boy. Your call.'

The game proceeded in a strained silence. Garnet got his bid, and when he played his cards so badly that he went three down not a word was said. Another rubber was begun and in the second game Garnet denied a suit.

'Having none?' his partner asked him.

Garnet's irritability was such that he did not even reply, and when at the end of the hand it appeared that he had revoked, and that his revoke cost the rubber, it was not to be expected that his partner should let his carelessness go without remark.

'What the devil's the matter with you, Henry?' he said. 'You're playing like a fool.'

Garnet was disconcerted. He did not so much mind losing a big rubber himself, but he was sore that his inattention should have made his partner lose too. He pulled himself together.

'I'd better not play any more. I thought a few rubbers would calm me, but the fact is I can't give my mind to the game. To tell you the truth I'm in a hell of a temper.'

They all burst out laughing.

'You don't have to tell us that, old boy. It's obvious.'

Garnet gave them a rueful smile.

'Well, I bet you'd be in a temper if what's happened to me

had happened to you. As a matter of fact I'm in a damned awkward situation, and if any of you fellows can give me any advice how to deal with it I'd be grateful.'

'Let's have a drink and you tell us all about it. With a K.C., a Home Office official and an eminent surgeon – if we can't tell you how to deal with a situation, nobody can.'

The K.C. got up and rang the bell for a waiter.

'It's about that damned boy of mine,' said Henry Garnet.

Drinks were ordered and brought. And this is the story that Henry Garnet told them.

The boy of whom he spoke was his only son. His name was Nicholas and of course he was called Nicky. He was eighteen. The Garnets had two daughters besides, one of sixteen and the other of twelve, but however unreasonable it seemed, for a father is generally supposed to like his daughters best, and though he did all he could not to show his preference, there was no doubt that the greater share of Henry Garnet's affection was given to his son. He was kind, in a chaffing, casual way, to his daughters, and gave them handsome presents on their birthdays and at Christmas; but he doted on Nicky. Nothing was too good for him. He thought the world of him. He could hardly take his eyes off him. You could not blame him, for Nicky was a son that any parent might have been proud of. He was six foot two, lithe but muscular, with broad shoulders and a slim waist, and he held himself gallantly erect; he had a charming head, well placed on the shoulders, with pale brown hair that waved slightly, blue eyes with long dark lashes under well-marked eyebrows, a full red mouth, and a tanned, clean skin. When he smiled he showed very regular and very white teeth. He was not shy, but there was a modesty in his demeanour that was attractive. In social intercourse he was easy, polite, and quietly gay. He was the offspring of nice, healthy, decent parents, he had been well brought up in a good home, he had been sent to a good school, and the general result was as engaging a specimen of young manhood as you were likely to find in a long time. You felt that he was as honest, open, and virtuous as he looked. He had never given his parents a moment's uneasiness. As a child he was seldom ill and never naughty. As a boy he did everything that was expected of him. His school reports were excellent. He was wonderfully popular, and he ended his career, with a creditable number of prizes, as head of the school and captain of the football team. But this was not all. At the age of fourteen Nicky had developed an unexpected gift for lawn tennis. This was a game that his father not only was fond of, but played very well, and when he discerned in the boy the promise of a tennis-player he fostered it. During the holidays he had him taught by the best professionals and by the time he was sixteen he had won a number of tournaments for boys of his age. He could beat his father so badly that only parental affection reconciled the older player to the poor show he put up. At eighteen Nicky went to Cambridge and Henry Garnet conceived the ambition that before he was through with the university he should play for it. Nicky had all the qualifications for becoming a great tennis-player. He was tall, he had a long reach, he was quick on his feet, and his timing was perfect. He realized instinctively where the ball was coming and, seemingly without hurry, was there to take it. He had a powerful serve, with a nasty break that made it difficult to return, and his forehand drive, low, long, and accurate, was deadly. He was not so good on the backhand and his volleying was wild, but all through the summer before he went to Cambridge Henry Garnet made him work on these points under the best teacher in England. At the back of his mind, though he did not even mention it to Nicky, he cherished a further ambition, to see his son play at Wimbledon, and who could tell, perhaps be chosen to represent his country in the Davis Cup. A great lump came into Henry Garnet's throat as he saw in fancy his son leap over the net to shake hands with the American champion whom he had just defeated, and walk off the court to the deafening plaudits of the multitude.

As an assiduous frequenter of Wimbledon Henry Garnet had a good many friends in the tennis world, and one evening he found himself at a City dinner sitting next to one of them, a Colonel Brabazon, and in due course began talking to him of Nicky and what chance there might be of his being chosen to play for his university during the following season.

'Why don't you let him go down to Monte Carlo and play in the spring tournament there?' said the Colonel suddenly.

'Oh, I don't think he's good enough for that. He's not nineteen yet, he only went up to Cambridge last October; he wouldn't stand a chance against all those cracks.'

'Of course, Austin and von Cramm and so on would knock spots off him, but he might snatch a game or two; and if he got up against some of the smaller fry there's no reason why he shouldn't win two or three matches. He's never been up against any of the first-rate players and it would be wonderful practice for him. He'd learn a lot more than he'll ever learn in the seaside tournaments you enter him for.'

'I wouldn't dream of it. I'm not going to let him leave Cambridge in the middle of a term. I've always impressed upon him that tennis is only a game and it mustn't interfere with work.'

Colonel Brabazon asked Garnet when the term ended.

'That's all right. He'd only have to cut about three days. Surely that could be arranged. You see, two of the men we were depending on have let us down, and we're in a hole. We want to send as good a team as we can. The Germans are sending their best players and so are the Americans.'

'Nothing doing, old boy. In the first place Nicky's not good enough, and secondly, I don't fancy the idea of sending a kid like that to Monte Carlo without anyone to look after him. If I could get away myself I might think of it, but that's out of the question.'

'I shall be there. I'm going as the non-playing captain of the English team. I'll keep an eye on him.'

'You'll be busy, and besides, it's not a responsibility I'd like to ask you to take. He's never been abroad in his life, and to tell you the truth, I shouldn't have a moment's peace all the time he was there.'

They left it at that and presently Henry Garnet went home. He was so flattered by Colonel Brabazon's suggestion that he could not help telling his wife.

'Fancy his thinking Nicky's as good as that. He told me he'd seen him play and his style was fine. He only wants more practice to get into the first flight. We shall see the kid playing in the semi-finals at Wimbledon yet, old girl.'

To his surprise Mrs Garnet was not so much opposed to the notion as he would have expected.

'After all the boy's eighteen. Nicky's never got into mischief yet and there's no reason to suppose he will now.'

'There's his work to be considered; don't forget that. I think it would be a very bad precedent to let him cut the term.'

'But what can three days matter? It seems a shame to rob him of a chance like that. I'm sure he'd jump at it if you asked him.'

'Well, I'm not going to. I haven't sent him to Cambridge just to play tennis. I know he's steady, but it's silly to put temptation in his way. He's much too young to go to Monte Carlo by himself.'

'You say he won't have a chance against these crack players, but you can't tell.'

Henry Garnet sighed a little. On the way home in the car it had struck him that Austin's health was uncertain and that von Cramm had his off-days. Supposing, just for the sake of argument, that Nicky had a bit of luck like that – then there would be no doubt that he would be chosen to play for Cambridge. But of course that was all nonsense.

'Nothing doing, my dear. I've made up my mind and I'm not going to change it.'

Mrs Garnet held her peace. But next day she wrote to Nicky, telling him what had happened, and suggested to him what she would do in his place if, wanting to go, he wished to get his father's consent. A day or two later Henry Garnet received a letter from his son. He was bubbling over with excitement. He had seen his tutor, who was a tennis-player himself, and the

Provost of his college, who happened to know Colonel Brabazon, and no objection would be made to his leaving before the end of term; they both thought it an opportunity that shouldn't be missed. He didn't see what harm he could come to, and if only, just this once, his father would stretch a point, well, next term, he promised faithfully, he'd work like blazes. It was a very pretty letter. Mrs Garnet watched her husband read it at the breakfast table; she was undisturbed by the frown on his face. He threw it over to her.

'I don't know why you thought it necessary to tell Nicky something I told you in confidence. It's too bad of you. Now you've thoroughly unsettled him.'

'I'm sorry. I thought it would please him to know that Colonel Brabazon had such a high opinion of him. I don't see why one should only tell people the disagreeable things that are said about them. Of course I made it quite clear that there could be no question of his going.'

'You've put me in an odious position. If there's anything I hate it's for the boy to look upon me as a spoil-sport and a tyrant.'

'Oh, he'll never do that. He may think you rather silly and unreasonable, but I'm sure he'll understand that it's only for his own good that you're being so unkind.'

'Christ,' said Henry Garnet.

His wife had a great inclination to laugh. She knew the battle was won. Dear, oh dear, how easy it was to get men to do what you wanted. For appearance sake Henry Garnet held out for forty-eight hours, but then he yielded, and a fortnight later Nicky came to London. He was to start for Monte Carlo next morning, and after dinner, when Mrs Garnet and her elder daughter had left them, Henry took the opportunity to give his son some good advice.

'I don't feel quite comfortable about letting you go off to a place like Monte Carlo at your age practically by yourself,' he finished, 'but there it is and I can only hope you'll be sensible. I don't want to play the heavy father, but there are three things especially that I want to warn you against: one is gambling, don't gamble; the second is money, don't lend anyone money; and the third is women, don't have anything to do with women. If you don't do any of those three things you can't come to much harm, so remember them well.'

'All right, father,' Nicky smiled.

'That's my last word to you. I know the world pretty well and believe me, my advice is sound.'

'I won't forget it. I promise you.'

'That's a good chap. Now let's go up and join the ladies.'

Nicky beat neither Austin nor von Cramm in the Monte Carlo tournament, but he did not disgrace himself. He snatched an unexpected victory over a Spanish player and gave one of the Austrians a closer match than anyone had thought possible. In the mixed doubles he got into the semi-finals. His charm conquered everyone and he vastly enjoyed himself. It was generally allowed that he showed promise, and Colonel Brabazon told him that when he was a little older and had had more practice with first-class players he would be a credit to his father. The tournament came to an end and the day following he was to fly back to London. Anxious to play his best he had lived very carefully, smoking little and drinking nothing, and going to bed early; but on his last evening he thought he would like to see something of the life in Monte Carlo of which he had heard so much. An official dinner was given to the tennis-players and after dinner with the rest of them he went into the Sporting Club. It was the first time he had been there. Monte Carlo was very full and the rooms were crowded. Nicky had never before seen roulette played except in the pictures; in a maze he stopped at the first table he came to; chips of different sizes were scattered over the green cloth in what looked like a hopeless muddle; the croupier gave the wheel a sharp turn and with a flick threw in the little white ball. After what seemed an endless time the ball stopped and another croupier with a broad, indifferent gesture raked in the chips of those who had lost.

Presently Nicky wandered over to where they were playing *trente et quarante*, but he couldn't understand what it was all about and he thought it dull. He saw a crowd in another room and sauntered in. A big game of baccara was in progress and he was immediately conscious of the tension. The players were protected from the thronging bystanders by a brass rail; they sat round the table, nine on each side, with the dealer in the middle and the croupier facing him. Big money was changing hands. The dealer was a member of the Greek Syndicate. Nicky looked at his impassive face. His eyes were watchful, but his expression never changed whether he won or lost. It was a terrifying, strangely impressive sight. It gave Nicky, who had been thriftily brought up, a peculiar thrill to see someone risk a thousand pounds on the turn of a card and when he lost make a little joke and laugh. It was all terribly exciting. An acquaintance came up to him.

'Been doing any good?' he asked.

'I haven't been playing.'

'Wise of you. Rotten game. Come and have a drink.'

'All right.'

While they were having it Nicky told his friends that this was the first time he had ever been in the rooms.

'Oh, but you must have one little flutter before you go. It's idiotic to leave Monte without having tried your luck. After all it won't hurt you to lose a hundred francs or so.'

'I don't suppose it will, but my father wasn't any too keen on my coming at all and one of the three things he particularly advised me not to do was to gamble.'

But when Nicky left his companion he strolled back to one of the tables where they were playing roulette. He stood for a while looking at the losers' money being raked-in by the croupier and the money that was won paid out to the winners. It was impossible to deny that it was thrilling. His friend was right, it did seem silly to leave Monte without putting something on the table just once. It would be an experience, and at his age you had to have all the experience you could get. He reflected that he hadn't promised his father not to gamble, he'd promised him not to forget his advice. It wasn't quite the same, was it? He took a hundred-franc note out of his pocket and rather shyly put it on number eighteen. He chose it because that was his age. With a wildly beating heart he watched the wheel turn; the little white ball whizzed about like a small demon of mischief; the wheel went round more slowly, the little white ball hesitated, it seemed about to stop, it went on again; Nicky could hardly believe his eyes when it fell into number eighteen. A lot of chips were passed over to him and his hands trembled as he took them. It seemed to amount to a lot of money. He was so confused that he never thought of putting anything on the following round; in fact he had no intention of playing any more, once was enough; and he was surprised when eighteen again came up. There was only one chip on it.

'By George, you've won again,' said a man who was standing near to him.

'Me? I hadn't got anything on.'

'Yes, you had. Your original stake. They always leave it on unless you ask for it back. Didn't you know?'

Another packet of chips was handed over to him. Nicky's head reeled. He counted his gains: seven thousand francs. A queer sense of power seized him; he felt wonderfully clever. This was the easiest way of making money that he had ever heard of. His frank, charming face was wreathed in smiles. His bright eyes met those of a woman standing by his side. She smiled.

'You're in luck,' she said.

She spoke English, but with a foreign accent.

'I can hardly believe it. It's the first time I've ever played.'

'That explains it. Lend me a thousand francs, will you? I've lost everything I've got. I'll give it you back in half an hour.'

'All right.'

She took a large red chip from his pile and with a word of

thanks disappeared. The man who had spoken to him before grunted.

'You'll never see that again.'

Nicky was dashed. His father had particularly advised him not to lend anyone money. What a silly thing to do! And to somebody he'd never seen in his life. But the fact was, he felt at that moment such a love for the human race that it had never occurred to him to refuse. And that big red chip, it was almost impossible to realize that it had any value. Oh well, it didn't matter, he still had six thousand francs, he'd just try his luck once or twice more and if he didn't win he'd go home. He put a chip on sixteen, which was his elder sister's age, but it didn't come up; then on twelve, which was his younger sister's, and that didn't come up either; he tried various numbers at random, but without success. It was funny, he seemed to have lost his knack. He thought he would try just once more and then stop; he won. He had made up all his losses and had something over. At the end of an hour, after various ups and downs, having experienced such thrills as he had never known in his life, he found himself with so many chips that they would hardly go in his pockets. He decided to go. He went to the changers' office and he gasped when twenty thousand-franc notes were spread out before him. He had never had so much money in his life. He put it in his pocket and was turning away when the woman to whom he had lent the thousand francs came up to him.

'I've been looking for you everywhere,' she said. 'I was afraid you'd gone. I was in a fever, I didn't know what you'd think of me. Here's your thousand francs and thank you so much for the loan.'

Nicky, blushing scarlet, stared at her with amazement. How he had misjudged her! His father had said, don't gamble; well, he had, and he'd made twenty thousand francs; and his father had said, don't lend anyone money; well, he had, he'd lent quite a lot to a total stranger, and she'd returned it. The fact was that he wasn't nearly such a fool as his father thought: he'd had an instinct that he could lend her the money with safety, and you see, his instinct was right. But he was so obviously taken aback that the little lady was forced to laugh.

'What is the matter with you?' she asked.

'To tell you the truth I never expected to see the money back.'

'What did you take me for? Did you think I was a – cocotte?'

Nicky reddened to the roots of his wavy hair.

'No, of course not.'

'Do I look like one?'

'Not a bit.'

She was dressed very quietly, in black, with a string of gold beads round her neck; her simple frock showed off a neat, slight figure; she had a pretty little face and a trim head. She was made up, but not excessively, and Nicky supposed that she was not more than three or four years older than himself. She gave him a friendly smile.

'My husband is in the administration in Morocco, and I've come to Monte Carlo for a few weeks because he thought I wanted a change.'

'I was just going,' said Nicky because he couldn't think of anything else to say.

'Already!'

'Well, I've got to get up early tomorrow, I'm going back to London by air.'

'Of course. The tournament ended today, didn't it? I saw you play, you know, two or three times.'

'Did you? I don't know why you should have noticed me.'

'You've got a beautiful style. And you looked very sweet in your shorts.'

Nicky was not an immodest youth, but it did cross his mind that perhaps she had borrowed that thousand francs in order to scrape acquaintance with him.

'Do you ever go to the Knickerbocker?' she asked.

'No I never have.'

'Oh, but you mustn't leave Monte Carlo without having

been there. Why don't you come and dance a little? To tell you the truth, I'm starving with hunger and I should adore some bacon and eggs.'

Nicky remembered his father's advice not to have anything to do with women, but this was different; you had only to look at the pretty little thing to know at once that she was perfectly respectable. Her husband was in what corresponded, he supposed, to the Civil Service. His father and mother had friends who were Civil Servants and they and their wives sometimes came to dinner. It was true that the wives were neither so young nor so pretty as this one, but she was just as ladylike as they were. And after winning twenty thousand francs he thought it wouldn't be a bad idea to have a little fun.

'I'd love to go with you,' he said. 'But you won't mind if I don't stay very long. I've left instructions at my hotel that I'm to be called at seven.'

'We'll leave as soon as ever you like.'

Nicky found it very pleasant at the Knickerbocker. He ate his bacon and eggs with appetite. They shared a bottle of champagne. They danced, and the little lady told him he danced beautifully. He knew he danced pretty well, and of course she was easy to dance with. As light as a feather. She laid her cheek against his and when their eyes met there was in hers a smile that made his heart go pit-a-pat. A coloured woman sang in a throaty, sensual voice. The floor was crowded.

'Have you ever been told that you're very good-looking?' she asked.

'I don't think so,' he laughed. 'Gosh,' he thought, 'I believe she's fallen for me.'

Nicky was not such a fool as to be unaware that women often liked him, and when she made that remark he pressed her to him a little more closely. She closed her eyes and a faint sigh escaped her lips.

'I suppose it wouldn't be quite nice if I kissed you before all these people,' he said.

'What do you think they would take me for?'

It began to grow late and Nicky said that really he thought he ought to be going.

'I shall go too,' she said, 'Will you drop me at my hotel on your way?'

Nicky paid the bill. He was rather surprised at its amount, but with all that money he had in his pocket he could afford not to care, and they got into a taxi. She snuggled up to him and he kissed her. She seemed to like it.

'By Jove,' he thought, 'I wonder if there's anything doing.'

It was true that she was a married woman, but her husband was in Morocco, and it certainly did look as if she'd fallen for him. Good and proper. It was true also that his father had warned him to have nothing to do with women, but, he reflected again, he hadn't actually promised he wouldn't, he'd only promised not to forget his advice. Well, he hadn't; he was bearing it in mind that very minute. But circumstances alter cases. She was a sweet little thing; it seemed silly to miss the chance of an adventure when it was handed to you like that on a tray. When they reached the hotel he paid off the taxi.

'I'll walk home,' he said. 'The air will do me good after the stuffy atmosphere of that place.'

'Come up a moment,' she said. 'I'd like to show you the photo of my little boy.'

'Oh, have you got a little boy?' he exclaimed, a trifle dashed.

'Yes, a sweet little boy.'

He walked upstairs after her. He didn't in the least want to see the photograph of her little boy, but he thought it only civil to pretend he did. He was afraid he'd made a fool of himself; it occurred to him that she was taking him up to look at the photograph in order to show him in a nice way that he'd made a mistake. He'd told her he was eighteen.

'I suppose she thinks I'm just a kid.'

He began to wish he hadn't spent all that money on champagne at the night-club.

But she didn't show him the photograph of her little boy

after all. They had no sooner got into her room than she turned to him, flung her arms round his neck, and kissed him full on the lips. He had never in all his life been kissed so passionately.

'Darling,' she said.

For a brief moment his father's advice once more crossed Nicky's mind and then he forgot it.

Nicky was a light sleeper and the least sound was apt to wake him. Two or three hours later he awoke and for a moment could not imagine where he was. The room was not quite dark, for the door of the bathroom was ajar, and the light in it had been left on. Suddenly he was conscious that someone was moving about the room. Then he remembered. He saw that it was his little friend, and he was on the point of speaking when something in the way she was behaving stopped him. She was walking very cautiously, as though she were afraid of waking him; she stopped once or twice and looked over at the bed. He wondered what she was after. He soon saw. She went over to the chair on which he had placed his clothes and once more looked in his direction. She waited for what seemed to him an interminable time. The silence was so intense that Nicky thought he could hear his own heart beating. Then, very slowly, very quietly, she took up his coat, slipped her hand into the inside pocket and drew out all those beautiful thousand-franc notes that Nicky had been so proud to win. She put the coat back and placed some other clothes on it so that it should look as though it had not been disturbed, then, with the bundle of notes in her hand, for an appreciable time stood once more stock-still. Nicky had repressed an instinctive impulse to jump up and grab her, it was partly surprise that had kept him quiet, partly the notion that he was in a strange hotel, in a foreign country, and if he made a row he didn't know what might happen. She looked at him. His eyes were partly closed and he was sure that she thought he was asleep. In the silence she could hardly fail to hear his regular breathing. When she had reassured herself that her movements had not disturbed him she stepped, with infinite caution, across the room. On a small table in the window a cineraria was growing in a pot. Nicky watched her now with his eyes wide open. The plant was evidently placed quite loosely in the pot, for taking it by the stalks she lifted it out; she put the banknotes in the bottom of the pot and replaced the plant. It was an excellent hiding-place. No one could have guessed that anything was concealed under that richly-flowering plant. She pressed the earth down with her fingers and then, very slowly, taking care not to make the smallest noise, crept across the room and slipped back into bed.

'*Chéri*,' she said, in a caressing voice.

Nicky breathed steadily, like a man immersed in deep sleep. The little lady turned over on her side and disposed herself to slumber. But though Nicky lay so still his thoughts worked busily. He was extremely indignant at the scene he had just witnessed, and to himself he spoke his thoughts with vigour.

'She's nothing but a damned tart. She and her dear little boy and her husband in Morocco. My eye! She's a rotten thief, that's what she is. Took me for a mug. If she thinks she's going to get away with anything like that, she's mistaken.'

He had already made up his mind what he was going to do with the money he had so cleverly won. He had long wanted a car of his own, and had thought it rather mean of his father not to have given him one. After all, a feller doesn't always want to drive about in the family bus. Well, he'd just teach the old man a lesson and buy one himself. For twenty thousand francs, two hundred pounds roughly, he could get a very decent second-hand car. He meant to get the money back, but just then he didn't quite know how. He didn't like the idea of kicking up a row, he was a stranger, in a hotel he knew nothing of; it might very well be that the beastly woman had friends there, he didn't mind facing anyone in a fair fight, but he'd look pretty foolish if someone pulled a gun on him. He reflected besides, very sensibly, that he had no proof the money was his. If it came to a show-down and she swore it was hers, he might very easily find himself hauled off to a police-station. He really didn't know what to do. Presently by her regular breathing he knew that the little lady was asleep. She must have fallen asleep with an easy mind, for she had done her job without a hitch. It infuriated Nicky that she should rest so peacefully while he lay awake worried to death. Suddenly an idea occurred to him. It was such a good one that it was only by the exercise of all his self-control that he prevented himself from jumping out of bed and carrying it out at once. Two could play at her game. She'd stolen his money; well he'd steal it back again, and they'd be all square. He made up his mind to wait quite quietly until he was sure that deceitful woman was sound asleep. He waited for what seemed to him a very long time. She did not stir. Her breathing was as regular as a child's.

'Darling,' he said at last.

No answer. No movement. She was dead to the world. Very slowly, pausing after every movement, very silently, he slipped out of bed. He stood still for a while, looking at her to see whether he had disturbed her. Her breathing was as regular as before. During the time he was waiting he had taken note carefully of the furniture in the room so that in crossing it he should not knock against a chair or a table and make a noise. He took a couple of steps and waited, he took a couple of steps more; he was very light on his feet and made no sound as he walked; he took fully five minutes to get to the window, and here he waited again. He started, for the bed slightly creaked, but it was only because the sleeper turned in her sleep. He forced himself to wait till he had counted one hundred. She was sleeping like a log. With infinite care he seized the cineraria by the stalks and gently pulled it out of the pot; he put his other hand in, his heart beat nineteen to the dozen as his fingers touched the notes, his hand closed on them and he slowly drew them out. He replaced the plant and in his turn carefully pressed down the earth. While he was doing all this he had kept one eye on the form lying in the bed. It remained still. After another pause he crept softly to the chair on which his clothes were lying. He first put the bundle of notes in his coat pocket and then proceeded to dress. It took him a good quarter of an hour, because he could afford to make no sound. He had been wearing a soft shirt with his dinner jacket, and he congratulated himself on this, because it was easier to put on silently than a stiff one. He had some difficulty in tying his tie without a looking-glass, but he very wisely reflected that it didn't really matter if it wasn't tied very well. His spirits were rising. The whole thing now began to seem rather a lark. At length he was completely dressed except for his shoes, which he took in his hand; he thought he would put them on when he got into the passage. Now he had to cross the room to get to the door. He reached it so quietly that he could not have disturbed the lightest sleeper. But the door had to be unlocked. He turned the key very slowly; it creaked.

'Who's that?'

The little woman suddenly sat up in bed. Nicky's heart jumped to his mouth. He made a great effort to keep his head.

'It's only me. It's six o'clock and I've got to go. I was trying not to wake you.'

'Oh, I forgot.'

She sank back on to the pillow.

'Now that you're awake I'll put on my shoes.'

He sat down on the edge of the bed and did this.

'Don't make a noise when you go out. The hotel people don't like it. Oh, I'm so sleepy.'

'You go right off to sleep again.'

'Kiss me before you go.' He bent down and kissed her. 'You're a sweet boy and a wonderful lover. *Bon voyage.*'

Nicky did not feel quite safe till he got out of the hotel. The dawn had broken. The sky was unclouded, and in the harbour the yachts and the fishing-boats lay motionless on the still water. On the quay fisherman were getting ready to start on their day's work. The streets were deserted. Nicky took a long breath of the sweet morning air. He felt alert and well. He also felt as pleased as Punch. With a swinging stride, his shoulders well thrown back, he walked up the hill and along the gardens in front of the Casino – the flowers in that clear light had a dewy brilliance that was delicious – till he came to his hotel. Here the day had already begun. In the hall porters with mufflers round their necks and berets on their heads were busy sweeping. Nicky went up to his room and had a hot bath. He lay in it and thought with satisfaction that he was not such a mug as some people might think. After his bath he did his exercises, dressed, packed, and went down to breakfast. He had a grand appetite. No continental breakfast for him! He had grapefruit, porridge, bacon and eggs, rolls fresh from the oven, so crisp and delicious they melted in your mouth, marmalade, and three cups of coffee. Though feeling perfectly well before, he felt better after that. He lit the pipe he had recently learnt to smoke, paid his bill and stepped into the car that was waiting to take him to the aerodrome on the other side of Cannes. The road as far as Nice ran over the hills and below him was the blue sea and the coast-line. He couldn't help thinking it damned pretty. They passed through Nice, so gay and friendly in the early morning, and presently they came to a long stretch of straight road that ran by the sea. Nicky had paid his bill, not with the money he had won the night before, but with the money his father had given him; he had changed a thousand francs to pay for supper at the Knickerbocker, but the deceitful little woman had returned him the thousand francs he had lent her, so that he still had twenty thousand-franc notes in his pocket. He thought he would like to have a look at them. He had so nearly lost them that they had a double value for him. He took them out of his hip-pocket into which for safety's sake he had stuffed them when he put on the suit he was travelling in, and counted them one by one. Something very strange had happened to them. Instead of there being twenty notes as there should have been there were twenty-six. He couldn't understand it at all. He counted them twice more. There was no doubt about it; somehow or other he had twenty-six thousand francs instead of the twenty he should have had. He couldn't make it out. He asked himself if it was possible that he had won more at the Sporting Club than he had realized. But no, that was out of the question; he distinctly remembered the man at the desk laying the notes out in four rows of five, and he had counted them himself. Suddenly the explanation occurred to him; when he had put his hand into the flower-pot, after taking out the cineraria, he had grabbed everything he felt there. The flower-pot was the little hussy's money-box and he had taken out not only his own money, but her savings as well. Nicky leant back in the car and burst into a roar of laughter. It was the funniest thing he had ever heard in his life. And when he thought of her going to the flower-pot some time later in the morning when she awoke, expecting to find the money she had so cleverly got away with, and finding, not only that it wasn't there, but that her own had gone too, he laughed more than ever. And so far as he was concerned there was nothing to do about it; he neither knew her name, nor the name of the hotel to which she had taken him. He couldn't return her money even if he wanted to.

'It serves her damned well right,' he said.

This then was the story that Henry Garnet told his friends over the bridge-table, for the night before, after dinner when his wife and daughter had left them to their port, Nicky had narrated it in full.

'And you know what infuriated me is that he's so damned pleased with himself. Talk of a cat swallowing a canary. And d'you know what he said to me when he'd finished? He looked at me with those innocent eyes of his and said: 'You know, father, I can't help thinking there was something wrong about the advice you gave me. You said, don't gamble; well, I did, and I made a packet; you said, don't lend money; well, I did, and I got it back; and you said, don't have anything to do with women; well, I did, and I made six thousand francs on the deal.'

It didn't make it any better for Henry Garnet that his three companions burst out laughing.

'It's all very well for you fellows to laugh, but you know, I'm in a damned awkward position. The boy looked up to me, he respected me, he took whatever I said as gospel truth, and now, I saw it in his eyes, he just looks upon me as a drivelling old fool. It's no good my saying one swallow doesn't make a summer; he doesn't see that it was just a fluke, he thinks the whole thing was due to his own cleverness. It may ruin him.'

'You do look a bit of a damned fool, old man,' said one of the others. 'There's no denying that, is there?'

'I know I do, and I don't like it, It's so dashed unfair. Fate has no right to play one tricks like that. After all, you must admit that my advice was good.'

'Very good.'

'And the wretched boy ought to have burnt his fingers. Well, he hasn't. You're all men of the world, you tell me how I'm to deal with the situation now.'

But they none of them could.

'Well, Henry, if I were you I wouldn't worry,' said the lawyer. 'My belief is that your boy's born lucky, and in the long run that's better than to be born clever or rich.'

The Unconquered

HE CAME BACK into the kitchen. The man was still on the floor, lying where he had hit him, and his face was bloody. He was moaning. The woman had backed against the wall and was staring with terrified eyes at Willi, his friend, and when he came in she gave a gasp and broke into loud sobbing. Willi was sitting at the table, his revolver in his hand, with a half empty glass of wine beside him. Hans went up to the table, filled his glass and emptied it at a gulp.

'You look as though you'd had trouble, young fellow,' said Willi with a grin.

Hans's face was blood-stained and you could see the gashes of five sharp finger-nails. He put his hand gingerly to his cheek.

'She'd have scratched my eyes out if she could, the bitch. I shall have to put some iodine on. But she's all right now. You go along.'

'I don't know. Shall I? It's getting late.'

'Don't be a fool. You're a man, aren't you? What if it is getting late? We lost our way.'

It was still light and the westering sun streamed into the kitchen windows of the farm-house. Willi hesitated a moment. He was a little fellow, dark and thin-faced, a dress designer in civil life, and he didn't want Hans to think him a cissy. He got up and went towards the door through which Hans had come. When the woman saw what he was going to do she gave a shriek and sprang forwards.

'*Non, non,*' she cried.

With one step Hans was in front of her. He seized her by the shoulders and flung her violently back. She tottered and fell. He took Willi's revolver.

'Stop still, both of you,' he rasped in French, but with his guttural German accent. He nodded his head towards the door.

'Go on. I'll look after them.'

Willi went out, but in a moment was back again.

'She's unconscious.'

'Well, what of it?'

'I can't. It's no good.'

'Stupid, that's what you are. *Ein Weibchen.* A woman.'

Willi flushed.

'We'd better be getting on our way.'

Hans shrugged a scornful shoulder.

'I'll just finish the bottle of wine and then we'll go.'

He was feeling at ease and it would have been pleasant to linger. He had been on the job since morning and after so many hours on his motor-cycle his limbs ached. Luckily they hadn't far to go, only to Soissons – ten or fifteen kilometres. He wondered if he'd have the luck to get a bed to sleep in. Of course all this wouldn't have happened if the girl hadn't been a fool. They had lost their way, he and Willi, they had stopped a peasant working in a field and he had deliberately misled them, and they found themselves on a side road. When they came to the farm they stopped to ask for a direction. They'd asked very politely, for orders were to treat the French population well as long as they behaved themselves. The door was opened for them by the girl and she said she didn't know the way to Soissons, so they pushed in; then the woman, her mother, Hans guessed, told them. The three of them, the farmer, his wife and daughter, had just finished supper and there was a bottle of wine on the table. It reminded Hans that he was as thirsty as the devil. The day had been sweltering and he hadn't had a drink since noon. He asked them for a bottle of wine and Willi had added that they would pay them well for it. Willi was a good little chap, but soft. After all, they were the victors. Where was the French army? In head-long flight. And the English, leaving everything behind, had scuttled like rabbits back to their island. The conquerors took what they wanted, didn't they? But Willi had worked at a Paris dressmaker's for two years. It's true he spoke French well, that's why he had his present job, but it had done something to him. A decadent people. It did a German no good to live among them.

The farmer's wife put a couple of bottles of wine on the table and Willi took twenty francs out of his pocket and gave it to her. She didn't even say thank you. Hans's French wasn't as good as Willi's, but he could make himself understood, and he and Willi spoke it together all the time. Willi corrected his mistakes. It was because Willi was so useful to him in this way that he had made him his friend, and he knew that Willi admired him. He admired him because he was so tall, slim, and broad-shouldered, because his curly hair was so fair and his eyes so blue. He never lost an opportunity to practise his French, and he tried to talk now, but those three French people wouldn't meet him half-way. He told them that he was a farmer's son himself and when the war was over was going back to the farm. He had been sent to school in Munich because his mother wanted him to go into business, but his heart wasn't in it, and so after matriculating he had gone to an agricultural college.

'You came here to ask your way and now you know it,' said the girl. 'Drink up your wine and go.'

He had hardly looked at her before. She wasn't pretty, but she had fine dark eyes and a straight nose. Her face was very pale. She was plainly dressed, but somehow she didn't look quite like what she evidently was. There was a sort of distinction about her. Ever since the war started he'd heard fellows talk about the French girls. They had something the German girls hadn't. Chic, Willi said it was, but when he asked him just what he meant by that Willi could only say that you had to see it to understand. Of course he'd heard others say that they were mercenary and hard as nails. Well, they'd be in Paris in a week and he'd find out for himself. They said the High Command had already arranged for houses for the men to go to.

'Finish your wine and let's go,' said Willi.

But Hans was feeling comfortable and didn't want to be hurried.

'You don't look like a farmer's daughter,' he said to the girl.

'And so what?' she answered.

'She's a teacher,' said her mother.

'Then you've had a good education.' She shrugged her shoulders, but he went on good-humouredly in his bad French. 'You ought to understand that this is the best thing that has ever happened to the French people. We didn't declare war. You declared war. And now we're going to make France a decent country. We're going to put order into it. We're going to teach you to work. You'll learn obedience and discipline.'

She clenched her fists and looked at him, her eyes black with hatred. But she did not speak.

'You're drunk, Hans,' said Willi.

'I'm as sober as a judge. I'm only telling them the truth and they may just as well know it at once.'

'He's right,' she cried out, unable any longer to contain herself. 'You're drunk. Now go. Go.'

'Oh, you understand German, do you? All right, I'll go. But you must give me a kiss first.'

She took a step back to avoid him, but he seized her wrist.

'Father,' she cried. 'Father.'

The farmer flung himself on the German. Hans let go of her and with all his might hit him in the face. He crumpled up on the floor. Then, before she could escape him, he caught the girl in his arms. She gave him a swinging blow on the cheek. . . . He chuckled grimly.

'Is that how you take it when a German soldier wants to kiss you? You'll pay for this.'

With his great strength he pinioned her arms and was dragging her out of the door, but her mother rushed at him and catching him by the clothes tried to pull him away. With one arm holding the girl close to him, with the flat of his other hand he gave the woman a great push and she staggered back to the wall.

'Hans, Hans,' cried Willi.

'Shut up, damn you.'

He put his hands over the girl's mouth to stop her shrieking and carried her out of the room. That was how it had happened and you had to admit that she'd brought it on herself. She shouldn't have slapped him. If she'd given him the kiss he'd asked for he'd have gone away. He gave a glance at the farmer still lying where he had fallen and he could hardly help laughing at his funny face. There was a smile in his eyes when he looked at the woman cowering against the wall. Was she afraid it was her turn next? Not likely. He remembered a French proverb.

'*C'est le premier pas qui coûte*. There's nothing to cry about, old woman. It had to come sooner or later.' He put his hand to his hip pocket and pulled out a wallet. 'Look, here's a hundred francs so that mademoiselle can buy herself a new dress. There's not much left of that one.' He placed the note on the table and put his helmet back on his head. 'Let's go.'

They slammed the door behind them and got on their motor-cycles. The woman went into the parlour. Her daughter was lying on the divan. She was lying as he had left her and she was weeping bitterly.

Three months later Hans found himself in Soissons again. He had been in Paris with the conquering army and had ridden through the Arc de Triomphe on his motor-cycle. He had advanced with the army first to Tours and then to Bordeaux. He'd seen very little fighting. The only French soldiers he'd seen were prisoners. The campaign had been the greatest spree he could ever have imagined. After the armistice he had spent a month in Paris. He'd sent picture postcards to his family in Bavaria and bought them all presents. Willi, because he knew the city like the palm of his hand, had stayed on, but he and the rest of his unit were sent to Soissons to join the force that was holding it. It was a nice little town and he was comfortably billeted. Plenty to eat and champagne for less than a mark a bottle in German money. When he was ordered to proceed there it had occurred to him that it would be fun to go and have a look at the girl he'd had. He'd take her a pair of silk stockings to show there was no ill-feeling. He had a good bump of locality and he thought he would be able to find the farm without difficulty. So one afternoon, when he had nothing to do, he put the silk stockings in his pocket and got on his machine. It was a lovely autumn day, with hardly a cloud in the sky, and it was pretty, undulating country that he rode through. It had been fine and dry for so long that, though it was September, not even the restless poplars gave sign that the summer was drawing to an end. He took one wrong turning, which delayed him, but for all that he got to the place he sought in less than half an hour. A mongrel dog barked at him as he walked up to the door. He did not knock, but turned the handle and stepped in. The girl was sitting at the table peeling potatoes. She sprang to her feet when she saw the uniformed man.

'What d'you want?' Then she recognized him. She backed to the wall, clutching the knife in her hands. 'It's you. *Cochon.*'

'Don't get excited. I'm not going to hurt you. Look. I've brought you some silk stockings.'

'Take them away and take yourself off with them.'

'Don't be silly. Drop that knife. You'll only get hurt if you try to be nasty. You needn't be afraid of me.'

'I'm not afraid of you,' she said.

She let the knife fall to the floor. He took off his helmet and sat down. He reached out with his foot and drew the knife towards him.

'Shall I peel some of your potatoes for you?' She did not answer. He bent down for the knife and then took a potato out of the bowl and went to work on it. Her face hard, her eyes hostile, she stood against the wall and watched him. He smiled at her disarmingly. 'Why do you look so cross? I didn't do you much harm, you know. I was excited, we all were, they'd talked of the invincible French army and the Maginot line . . .' he finished the sentence with a chuckle. 'And the wine went to my head. You might have fared worse. Women have told me that I'm not a bad-looking fellow.'

She looked him up and down scornfully.

'Get out of here.'

'Not until I choose.'

'If you don't go my father will go to Soissons and complain to the general.'

'Much he'll care. Our orders are to make friends with the population. What's your name?'

'That's not your business.'

There was a flush in her cheeks now and her angry eyes were blazing. She was prettier than he remembered her. He hadn't done so badly. She had a refinement that suggested the city-dweller rather than the peasant. He remembered her mother saying she was a teacher. Because she was almost a lady it amused him to torment her. He felt strong and healthy. He passed his hand through his curly blond hair, and giggled when he thought that many girls would have jumped at the chance she had had. His face was so deeply tanned by the summer that his eyes were startlingly blue.

'Where are your father and mother?'

'Working in the fields.'

'I'm hungry. Give me a bit of bread and cheese and a glass of wine. I'll pay.'

She gave a harsh laugh.

'We haven't seen cheese for three months. We haven't enough bread to stay our hunger. The French took our horses a year ago and now the Boches have taken our cows, our pigs, our chickens, everything.'

'Well, they paid you for them.'

'Can we eat the worthless paper they gave us?'

She began to cry.

'Are you hungry?'

'Oh, no,' she answered bitterly, 'we can eat like kings on potatoes and bread and turnips and lettuce. Tomorrow my father's going to Soissons to see if he can buy some horse meat.'

'Listen, Miss. I'm not a bad fellow. I'll bring you a cheese, and I think I can get hold of a bit of ham.'

'I don't want your presents. I'll starve before I touch the food you swine have stolen from us.'

'We'll see,' he said good-humouredly.

He put on his hat, got up, and with an *Au revoir, mademoiselle*, walked out.

He wasn't supposed to go joy-riding round the country and he had to wait to be sent on an errand before he was able to get to the farm again. It was ten days later. He walked in as unceremoniously as before and this time he found the farmer and his wife in the kitchen. It was round about noon and the woman was stirring a pot on the stove. The man was seated at table. They gave him a glance when he came in, but there was no surprise in it. Their daughter had evidently told them of his visit. They did not speak. The woman went on with her cooking, and the man, a surly look on his face, stared at the oil-cloth on the table. But it required more than this to disconcert the good-humoured Hans.

'*Bonjour, la compagnie*,' he said cheerfully. 'I've brought you a present.'

He undid the package he had with him and set out a sizable piece of Gruyère cheese, a piece of pork, and a couple of tins of sardines. The woman turned round and he smiled when he saw the light of greed in her eyes. The man looked at the foodstuff sullenly. Hans gave him his sunny grin.

'I'm sorry we had a misunderstanding the first time I came here. But you shouldn't have intefered.'

At that moment the girl came in.

'What are you doing here?' she cried harshly. Then her eyes fell on the things he had brought. She swept them together and flung them at him. 'Take them away. Take them.'

But her mother sprang forward.

'Annette, you're crazy.'

'I won't take his presents.'

'It's our own food that they've stolen from us. Look at the sardines. They're Bordeaux sardines.'

She picked the things up. Hans looked at the girl with a mocking smile in his light blue eyes.

'Annette's your name, is it? A pretty name. Do you grudge your parents a little food? You said you hadn't had cheese for three months. I couldn't get any ham; I did the best I could.'

The farmer's wife took the lump of meat in her hands and pressed it to her bosom. You felt that she could have kissed it. Tears ran down Annette's cheeks.

'The shame of it,' she groaned.

'Oh, come now, there's no shame in a bit of Gruyère and a piece of pork.'

Hans sat down and lit a cigarette. Then he passed the packet over to the old man. The farmer hesitated for a moment, but the temptation was too strong for him; he took one and handed back the packet.

'Keep it,' said Hans. 'I can get plenty more.' He inhaled the smoke and blew a cloud of it from his nostrils. 'Why can't we be friends? What's done can't be undone. War is war, and, well, you know what I mean. I know Annette's an educated girl and I want her to think well of me. I expect we shall be in Soissons for quite a while and I can bring you something now and then to help out. You know, we do all we can to make friends with the townspeople, but they won't let us. They won't even look at us when we pass them in the street. After all, it was an accident, what happened that time I came here with Willi. You needn't be afraid of me. I'll respect Annette as if she was my own sister.'

'Why do you want to come here? Why can't you leave us alone?' asked Annette.

He really didn't know. He didn't like to say that he wanted a little human friendship. The silent hostility that surrounded them all at Soissons got on his nerves so that sometimes he wanted to go up to a Frenchman who looked at him as if he wasn't there and knock him down, and sometimes it affected him so that he was almost inclined to cry. It would be nice if he had some place to go where he was welcome. He spoke the truth when he said he had no desire for Annette. She wasn't the sort of woman he fancied. He liked women to be tall and full-breasted, blue-eyed, and fair-haired like himself; he liked them to be strong and hefty and well-covered. That refinement which he couldn't account for, that thin fine nose and those dark eyes, the long pale face – there was something intimidating about the girl, so that if he hadn't been excited by the great victories of the German armies, if he hadn't been so tired and yet so elated, if he hadn't drunk all that wine on an empty stomach, it would never have crossed his mind that he could have anything to do with her.

For a fortnight after that Hans couldn't get away. He'd left the food at the farm and he had no doubt that the old people had wolfed it. He wondered if Annette had eaten it too; he wouldn't have been surprised to discover that the moment his back was turned she had set to with the others. These French people, they couldn't resist getting something for nothing. They were weak and decadent. She hated him, yes, God, how she hated him, but pork was pork, and cheese was cheese. He thought of her quite a lot. It tantalized him that she should have such a loathing for him. He was used to being liked by women. It would be funny if one of these days she fell in love with him. He'd been her first lover and he'd heard the students at Munich over their beer saying that it was her first lover a woman loved, after that it was love. When he'd set his mind on getting a girl he'd never failed yet. Hans laughed to himself and a sly look came into his eyes.

At last he got his chance to go to the farm. He got hold of cheese and butter, sugar, a tin of sausages, and some coffee, and set off on his motor-cycle. But that time he didn't see Annette. She and her father were at work in the fields. The old woman was in the yard and her face lit up when she saw the parcel he was bringing. She led him into the kitchen. Her hands trembled a little as she untied the string and when she saw what he had brought her eyes filled with tears.

'You're very good,' she said.

'May I sit down?' he asked politely.

'Of course.' She looked out of the window and Hans guessed that she wanted to make sure that Annette was not coming. 'Can I offer you a glass of wine.'

'I'd be glad of it.'

He was sharp enough to see that her greed for food had made her, if not friendly to him, at least willing to come to terms with him. That look out of the window made them almost fellow conspirators.

'Did you like the pork?' he asked.

'It was a treat.'

'I'll try to bring you some more next time I come. Did Annette like it?'

'She wouldn't touch a thing you'd left. She said she'd rather starve.'

'Silly.'

'That's what I said to her. As long as the food is there, I said, there's nothing to be gained by not eating it.'

They chatted quite amicably while Hans sipped his wine. He discovered that she was called Madame Périer. He asked her whether there were any other members of the family. She sighed. No, they'd had a son, but he'd been mobilized at the beginning of the war and he'd died. He hadn't been killed, he'd got pneumonia and died in the hospital at Nancy.

'I'm sorry,' said Hans.

'Perhaps he's better off than if he'd lived. He was like Annette in many ways. He could never have borne the shame of defeat.' She sighed again. 'Oh, my poor friend, we've been betrayed.'

'Why did you want to fight for the Poles? What were they to you?'

'You're right. If we had let your Hitler take Poland he would have left us alone.'

When Hans got up to go he said he would come again soon
'I shan't forget the pork.'

Then Hans had a lucky break; he was given a job that took him twice a week to a town in the vicinity so that he was able to get to the farm much oftener. He took care never to come without bringing something. But he made no headway with Annette. Seeking to ingratiate himself with her, he used the simple wiles that he had discovered went down with women; but they only excited her derision. Thin-lipped and hard, she looked at him as though he were dirt. On more than one occasion she made him so angry that we would have liked to take her by the shoulders and shake the life out of her. Once he found her alone, and when she got up to go he barred her passage.

'Stop where you are. I want to talk to you.'

'Talk. I am a woman and defenceless.'

'What I want to say is this: for all I know I may be here for a long time. Things aren't going to get easier for you French, they're going to get harder. I can be useful to you. Why don't you be reasonable like your father and mother?'

It was true that old Périer had come round. You couldn't say that he was cordial, he was indeed cold and gruff, but he was civil. He had even asked Hans to bring him some tobacco, and when he wouldn't accept payment for it had thanked him. He was pleased to hear the news of Soissons and grabbed the paper that Hans brought him. Hans, a farmer's son, could talk about the farm as one who knew. It was a good farm, not too big and not too small, well watered, for a sizable brook ran through it, and well wooded, with arable land and pasture. Hans listened with understanding sympathy when the old man bewailed himself because without labour, without fertilizers, his stock taken from him, it was all going to rack and ruin.

'You ask me why I can't be reasonable like my father and mother,' said Annette.

She pulled her dress tight and showed herself to him. He couldn't believe his eyes. What he saw caused such a convulsion in his soul as he had never known. The blood rushed to his cheeks.

'You're pregnant.'

She sank back on her chair and leaning her head on her hands began to weep as though her heart would break.

'The shame of it. The shame.'

He sprang towards her to take her in his arms.

'My sweet,' he cried.

But she sprang to her feet and pushed him away.

'Don't touch me. Go away. Go away. Haven't you done me enough harm already?'

She flung out of the room. He waited by himself for a few minutes. He was bewildered. His thoughts in a whirl, he rode slowly back to Soissons, and when he went to bed he couldn't get to sleep for hours. He could think of nothing but Annette and her swollen body. She had been unbearably pathetic as she sat there at the table crying her eyes out. It was his child she bore in her womb. He began to feel drowsy, and then with a start he was once more wide awake, for suddenly it came to him, it came to him with the shattering suddenness of gun-fire: he was in love with her. It was such a surprise, such a shock that he couldn't cope with it. Of course he'd thought of her a lot, but never in that way, he'd thought it would be a great joke if he made her fall in love with him, it would be a triumph if the time came when she offered what he had taken by force; but not for a moment had it occurred to him that she was anything to him but a woman like another. She wasn't his type. She wasn't very pretty. There was nothing to her. Why should he have all of a sudden this funny feeling for her? It wasn't a pleasant feeling either, it was a pain. But he knew what it was all right; it was love, and it made him feel happier than he had ever felt in his life. He wanted to take her in his arms, he wanted to pet her, he wanted to kiss those tear-stained eyes of hers. He didn't desire her, he thought, as a man desires a woman, he wanted to comfort her, he wanted her to smile at him – strange, he had never seen her smile, he wanted to see her eyes – fine eyes they were, beautiful eyes – soft with tenderness.

For three days he could not leave Soissons and for three days, three days and three nights, he thought of Annette and the child she would bear. Then he was able to go to the farm. He wanted to see Madame Périer by herself, and luck was with him, for he met her on the road some way from the house. She had been gathering sticks in the wood and was going home with a great bundle on her back. He stopped his motor-cycle. He knew that the friendliness she showed him was due only to the provisions he brought with him, but he didn't care; it was enough that she was mannerly, and that she was prepared to be so as long as she could get something out of him. He told her he wanted to talk to her and asked her to put her bundle down. She did as he bade. It was a grey, cloudy day, but not cold.

'I know about Annette,' he said.

She started.

'How did you find out? She was set on your not knowing.'

'She told me.'

'That was a pretty job of work you did that evening.'

'I didn't know. Why didn't you tell me sooner?'

She began to talk, not bitterly, not blaming him even, but as though it were a misfortune of nature, like a cow dying in giving birth to a calf or a sharp spring frost nipping the fruit trees and ruining the crop, a misfortune that human kind must accept with resignation and humility. After that dreadful night Annette had been in bed for days with a high fever. They thought she was going out of her mind. She would scream for hours on end. There were no doctors to be got. The village doctor had been called to the colours. Even in Soissons there were only two doctors left, old men both of them, and how could they get to the farm even if it had been possible to send for them? They weren't allowed to leave the town. Even when the fever went down Annette was too ill to leave her bed, and when she got up she was so weak, so pale, it was pitiful. The shock had been terrible, and when a month went by, and another month, without her being unwell she paid no attention. She had always been irregular. It was Madame Périer who first suspected that something was wrong. She questioned Annette. They were terrified, both of them, but they weren't certain and they said nothing to Périer. When the third month came it was impossible to doubt any longer. Annette was pregnant.

They had an old Citroën in which before the war Madame Périer had taken the farm produce into the market at Soissons two mornings a week, but since the German occupation they had had nothing to sell that made the journey worth while. Petrol was almost unobtainable. But now they got it out and drove into town. The only cars to be seen were the military cars of the Germans. German soldiers lounged about. There were German signs in the streets, and on public buildings proclamations in French signed by the Officer Commanding. Many shops were closed. They went to the old doctor they knew, and he confirmed their suspicions. But he was a devout Catholic and would not help them. When they wept he shrugged his shoulders.

'You're not the only one,' he said. '*Il faut souffrir.*'

They knew about the other doctor too and went to see him. They rang the bell and for a long time no one answered. At last the door was opened by a sad-faced woman in black, but when they asked to see the doctor she began to cry. He had been arrested by the Germans because he was a freemason, and was held as a hostage. A bomb had exploded in a café frequented by German officers and two had been killed and several wounded. If the guilty were not handed over before a certain date he was to be shot. The woman seemed kindly and Madame Périer told her of their trouble.

'The brutes,' she said. She looked at Annette with compassion. 'My poor child.'

She gave them the address of a midwife in the town, and told them to say that they had come from her. The midwife gave them some medicine. It made Annette so ill that she thought she was going to die, but it had no further effect. Annette was still pregnant.

That was the story that Madame Périer told Hans. For a while he was silent.

'It's Sunday tomorrow,' he said then. 'I shall have nothing to do. I'll come and we'll talk. I'll bring something nice.'

'We have no needles. Can you bring some?'

'I'll try.'

She hoisted the bundle of sticks on her back and trudged down the road. Hans went back to Soissons. He dared not use his motor-cycle, so next day he hired a push-bike. He tied his parcel of food on the carrier. It was a larger parcel than usual because he had put a bottle of champagne into it. He got to the farm when the gathering darkness made it certain that they would all be home from work. It was warm and cosy in the kitchen when he walked in. Madame Périer was cooking and her husband was reading a *Paris-Soir*. Annette was darning stockings.

'Look, I've brought you some needles,' he said, as he undid his parcel. 'And here's some material for you, Annette.'

'I don't want it.'

'Don't you?' he grinned. 'You'll have to begin making things for the baby.'

'That's true, Annette,' said her mother, 'and we have nothing.' Annette did not look up from her sewing. Madame Périer's greedy eyes ran over the contents of the parcel. 'A bottle of champagne.'

Hans chuckled.

'I'll tell you what that's for presently. I've had an idea.' He hesitated for a moment, then drew up a chair and sat down facing Annette. 'I don't know quite how to begin. I'm sorry for what I did that night, Annette. It wasn't my fault, it was the circumstances. Can't you forgive me?'

She threw him a look of hatred.

'Never. Why don't you leave me alone? Isn't it enough that you've ruined my life?'

'Well, that's just it. Perhaps I haven't. When I knew you were going to have a baby it had a funny effect on me. It's all different now. It's made me so proud.'

'Proud?' she flung at him viciously.

'I want you to have the baby, Annette. I'm glad you couldn't get rid of it.'

'How dare you say that?'

'But listen to me. I've been thinking of nothing else since I knew. The war will be over in six months. We shall bring the English to their knees in the spring. They haven't got a chance. And then I shall be demobilized and I'll marry you.'

'You? Why?'

He blushed under his tan. He could not bring himself to say it in French, so he said it in German. He knew she understood it.

'*Ich liebe dich.*'

'What does he say?' asked Madame Périer.

'He says he loves me.'

Annette threw back her head and broke into a peal of harsh laughter. She laughed louder and louder and she couldn't stop and tears streamed from her eyes. Madame Périer slapped her sharply on both cheeks.

'Don't pay any attention,' she said to Hans. 'It's hysteria. Her condition, you know.'

Annette gasped. She gained control over herself.

'I brought the bottle of champagne to celebrate our engagement,' said Hans.

'That's the bitterest thing of all,' said Annette, 'that we were beaten by fools, by such fools.'

Hans went on speaking in German.

'I didn't know I loved you till that day when I found out that you were going to have a baby. It came like a clap of thunder, but I think I've loved you all the time.'

'What does he say?' asked Madame Périer.

'Nothing of importance.'

He fell back into French. He wanted Annette's parents to hear what he had to say.

'I'd marry you now, only they wouldn't let me. And don't think I'm nothing at all. My father's well-to-do and we're well thought of in our commune. I'm the eldest son and you'd want for nothing.'

'Are you a Catholic?' asked Madame Périer.

'Yes, I'm a Catholic.'

'That's something.'

'It's pretty, the country where we live and the soil's good. There's not better farming land between Munich and Innsbruck, and it's our own. My grandfather bought it after the war of '70. And we've got a car and a radio, and we're on the telephone.'

Annette turned to her father.

'He has all the tact in the world, this gentleman,' she cried ironically. She eyed Hans. 'It would be a nice position for me, the foreigner from the conquered country with a child born out of wedlock. It offers me a chance of happiness, doesn't it? A fine chance.'

Périer, a man of few words, spoke for the first time.

'No, I don't deny that it's a fine gesture you're making. I went through the last war and we all did things we wouldn't have done in peace time. Human nature is human nature. But now that our son is dead, Annette is all we have. We can't let her go.'

'I thought you might feel that way,' said Hans, 'and I've got my answer to that. I'll stay here.'

Annette gave him a quick look.

'What do you mean?' asked Madame Périer.

'I've got another brother. He can stay and help my father. I like this country. With energy and initiative a man could make a good thing of your farm. When the war's over a lot of Germans will be settling here. It's well known that you haven't got enough men in France to work the land you've got. A fellow gave us a lecture the other day at Soissons. He said that a third of the farms were left uncultivated because there aren't the men to work them.'

Périer and his wife exchanged glances and Annette saw that they were wavering. That was what they'd wanted since their son had died, a son-in-law who was strong and hefty and could take over when they grew too old to do more than potter about.

'That changes the case,' said Madame Périer. 'It's a proposition to consider.'

'Hold your tongue,' cried Annette roughly. She leant forward and fixed her burning eyes on the German. 'I'm engaged to a teacher who worked in the boys' school in the town where I taught, we were to be married after the war. He's not strong and big like you, or handsome; he's small and frail. His only beauty is the intelligence that shines in his face, his only strength is the greatness of his soul. He's not a barbarian, he's civilized; he has a thousand years of civilization behind him. I love him. I love him with all my heart and soul.'

Han's face grew sullen. It had never occurred to him that Annette might care for anyone else.

'Where is he now?'

'Where do you suppose he is? In Germany. A prisoner and starving. While you eat the fat of our land. How many times have I got to tell you that I hate you? You ask me to forgive you. Never. You want to make reparation. You fool.' She threw her head back and there was a look of intolerable anguish on her face. 'Ruined. Oh, he'll forgive me. He's tender. But I'm tortured by the thought that one day the suspicion may come to him that perhaps I hadn't been forced – that perhaps I'd given myself to you for butter and cheese and silk stockings. I shouldn't be the only one. And what would our life be with that child between us, your child, a German child? Big like you, and blond like you, and blue-eyed like you. Oh, my God, why do I have to suffer this?'

She got up and went swiftly out of the kitchen. For a minute the three were left in silence. Hans looked ruefully at his bottle of champagne. He sighed and rose to his feet. When he went out Madame Périer accompanied him.

'Did you mean it when you said you would marry her?' she asked him, speaking in a low voice.

'Yes. Every word. I love her.'

'And you wouldn't take her away? You'd stay here and work on the farm?'

'I promise you.'

'Evidently my old man can't last for ever. At home you'd have to share with your brother. Here you'd share with nobody.'

'There's that too.'

'We never were in favour of Annette marrying that teacher, but our son was alive then and he said, if she wants to marry him, why shouldn't she? Annette was crazy about him. But now that our son's dead, poor boy, it's different. Even if she wanted to, how could she work the farm alone?'

'It would be a shame if it was sold. I know how one feels about one's own land.'

They had reached the road. She took his hand and gave it a little squeeze.

'Come again soon.'

Hans knew that she was on his side. It was a comfort to him to think that as he rode back to Soissons. It was a bother that Annette was in love with somebody else. Fortunately he was a prisoner; long before he was likely to be released the baby would be born. That might change her; you could never tell with a woman. Why, in his village there'd been a woman who was so much in love with her husband that it had been a joke, and then she had a baby and after that she couldn't bear the sight of him. Well, why shouldn't the contrary happen too? And now that he'd offered to marry her she must see that he was a decent sort of fellow. God, how pathetic she'd looked with her head flung back, and how well she'd spoken! What language! An actress on the stage couldn't have expressed herself better, and yet it had all sounded so natural. You had to admit that, these French people knew how to talk. Oh, she was clever. Even when she lashed him with that bitter tongue it was a joy to listen to her. He hadn't had a bad education himself, but he couldn't hold a candle to her. Culture, that's what she had.

'I'm a donkey,' he said out loud as he rode along. She'd said he was big and strong and handsome. Would she have said that if it hadn't meant something to her? And she'd talked of the baby having fair hair and blue eyes like his own. If that didn't mean that his colouring had made an impression on her he was a Dutchman. He chuckled. 'Give me time. Patience, and let nature go to work.'

The weeks went by. The C.O. at Soissons was an elderly, easy-going fellow and in view of what the spring had in store for them he was content not to drive his men too hard. The German papers told them that England was being wrecked by the Luftwaffe and the people were in a panic. Submarines were sinking British ships by the score and the country was starving. Revolution was imminent. Before summer it would be all over and the Germans would be masters of the world. Hans wrote home and told his parents that he was going to marry a French girl and with her a fine farm. He proposed that his brother should borrow money to buy him out of his share of the family property so that he could increase the size of his own holding while land, owing to the war and the exchange, could still be bought for a song. He went over the farm with Périer. The old man listened quietly when Hans told him his ideas: the farm would have to be restocked and as a German he would have a pull; the motor tractor was old, he would get a fine new one from Germany, and a motor plough. To make a farm pay you had to take advantage of modern inventions. Madame Périer told him afterwards that her husband had said he wasn't a bad lad and seemed to know a lot. She was very friendly with him now and insisted that he should share their midday meal with them on Sundays. She translated his name into French and called him Jean. He was always ready to give a hand, and as time went on and Annette could do less and less it was useful to have a man about who didn't mind doing a job of work.

Annette remained fiercely hostile. She never spoke to him except to answer his direct questions and as soon as it was possible went to her own room. When it was so cold that she couldn't stay there she sat by the side of the kitchen stove, sewing or reading, and took no more notice of him than if he hadn't been there. She was in radiant health. There was colour in her cheeks and in Hans's eyes she was beautiful. Her approaching maternity had given her a strange dignity and he was filled with exultation when he gazed upon her. Then one day when he was on his way to the farm he saw Madame Périer in the road waving to him to stop. He put his brakes on hard.

'I've been waiting for an hour. I thought you'd never come. You must go back. Pierre is dead.'

'Who's Pierre?'

'Pierre Gavin. The teacher Annette was going to marry.'

Hans's heart leapt. What luck! Now he'd have his chance.

'Is she upset?'

'She's not crying. When I tried to say something she bit my head off. If she saw you today she's capable of sticking a knife into you.'

'It's not my fault if he died. How did you hear?'

'A prisoner, a friend of his, escaped through Switzerland and he wrote to Annette. We got the letter this morning. There was a mutiny in the camp because they weren't given enough to eat, and the ringleaders were shot. Pierre was one of them.'

Hans was silent. He could only think it served the man right. What did they think that a prison camp was – the Ritz?

'Give her time to get over the shock,' said Madame Périer. 'When she's calmer I'll talk to her. I'll write you a letter when you can come again.'

'All right. You will help me, won't you?'

'You can be sure of that. My husband and I, we're agreed. We talked it over and we came to the conclusion that the only thing to do was to accept the situation. He's no fool, my husband, and he says the best chance for France now is to collaborate. And take it all in all I don't dislike you. I shouldn't wonder if you didn't make Annette a better husband than that teacher. And with the baby coming and all.'

'I want it to be a boy,' said Hans.

'It's going to be a boy. I know for certain. I've seen it in the coffee grounds and I've put out the cards. The answer is a boy every time.'

'I almost forgot, here are some papers for you,' said Hans, as he turned his cycle and prepared to mount.

He handed her three numbers of *Paris-Soir*. Old Périer read every evening. He read that the French must be realistic and accept the new order that Hitler was going to create in Europe. He read that the German submarines were sweeping the sea. He read that the General Staff had organized to the last detail the campaign that would bring England to her knees and that the Americans were too unprepared, too soft and too divided to come to her help. He read that France must take the heaven-sent opportunity and by loyal collaboration with the Reich regain her honoured position in the new Europe. And it wasn't Germans who wrote it all; it was Frenchmen. He nodded his head with approval when he read that the plutocrats and the Jews would be destroyed and the poor man in France would at last come into his own. They were quite right, the clever fellows who said that France was essentially an agricultural country and its backbone was its industrious farmers. Good sense, that was.

One evening, when they were finishing their supper, ten days after the news had come of Pierre Gavin's death, Madame Périer by arrangement with her husband, said to Annette:

'I wrote a letter to Hans a few days ago telling him to come here tomorrow.'

'Thank you for the warning. I shall stay in my room.'

'Oh, come, daughter, the time has passed for foolishness. You must be realistic. Pierre is dead. Hans loves you and wants to marry you. He's a fine-looking fellow. Any girl would be proud of him as a husband. How can we restock the farm without his help? He's going to buy a tractor and a plough with his own money. You must let bygones be bygones.'

'You're wasting your breath, Mother. I earned my living before. I can earn my living again. I hate him. I hate his vanity and his arrogance. I could kill him: his death wouldn't satisfy me. I should like to torture him as he's tortured me. I think I should die happy if I could find a way to wound him as he's wounded me.'

'You're being very silly, my poor child.'

'Your mother's right, my girl,' said Périer. 'We've been defeated and we must accept the consequences. We've got to make the best arrangement we can with the conquerors. We're cleverer than they are and if we play our cards well we shall come out on top. France was rotten. It's the Jews and the plutocrats who ruined the country. Read the papers and you'll see for yourself!'

'Do you think I believe a word in that paper? Why do you think he brings it to you except that it's sold to the Germans? The men who write in it – traitors, traitors. Oh God, may I live to see them torn to pieces by the mob. Bought, bought every one of them – bought with German money. The swine.'

Madame Périer was getting exasperated.

'What have you got against the boy? He took you by force – yes. he was drunk at the time. It's not the first time that's happened to a woman and it won't be the last time. He hit your father and he bled like a pig, but does your father bear him malice?'

'It was an unpleasant incident, but I've forgotten it,' said Périer.

Annette burst into harsh laughter.

'You should have been a priest. You forgive injuries with a spirit truly Christian.'

'And what is there wrong about that?' asked Madame Périer

angrily. 'Hasn't he done everything he could to make amends? Where would your father have got his tobacco all these months if it hadn't been for him? If we haven't gone hungry it's owing to him.'

'If you'd had any pride, if you'd had any sense of decency, you'd have thrown his presents in his face.'

'You've profited by them, haven't you?'

'Never. Never.'

'It's a lie and you know it. You've refused to eat the cheese he brought and the butter and the sardines. But the soup you've eaten, you know I put the meat in it that he brought; and the salad you ate tonight, if you didn't have to eat it dry, it's because he brought me oil.'

Annette sighed deeply. She passed her hand over her eyes.'

' know. I tried not to, I couldn't help myself, I was so hungry. Yes, I knew his meat went into the soup and I ate it. I knew the salad was made with his oil. I wanted to refuse it; I had such a longing for it, it wasn't I that ate it, it was a ravenous beast within me.'

'That's neither here nor there. You ate it.'

'With shame. With despair. They broke our strength first with their tanks and their planes, and now when we're defenceless they're breaking our spirit by starving us.'

'You get nowhere by being theatrical, my girl. For an educated woman you have really no sense. Forget the past and give a father to your child, to say nothing of a good workman for the farm who'll be worth two hired men. That is sense.'

Annette shrugged her shoulders wearily and they lapsed into silence. Next day Hans came. Annette gave him a sullen look, but neither spoke nor moved. Hans smiled.

'Thank you for not running away,' he said.

'My parents asked you to come and they've gone down to the village. It suits me because I want to have a definite talk with you. Sit down.'

He took off his coat and his helmet and drew a chair to the table.

'My parents want me to marry you. You've been clever; with your presents, with your promises, you've got round them. They believe all they read in the papers you bring them. I want to tell you that I will never marry you. I wouldn't have thought it possible that I could hate a human being as I hate you.'

'Let me speak in German. You understand enough to know what I'm saying.'

'I ought to. I taught it. For two years I was governess to two little girls in Stuttgart.'

He broke into German, but she went on speaking French.

It's not only that I love you, I admire you, I admire your distinction and your grace. There's something about you I don't understand. I respect you. Oh, I can see that you don't want to marry me now even it it were possible. But Pierre is dead.'

'Don't speak of him,' she cried violently. 'That would be the last straw.'

'I only want to tell you that for your sake I'm sorry he died.'

'Shot in cold blood by his German jailers.'

'Perhaps in time you'll grieve for him less. You know, when someone you love dies, you think you'll never get over it, but you do. Won't it be better then to have a father for your child?'

'Even if there were nothing else do you think I could ever forget that you are a German and I'm a Frechwoman? If you weren't as stupid as only a German can be you'd see that that child must be a reproach to me as long as I live. Do you think I have no friends? How could I ever look them in the face with the child I had with a German soldier? There's only one thing I ask you; leave me alone with my disgrace. Go, go – for God's sake go and never come again.'

'But he's my child too. I want him.'

'You?' she cried in astonishment. 'What can a by-blow that you got in a moment of savage drunkenness mean to you?'

'You don't understand. I'm so proud and so happy. It was when I knew you were going to have a baby that I knew I loved you. At first I couldn't believe it; it was such a surprise to me. Don't you see what I mean? That child that's going to be born means everything in the world to me. Oh, I don't know how to put it; it's put feelings in my heart that I don't understand myself.'

She looked at him intently and there was a strange gleam in her eyes. You would have said it was a look of triumph. She gave a short laugh.

'I don't know whether I more loathe the brutality of you Germans or despise your sentimentality.'

He seemed not to have heard what she said.

'I think of him all the time.'

'You've made up your mind it'll be a boy?'

'I know it'll be a boy. I want to hold him in my arms and I want to teach him to walk. And then when he grows older I'll teach him all I know. I'll teach him to ride and I'll teach him to shoot. Are there fish in your brook? I'll teach him to fish. I'm going to be the proudest father in the world.'

She stared at him with hard, hard eyes. Her face was set and stern. An idea, a terrible idea was forming itself in her mind. He gave her a disarming smile.

'Perhaps when you see how much I love our boy, you'll come to love me too. I'll make you a good husband, my pretty.'

She said nothing. She merely kept on gazing at him sullenly.

'Haven't you one kind word for me?' he said.

She flushed. She clasped her hands tightly together.

'Others may despise me. I will never do anything that can make me despise myself. You are my enemy and you will always be my enemy. I only live to see the deliverance of France. It'll come, perhaps not next year or the year after, perhaps not for thirty years, but it'll come. The rest of them can do what they like, I will never come to terms with the invaders of my country. I hate you and I hate this child that you've given me. Yes, we've been defeated. Before the end comes you'll see that we haven't been conquered. Now go. My mind's made up and nothing on God's earth can change it.'

He was silent for a mintue or two.

'Have you made arrangements for a doctor? I'll pay all the expenses.'

'Do you suppose we want to spread our shame through the whole countryside? My mother will do all that's necessary.'

'But supposing there's an accident?'

'And supposing you mind your own business!'

He sighed and rose to his feet. When he closed the door behind him she watched him walk down the pathway that led to the road. She realized with rage that some of the things he said had aroused in her heart a feeling that she had never felt for him before.

'O God, give me strength,' she cried.

Then, as he walked along, the dog, an old dog they'd had for years, ran up to him barking angrily. He had tried for months to make friends with the dog, but it had never responded to his advances; when he tried to pat it, it backed away growling and showing its teeth. And now as the dog ran towards him, irritably giving way to his feelings of frustration, Hans gave it a savage brutal kick and the dog was flung into the bushes and limped yelping away.

'The beast,' she cried. 'Lies, lies, lies. And I was weak enough to be almost sorry for him.'

There was a looking-glass hanging by the side of the door and she looked at herself in it. She drew herself up and smiled at her reflection. But rather than a smile it was a finished grimace.

It was now March. There was a bustle of activity in the garrison at Soissons. There were inspections and there was intensive training. Rumour was rife. There was no doubt they were going somewhere, but the rank and file could only guess where. Some thought they were being got ready at last for the invasion of England, others were of opinion that they would be sent to the Balkans, and others again talked of the Ukraine. Hans was kept busy. It was not till the second Sunday afternoon that he was able to get out to the farm. It was a cold grey day, with sleet that looked as though it might turn to snow falling in sudden windy flurries. The country was grim and cheerless.

'You!' cried Madame Périer when he went in. 'We thought you were dead.'

'I couldn't come before. We're off any day now. We don't know when.'

'The baby was born this morning. It's a boy.'

Hans's heart gave a great leap in his breast. He hung his arms round the old woman and kissed her on both cheeks.

'A Sunday child, he ought to be lucky. Let's open the bottle of champagne. How's Annette?'

'She's as well as can be expected. She had a very easy time. She began to have pains last night and by five o'clock this morning it was all over.'

Old Périer was smoking his pipe sitting as near the stove as he could get. He smiled quietly at the boy's enthusiasm.

'One's first child, it has an effect on one,' he said.

'He has quite a lot of hair and it's as fair as yours; and blue eyes just like you said he'd have,' said Madame Périer. 'I've never seen a lovelier baby. He'll be just like his papa.'

'Oh, my God, I'm so happy,' cried Hans. 'How beautiful the world is! I want to see Annette.'

'I don't know if she'll see you. I don't want to upset her on account of the milk.'

'No, no, don't upset her on my account. If she doesn't want to see me it doesn't matter. But let me see the baby just for a minute.'

'I'll see what I can do. I'll try to bring it down.'

Madame Périer went out and they heard her heavy tread clumping up the stairs. But in a moment they heard her clattering down again. She burst into the kitchen.

'They're not there. She isn't in her room. The baby's gone.'

Périer and Hans cried out and without thinking what they were doing all three of them scampered upstairs. The harsh light of the winter afternoon cast over the shabby furniture, the iron bed, the cheap wardrobe, the chest of drawers, a dismal squalor. There was no one in the room.

'Where is she?' screamed Madame Périer. She ran into the narrow passage, opening doors, and called the girl's name. 'Annette, Annette. Oh, What madness!'

'Perhaps in the sitting-room.'

They ran downstairs to the unused parlour. An icy air met them as they opened the door. They opened the door of a store-room.

'She's gone out. Something awful has happened.'

'How could she have got out?' asked Hans sick with anxiety.

'Through the front door, you fool.'

Périer went up to it and looked.

'That's right. The bolt's drawn back.'

'Oh, my God, my God, what madness,' cried Madame Périer. 'It'll kill her.'

'We must look for her,' said Hans. Instinctively, because that was the way he always went in and out, he ran back into the kitchen and the others followed him. 'Which way?'

'The brook,' the old woman gasped.

He stopped as though turned to stone with horror. He stared at the old woman aghast.

'I'm frightened,' she cried. 'I'm frightened.'

Hans flung open the door, and as he did so Annette walked in. She had nothing on but her nightdress and a flimsy rayon dressing-gown. It was pink, with pale flowers. She was soaked, and her hair, dishevelled, clung damply to her head and hung down her shoulders in bedraggled wisps. She was deathly white. Madame Périer sprang towards her and took her in her arms.

'Where have you been? Oh, my poor child, you're wet through. What madness!'

But Annette pushed her away. She looked at Hans.

'You've come at the right moment, you.'

'Where's the baby?' cried Madame Périer.

'I had to do it at once. I was afraid if I waited I shouldn't have the courage.'

'Annette, what have you done?'

'I've done what I had to do. I took it down to the brook and held it under water till it was dead.'

Hans gave a great cry, the cry of an animal wounded to death; he covered his face with his hands, and staggering like a drunken man flung out of the door. Annette sank into a chair, and leaning her forehead on her two fists burst into passionate weeping.

Mr Know-All

I WAS PREPARED to dislike Max Kelada even before I knew him. The war had just finished and the passenger traffic in the ocean-going liners was heavy. Accommodation was very hard to get and you had to put up with whatever the agents chose to offer you. You could not hope for a cabin to yourself and I was thankful to be given one in which there were only two berths. But when I was told the name of my companion my heart sank. It suggested closed port-holes and the night air rigidly excluded. It was bad enough to share a cabin for fourteen days with anyone (I was going from San Francisco to Yokohama), but I should have looked upon it with less dismay if my fellow-passenger's name had been Smith or Brown.

When I went on board I found Mr Kelada's luggage already below. I did not like the look of it; there were too many labels on the suitcases, and the wardrobe trunk was too big. He had unpacked his toilet things, and I observed that he was a patron of the excellent Monsieur Coty; for I saw on the washing-stand his scent, his hair-wash, and his brilliantine. Mr Kelada's brushes, ebony with his monogram in gold, would have been all the better for a scrub. I did not at all like Mr Kelada. I made my way into the smoking-room. I called for a pack of cards and began to play patience. I had scarcely started before a man came up to me and asked me if he was right in thinking my name was so-and-so.

'I am Mr Kelada,' he added, with a smile that showed a row of flashing teeth, and sat down.

'Oh, yes, we're sharing a cabin, I think.'

'Bit of luck, I call it. You never know who you're going to be put in with. I was jolly glad when I heard you were English. I'm all for us English sticking together when we're abroad, if you understand what I mean.'

I blinked.

'Are you English?' I asked, perhaps tactlessly.

'Rather. You don't think I look an American, do you? British to the backbone, that's what I am.'

To prove it, Mr Kelada took out of his pocket a passport and airily waved it under my nose.

King George has many strange subjects. Mr Kelada was short and of a sturdy build, clean-shaven and dark-skinned, with a fleshy, hooked nose and very large, lustrous and liquid eyes. His long black hair was sleek and curly. He spoke with a fluency in which there was nothing English and his gestures were exuberant. I felt pretty sure that a closer inspection of that British passport would have betrayed the fact that Mr Kelada was born under a bluer sky than is generally seen in England.

'What will you have?' he asked me.

I looked at him doubtfully. Prohibition was in force and to all appearances the ship was bone-dry. When I am not thirsty I do not know which I dislike more, ginger-ale or lemon-squash. But Mr Kelada flashed an oriental smile at me.

'Whisky and soda or a dry Martini, you have only to say the word.'

From each of his hip-pockets he fished a flask and laid them on the table before me. I chose the Martini, and calling the steward he ordered a tumbler of ice and a couple of glasses.

'A very good cocktail,' I said.

'Well, there are plenty more where that came from, and if you've got any friends on board, you tell them you've got a pal who's got all the liquor in the world.'

Mr Kelada was chatty. He talked of New York and of San Francisco. He discussed plays, pictures, and politics. He was patriotic. The Union Jack is an impressive piece of drapery, but when it is flourished by a gentleman from Alexandria or Beirut, I cannot but feel that it loses somewhat in dignity. Mr Kelada was familiar. I do not wish to put on airs, but I cannot help feeling that it is seemly in a total stranger to put mister before my name when he addresses me. Mr Kelada, doubtless to set me at my ease, used no such formality. I did not like Mr Kelada. I had put aside the cards when he sat down, but now, thinking that for this first occasion our conversation had lasted long enough, I went on with my game.

'The three on the four,' said Mr Kelada.

There is nothing more exasperating when you are playing patience than to be told where to put the card you have turned up before you have had a chance to look for yourself.

'It's coming out, it's coming out,' he cried. 'The ten on the knave.'

With rage and hatred in my heart I finished. Then he seized the pack.

'Do you like card tricks?'

'No, I hate card tricks,' I answered.

'Well, I'll just show you this one.'

He showed me three. Then I said I would go down to the dining-room and get my seat at table.

'Oh, that's all right,' he said. 'I've already taken a seat for you. I thought that as we were in the same state-room we might just as well sit at the same table.'

I did not like Mr Kelada.

I not only shared a cabin with him and ate three meals a day at the same table, but I could not walk round the deck without his joining me. It was impossible to snub him. It never occurred to him that he was not wanted. He was certain that you were as glad to see him as he was to see you. In your own house you might have kicked him downstairs and slammed the door in his face without the suspicion dawning on him that he was not a welcome visitor. He was a good mixer, and in three days knew everyone on board. He ran everything. He managed the sweeps, conducted the auctions, collected money for prizes at the sports, got up quoit and golf matches, organized the concert, and arranged the fancy-dress ball. He was everywhere and always. He was certainly the best-hated man in the ship. We called him Mr Know-All, even to his face. He took it as a compliment. But it was at meal times that he was most intolerable.

For the better part of an hour then he had us at his mercy. He was hearty, jovial, loquacious and argumentative. He knew everything better than anybody else, and it was an affront to his overweening vanity that you should disagree with him. He would not drop a subject, however unimportant, till he had brought you round to his way of thinking. The possibility that he could be mistaken never occurred to him. He was the chap who knew. We sat at the doctor's table. Mr Kelada would certainly have had it all his own way, for the doctor was lazy and I was frigidly indifferent, except for a man called Ramsay who sat there also. He was as dogmatic as Mr Kelada and resented bitterly the Levantine's cocksureness. The discussions they had were acrimonious and interminable.

Ramsay was in the American Consular Service, and was stationed at Kobe. He was a great heavy fellow from the Middle West, with loose fat under a tight skin, and he bulged out of his ready-made clothes. He was on his way back to resume his post, having been on a flying visit to New York to fetch his wife, who had been spending a year at home. Mrs Ramsay was a very pretty little thing, with pleasant manners and a sense of humour. The Consular Service is ill paid, and she was dressed always very simply; but she knew how to wear her clothes. She achieved an effect of quiet distinction. I should not have paid any particular attention to her but that she possessed a quality that may be common enough in women, but nowadays is not obvious in their demeanour. You could not look at her without being struck by her modesty. It shone in her like a flower on a coat.

One evening at dinner the conversation by chance drifted to the subject of pearls. There had been in the papers a good deal of talk about the culture pearls which the cunning Japanese were making, and the doctor remarked that they must inevitably diminish the value of real ones. They were very good already; they would soon be perfect. Mr Kelada, as was his habit, rushed the new topic. He told us all that was to be known about pearls. I do not believe Ramsay knew anything about them at all, but he could not resist the opportunity to have a fling at the Levantine, and in five minutes we were in the middle of a heated argument. I had seen Mr Kelada vehement and voluble before, but never so voluble and vehement as now. At last something that Ramsay said stung him, for he thumped the table and shouted:

'Well, I ought to know what I am talking about. I'm going to Japan just to look into this Japanese pearl business. I'm in the trade and there's not a man in it who won't tell you that what I say about pearls goes. I know all the best pearls in the world, and what I don't know about pearls isn't worth knowing.'

Here was news for us, for Mr Kelada, with all his loquacity, had never told anyone what his business was. We only knew vaguely that he was going to Japan on some commercial errand. He looked round the table triumphantly.

'They'll never be able to get a culture pearl that an expert like me can't tell with half an eye.' He pointed to a chain that Mrs Ramsay wore. 'You take my word for it, Mrs Ramsay, that chain you're wearing will never be worth a cent less than it is now.'

Mrs Ramsay in her modest way flushed a little and slipped the chain inside her dress. Ramsay leaned forward. He gave us all a look and a smile flickered in his eyes.

'That's a pretty chain of Mrs Ramsay's, isn't it?'

'I noticed it at once,' answered Mr Kelada. 'Gee, I said to myself, those are pearls all right.'

'I didn't buy it myself, of course. I'd be interested to know how much you think it cost.'

'Oh, in the trade somewhere round fifteen thousand dollars. But if it was bought on Fifth Avenue I shouldn't be surprised to hear that anything up to thirty thousand was paid for it.'

Ramsay smiled grimly.

'You'll be surprised to hear that Mrs Ramsay bought that string at a department store the day before we left New York, for eighteen dollars.'

Mr Kelada flushed.

'Rot. It's not only real, but it's as fine a string for its size as I've ever seen.'

'Will you bet on it? I'll bet you a hundred dollars it's imitation.'

'Done.'

'Oh, Elmer, you can't bet on a certainty,' said Mrs Ramsay.

She had a little smile on her lips and her tone was gently deprecating.

'Can't I? If I get a chance of easy money like that I should be all sorts of a fool not to take it.'

'But how can it be proved?' she continued. 'It's only my word against Mr Kelada's.'

'Let me look at the chain, and if it's imitation I'll tell you quickly enough. I can afford to lose a hundred dollars,' said Mr Kelada.

'Take it off, dear. Let the gentleman look at it as much as he wants.'

Mrs Ramsay hesitated a moment. She put her hands to the clasp.

'I can't undo it,' she said, 'Mr Kelada will just have to take my word for it.'

I had a sudden suspicion that something unfortunate was about to occur but I could think of nothing to say.

Ramsay jumped up.

'I'll undo it.'

He handed the chain to Mr Kelada. The Levantine took a magnifying glass from his pocket and closely examined it. A smile of triumph spread over his smooth and swarthy face. He handed back the chain. He was about to speak. Suddenly he caught sight of Mrs Ramsay's face. It was so white that she looked as though she were about to faint. She was staring at him with wide and terrified eyes. They held a desperate appeal; it was so clear that I wondered why her husband did not see it.

Mr Kelada stopped with his mouth open. He flushed deeply.

You could almost *see* the effort he was making over himself.

'I was mistaken,' he said. 'It's a very good imitation, but of course as soon as I looked through my glass I saw that it wasn't real. I think eighteen dollars is just about as much as the damned thing's worth.'

He took out his pocket-book and from it a hundred-dollar note. He handed it to Ramsay without a word.

'Perhaps that'll teach you not to be so cocksure another time, my young friend,' said Ramsay as he took the note.

I noticed that Mr Kelada's hands were trembling.

The story spread over the ship as stories do, and he had to put up with a good deal of chaff that evening. It was a fine joke that Mr Know-All had been caught out. But Mrs Ramsay retired to her state-room with a headache.

Next morning I got up and began to shave. Mr Kelada lay on his bed smoking a cigarette. Suddenly there was a small scraping sound and I saw a letter pushed under the door. I opened the door and looked out. There was nobody there. I picked up the letter and saw that it was addressed to Max Kelada. The name was written in block letters. I handed it to him.

'Who's this from?' He opened it. 'Oh!'

He took out of the envelope, not a letter, but a hundred-dollar note. He looked at me and again he reddened. He tore the envelope into little bits and gave them to me.

'Do you mind just throwing them out of the port-hole?'

I did as he asked, and then I looked at him with a smile.

'No one likes being made to look a perfect damned fool,' he said.

'Were the pearls real?'

'If I had a pretty little wife I shouldn't let her spend a year in New York while I stayed at Kobe,' said he.

At that moment I did not entirely dislike Mr Kelada. He reached out for his pocket-book and carefully put in it the hundred-dollar note.

Lord Mountdrago

DR AUDLIN LOOKED at the clock on his desk. It was twenty minutes to six. He was surprised that his patient was late, for Lord Mountdrago prided himself on his punctuality; he had a sententious way of expressing himself which gave the air of an epigram to a commonplace remark, and he was in the habit of saying that punctuality is a compliment you pay to the intelligent and a rebuke you administer to the stupid. Lord Mountdrago's appointment was for five-thirty.

There was in Dr Audlin's appearance nothing to attract attention. He was tall and spare, with narrow shoulders and something of a stoop; his hair was grey and thin; his long, sallow face deeply lined. He was not more than fifty, but he looked older. His eyes, pale-blue and rather large, were weary. When you had been with him for a while you noticed that they moved very little; they remained fixed on your face, but so empty of expression were they that it was no discomfort. They seldom lit up. They gave no clue to his thoughts nor changed with the words he spoke. If you were of an observant turn it might have struck you that he blinked much less often than most of us. His hands were on the large side, with long, tapering fingers; they were soft, but firm, cool but not clammy. You could never have said what Dr Audlin wore unless you had made a point of looking. His clothes were dark. His tie was black. His dress made his sallow lined face paler, and his pale eyes more wan. He gave you the impression of a very sick man.

Dr Audlin was a psycho-analyst. He had adopted the profession by accident and practised it with misgiving. When the war broke out he had not been long qualified and was getting experience at various hospitals; he offered his services to the authorities, and after a time was sent out to France. It was then that he discovered his singular gift. He could allay certain pains by the touch of his cool, firm hands, and by talking to them often induce sleep in men who were suffering from sleeplessness. He spoke slowly. His voice had no particular colour, and its tone did not alter with the words he uttered, but it was musical, soft, and lulling. He told the men that they must rest, that they mustn't worry, that they must sleep; and rest stole into their jaded bones, tranquillity pushed their anxieties away, like a man finding a place for himself on a crowded bench, and slumber fell on their tired eyelids like the light rain of spring upon the fresh-turned earth. Dr Audlin found that by speaking to men with that low, monotonous voice of his, by looking at them with his pale, quiet eyes, by stroking their weary foreheads with his long firm hands, he could soothe their perturbations, resolve the conflicts that distracted them, and banish the phobias that made their lives a torment. Sometimes he effected cures that seemed miraculous. He restored speech to a man who, after being buried under the earth by a bursting shell, had been struck dumb, and he gave back the use of his limbs to another who had been paralysed after a crash in a plane. He could not understand his powers; he was of a sceptical turn, and though they say that in circumstances of this kind the first thing is to believe in yourself, he never quite succeeded in doing that; and it was only the outcome of his activities, patent to the most incredulous observer, that obliged him to admit that he had some faculty, coming from he knew not where, obscure and uncertain, that enabled him to do things for which he could offer no explanation. When the war was over he went to Vienna and studied there, and afterwards to Zürich; and then settled down in London to practise the art he had so strangely acquired. He had been practising now for fifteen years, and had attained, in the speciality he followed, a distinguished reputation. People told one another of the amazing things he had done, and though his fees were high, he had as many patients as he had time to see. Dr Audlin knew that he had achieved some very extraordinary results; he had saved men from suicide, others from the lunatic asylum, he had assuaged griefs that embittered useful lives, he had turned unhappy marriages into happy ones, he had eradicated abnormal instincts and thus delivered not a few from a hateful bondage, he had given health to the sick in spirit; he had done all this, and yet at the back of his mind remained the suspicion that he was little more than a quack.

It went against his grain to exercise a power that he could not understand, and it offended his honesty to trade on the faith of the people he treated when he had no faith in himself. He was rich enough now to live without working, and the work exhausted him; a dozen times he had been on the point of giving up practice. He knew all that Freud and Jung and the rest of them had written. He was not satisfied; he had an intimate conviction that all their theory was hocus-pocus, and yet there the results were, incomprehensible, but manifest. And what had he not seen of human nature during the fifteen years that patients had been coming to his dingy back room in Wimpole Street? The revelations that had been poured into his ears, sometimes only too willingly, sometimes with shame, with reservations, with anger, had long ceased to surprise him. Nothing could shock him any longer. He knew by now that men were liars, he knew how extravagant was their vanity; he knew far worse than that about them; but he knew that it was not for him to judge or to condemn. But year by year as these terrible confidences were imparted to him his face grew a little greyer, its lines a little more marked, and his pale eyes more weary. He seldom laughed, but now and again when for relaxation he read a novel he smiled. Did their authors really think the men and women they wrote of were like that? If they only knew how much more complicated they were, how much more unexpected, what irreconcilable elements coexisted within their souls and what dark and sinister contentions afflicted them!

It was a quarter to six. Of all the strange cases he had been called upon to deal with Dr Audlin could remember none stranger than that of Lord Mountdrago. For one thing the personality of his patient made it singular. Lord Mountdrago was an able and a distinguished man. Appointed Secretary for Foreign Affairs when still under forty, now after three years in office he has seen his policy prevail. It was generally acknowledged that he was the ablest politician in the Conservative Party and only the fact that his father was a peer, on whose death he would no longer be able to sit in the House of Commons, made it impossible for him to aim at the premiership. But if in these democratic times it is out of the question for a Prime Minister of England to be in the House of Lords, there was nothing to prevent Lord Mountdrago from continuing to be Secretary for Foreign Affairs in successive Conservative administrations and so for long directing the foreign policy of his country.

Lord Mountdrago had many good qualities. He had intelligence and industry. He was widely travelled, and spoke several languages fluently. From early youth he had specialized in foreign affairs, and had conscientiously made himself acquainted with the political and economic circumstances of other countries. He had courage, insight, and determination. He was a good speaker, both on the platform and in the House, clear, precise, and often witty. He was a brilliant debater and his gift of repartee was celebrated. He had a fine presence: he was a tall, handsome man, rather bald and somewhat too stout, but this gave him solidity and an air of maturity that were of service to him. As a young man he had been something of an athlete and had rowed in the Oxford boat, and he was known to be one of the best shots in England. At twenty-four he had married a girl of eighteen whose father was a duke and her mother a great American heiress, so that she had both position and wealth, and by her he had had two sons. For several years they had lived privately apart, but in public united, so that appearances were saved, and no other attachment on either side had given the gossips occasion to whisper. Lord Mountdrago indeed was too ambitious, too hard-working, and it must be added too patriotic, to be tempted by any pleasures that might interfere with his career. He had, in short, a great deal to make him a popular and successful figure. He had unfortunately great defects.

He was a fearful snob. You would not have been surprised at this if his father had been the first holder of the title. That the son of an ennobled lawyer, a manufacturer, or a distiller should attach an inordinate importance to his rank is understandable. The earldom held by Lord Mountdrago's father was created by Charles II, and the barony held by the first Earl dated from the Wars of the Roses. For three hundred years the successive holders of the title had allied themselves with the noblest families of England. But Lord Mountdrago was as conscious of his birth as a *nouveau riche* is conscious of his money. He never missed an opportunity of impressing it upon others. He had beautiful manners when he chose to display them, but this he did only with people whom he regarded as his equals. He was coldly insolent to those whom he looked upon as his social inferiors. He was rude to his servants and insulting to his secretaries. The subordinate officials in the government offices to which he had been successively attached feared and hated him. His arrogance was horrible. He knew that he was a great deal cleverer than most of the persons he had to do with, and never hesitated to apprise them of the fact. He had no patience with the infirmities of human nature. He felt himself born to command and was irritated with people who expected him to listen to their arguments or wished to hear the reasons for his decisions. He was immeasurably selfish. He looked upon any service that was rendered him as a right due to his rank and intelligence and therefore deserving of no gratitude. It never entered his head that he was called upon to do anything for others. He had many enemies: he despised them. He knew no one who merited his assistance, his sympathy, or his compassion. He had no friends. He was distrusted by his chiefs, because they doubted his loyalty; he was unpopular with his party, because he was over-bearing and discourteous; and yet his merit was so great, his patriotism so evident, his intelligence so solid, and his management of affairs so brilliant that they had to put up with him. And what made it possible to do this was that on occasion he could be enchanting: when he was with persons whom he considered his equals, or whom he wished to captivate, in the company of foreign dignitaries or women of distinction, he could be gay, witty, and debonair; his manners then reminded you that in his veins ran the same blood as had run in the veins of Lord Chesterfield; he could tell a story with point, he could be natural, sensible, and even profound. You were surprised at the extent of his knowledge and the sensitiveness of his taste. You thought him the best company in the world; you forgot that he had insulted you the day before and was quite capable of cutting you dead the next.

Lord Mountdrago almost failed to become Dr Audlin's patient. A secretary rang up the doctor and told him that his lordship, wishing to consult him, would be glad if he would come to his house at ten o'clock on the following morning. Dr Audlin answered that he was unable to go to Lord Mountdrago's house, but would be pleased to give him an appointment at his consulting-room at five o'clock on the next day but one. The secretary took the message and presently rang back to say that Lord Mountdrago insisted on seeing Dr Audlin in his own house and the doctor could fix his own fee. Dr Audlin replied that he only saw patients in his consulting-room and expressed his regret that unless Lord Mountdrago was prepared to come to him he could not give him his attention. In a quarter of an hour a brief message was delivered to him that his lordship would come not next day but one, but next day, at five.

When Lord Mountdrago was then shown in he did not come forward, but stood at the door and insolently looked the doctor up and down. Dr Audlin perceived that he was in a rage; he gazed at him, silently, with still eyes. He saw a big heavy man, with greying hair, receding on the forehead so that it gave nobility to his brow, a puffy face with bold regular features and an expression of haughtiness. He had somewhat the look of one of the Bourbon sovereigns of the eighteenth century.

'It seems that it is as difficult to see you as a Prime Minister, Dr Audlin. I'm an extremely busy man.'

'Won't you sit down?' said the doctor.

His face showed no sign that Lord Mountdrago's speech in any way affected him. Dr Audlin sat in his chair at the desk Lord Mountdrago still stood and his frown darkened.

'I think I should tell you that I am His Majesty's Secretary for Foreign Affairs,' he said acidly.

'Won't you sit down?' the doctor repeated.

Lord Mountdrago made a gesture, which might have suggested that he was about to turn on his heel and stalk out of the room; but if that was his intention he apparently thought better of it. He seated himself. Dr Audlin opened a large book and took up his pen. He wrote without looking at his patient.

'How old are you?'

'Forty-two.'

'Are you married?'

'Yes.'

'How long have you been married?'

'Eighteen years.'

'Have you any children?'

'I have two sons.'

Dr Audlin noted down the facts as Lord Mountdrago abruptly answered his questions. Then he leaned back in his chair and looked at him. He did not speak; he just looked, gravely, with pale eyes that did not move.

'Why have you come to see me?' he asked at length.

'I've heard about you. Lady Canute is a patient of yours, I understand. She tells me you've done her a certain amount of good.'

Dr Audlin did not reply. His eyes remained fixed on the other's face, but they were so empty of expression that you might have thought he did not even see him.

'I can't do miracles,' he said at length. Not a smile, but the shadow of a smile flickered in his eyes. 'The Royal College of Physicians would not approve of it if I did.'

Lord Mountdrago gave a brief chuckle. It seemed to lessen his hostility. He spoke more amiably.

'You have a very remarkable reputation. People seem to believe in you.'

'Why have you come to me?' repeated Dr Audlin.

Now it was Lord Mountdrago's turn to be silent. It looked as though he found it hard to answer. Dr Audlin waited. At last Lord Mountdrago seemed to make an effort. He spoke.

'I'm in perfect health. Just as a matter of routine I had myself examined by my own doctor the other day. Sir Augustus Fitzherbert, I dare say you've heard of him, and he tells me I have the physique of a man of thirty. I work hard, but I'm never tired, and I enjoy my work. I smoke very little and I'm an extremely moderate drinker. I take a sufficiency of exercise and I lead a regular life. I am a perfectly sound, normal, healthy man. I quite expect you to think it very silly and childish of me to consult you.'

Dr Audlin saw that he must help him.

'I don't know if I can do anything to help you. I'll try. You're distressed?'

Lord Mountdrago frowned.

'The work that I'm engaged in is important. The decisions I am called upon to make can easily affect the welfare of the country and even the peace of the world. It is essential that my judgement should be balanced and my brain clear. I look upon it as my duty to eliminate any cause of worry that may interfere with my usefulness.'

Dr Audlin had never taken his eyes off him. He saw a great deal. He saw behind his patient's pompous manner and arrogant pride an anxiety that he could not dispel.

'I asked you to be good enough to come here because I know by experience that it's easier for someone to speak openly in the dingy surroundings of a doctor's consulting-room than in his accustomed environment.'

'They're certainly dingy,' said Lord Mountdrago acidly. He paused. It was evident that this man who had so much self-assurance, so quick and decided a mind that he was never at a loss, at this moment was embarrassed. He smiled in order to show the doctor that he was at his ease, but his eyes betrayed his disquiet. When he spoke again it was with unnatural heartiness.

'The whole thing's so trivial that I can hardly bring myself to bother you with it. I'm afraid you'll just tell me not to be a fool and waste your valuable time.'

'Even things that seem very trivial may have their importance. They can be a symptom of a deep-seated derangement. And my time is entirely at your disposal.'

Dr Audlin's voice was low and grave. The monotone in which he spoke was strangely soothing. Lord Mountdrago at length made up his mind to be frank.

'The fact is I've been having some very tiresome dreams lately. I know it's silly to pay any attention to them, but – well, the honest truth is that I'm afraid they've got on my nerves.'

'Can you describe any of them to me?'

Lord Mountdrago smiled, but the smile that tried to be careless was only rueful.

'They're so idiotic, I can hardly bring myself to narrate them.'

'Never mind.'

'Well, the first I had was about a month ago. I dreamt that I was at a party at Connemara House. It was an official party. The King and Queen were to be there and of course decorations were worn. I was wearing my ribbon and my star. I went into a sort of cloakroom they have to take off my coat. There was a little man there called Owen Griffiths, who's a Welsh Member of Parliament, and to tell you the truth, I was surprised to see him. He's very common, and I said to myself: "Really, Lydia Connemara is going too far, whom will she ask next?" I thought he looked at me rather curiously, but I didn't take any notice of him; in fact I cut the little bounder and walked upstairs. I suppose you've never been there?'

'Never.'

'No, it's not the sort of house you'd ever be likely to go to. It's a rather vulgar house, but it's got a very fine marble staircase, and the Connemaras were at the top receiving their guests. Lady Connemara gave me a look of surprise when I shook hands with her, and began to giggle; I didn't pay much attention, she's a very silly, ill-bred woman and her manners are no better than those of her ancestor whom King Charles II made a duchess. I must say the reception rooms at Connemara House are stately. I walked through, nodding to a number of people and shaking hands; then I saw the German Ambassador talking with one of the Austrian Archdukes. I particularly wanted to have a word with him, so I went up and held out my hand. The moment the Archduke saw me he burst into a roar of laughter. I was deeply affronted. I looked him up and down sternly, but he only laughed the more. I was about to speak to him rather sharply, when there was a sudden hush and I realized that the King and Queen had come. Turning my back on the Archduke, I stepped forward, and then, quite suddenly, I noticed that I hadn't got any trousers on. I was in short silk drawers, and I wore scarlet sock-suspenders. No wonder Lady Connemara had giggled; no wonder the Archduke had laughed! I can't tell you what that moment was. An agony of shame. I awoke in a cold sweat. Oh, you don't know the relief I felt to find it was only a dream.'

'It's the kind of dream that's not so very uncommon,' said Dr Audlin.

'I dare say not. But an odd thing happened next day. I was in the lobby of the House of Commons, when that fellow Griffiths walked slowly past me. He deliberately looked down at my legs and then he looked me full in the face and I was almost certain he winked. A ridiculous thought came to me. He'd been there the night before and seen me make that ghastly exhibition of myself and was enjoying the joke. But of course I knew that was impossible because it was only a dream. I gave him an icy glare and he walked on. But he was grinning his head off.'

Lord Mountdrago took his handkerchief out of his pocket

and wiped the palms of his hands. He was making no attempt now to conceal his perturbation. Dr Audlin never took his eyes off him.

'Tell me another dream.'

'It was the night after, and it was even more absurd than the first one. I dreamt that I was in the House. There was a debate on foreign affairs which not only the country, but the world, had been looking forward to with the gravest concern. The government had decided on a change in their policy which vitally affected the future of the Empire. The occasion was historic. Of course the House was crowded. All the ambassadors were there. The galleries were packed. It fell to me to make the important speech of the evening. I had prepared it carefully. A man like me has enemies, there are a lot of people who resent my having achieved the position I have at an age when even the cleverest men are content with situations of relative obscurity, and I was determined that my speech should not only be worthy of the occasion, but should silence my detractors. It excited me to think that the whole world was hanging on my lips. I rose to my feet. If you've ever been in the House you'll know how members chat to one another during a debate, rustle papers and turn over reports. The silence was the silence of the grave when I began to speak. Suddenly I caught sight of that odious little bounder on one of the benches opposite, Griffiths the Welsh member; he put out his tongue at me. I don't know if you've ever heard a vulgar music-hall song called *A Bicycle Made for Two*. It was very popular a great many years ago. To show Griffiths how completely I despised him I began to sing it. I sang the first verse right through. There was a moment's surprise, and when I finished they cried, "Hear, hear," on the opposite benches. I put up my hand to silence them and sang the second verse. The House listened to me in stony silence and I felt the song wasn't going down very well. I was vexed, for I have a good baritone voice, and I was determined that they should do me justice. When I started the third verse the members began to laugh; in an instant the laughter spread; the ambassadors, the strangers in the Distinguished Strangers' Gallery, the ladies in the Ladies' Gallery, the reporters, they shook, they bellowed, they held their sides, they rolled in their seats; everyone was overcome with laughter except the ministers on the Front Bench immediately behind me. In that incredible, in that unprecedented uproar, they sat petrified. I gave them a glance, and suddenly the enormity of what I had done fell upon me. I had made myself the laughing-stock of the whole world. With misery I realized that I should have to resign. I woke and knew it was only a dream.'

Lord Mountdrago's grand manner had deserted him as he narrated this, and now having finished he was pale and trembling. But with an effort he pulled himself together. He forced a laugh to his shaking lips.

'The whole thing was so fantastic that I couldn't help being amused. I didn't give it another thought, and when I went into the House on the following afternoon I was feeling in very good form. The debate was dull, but I had to be there, and I read some documents that required my attention. For some reason I chanced to look up and I saw that Griffiths was speaking. He has an unpleasant Welsh accent and an unprepossessing appearance. I couldn't imagine that he had anything to say that it was worth my while to listen to, and I was about to return to my papers when he quoted two lines from *A Bicycle Made for Two*. I couldn't help glancing at him and I saw that his eyes were fixed on me with a grin of bitter mockery. I faintly shrugged my shoulders. It was comic that a scrubby little Welsh member should look at me like that. It was an odd coincidence that he should quote two lines from that disastrous song that I'd sung all through in my dream. I began to read my papers again, but I don't mind telling you that I found it difficult to concentrate on them. I was a little puzzled. Owen Griffiths had been in my first dream, the one at Connemara House, and I'd received a very definite impression afterwards that he knew the sorry figure I'd cut. Was it a mere coincidence that he had just quoted those two lines? I asked myself if it was possible that he was dreaming the same dreams as I was. But of course the idea was preposterous and I determined not to give it a second thought.'

There was a silence. Dr Audlin looked at Lord Mountdrago and Lord Mountdrago looked at Dr Audlin.

'Other people's dreams are very boring. My wife used to dream occasionally and insist on telling me her dreams next day with circumstantial detail. I found it maddening.'

Dr Audlin faintly smiled.

'You're not boring me.'

'I'll tell you one more dream I had a few days later. I dreamt that I went into a pulic-house at Limehouse. I've never been to Limehouse in my life and I don't think I've ever been in a public-house since I was at Oxford, and yet I saw the street and the place I went into as exactly as if I were at home there. I went into a room, I don't know whether they call it the saloon bar or the private bar; there was a fireplace and a large leather arm-chair on one side of it, and on the other a small sofa; a bar ran the whole length of the room and over it you could see into the public bar. Near the door was a round marble-topped table and two armchairs beside it. It was a Saturday night and the place was packed. It was brightly lit, but the smoke was so thick that it made my eyes smart. I was dressed like a rough, with a cap on my head and a handkerchief round my neck. It seemed to me that most of the people there were drunk. I thought it rather amusing. There was a gramophone going, or the radio, I don't know which, and in front of the fireplace two women were doing a grotesque dance. There was a little crowd round them, laughing, cheering, and singing. I went up to have a look and some man said to me: " 'Ave a drink, Bill?" There were glasses on the table full of a dark liquid which I understand is called brown ale. He gave me a glass and not wishing to be conspicuous I drank it. One of the women who were dancing broke away from the other and took hold of the glass. " 'Ere, what's the idea?" she said. "That's my beer you're putting away." "Oh, I'm sorry," I said, "this gentleman offered it me and I very naturally thought it was his to offer." "All right, mate," she said, "I don't mind. You come an' 'ave a dance with me." Before I could protest she'd caught hold of me and we were dancing together. And then I found myself sitting in the arm-chair with the woman on my lap and we were sharing a glass of beer. I should tell you that sex has never played any great part in my life. I married young because in my position it was desirable that I should marry, but also in order to settle once for all the question of sex. I had the two sons I had made up my mind to have, and then I put the whole matter on one side. I've always been too busy to give much thought to that kind of thing, and living so much in the public eye as I do it would have been madness to do anything that might give rise to scandal. The greatest asset a politician can have is a blameless record as far as women are concerned. I have no patience with the men who smash up their careers for women. I only despise them. The woman I had on my knees was drunk; she wasn't pretty and she wasn't young; in fact, she was just a blowsy old prostitute. She filled me with disgust, and yet when she put her mouth to mine and kissed me, though her breath stank of beer and her teeth were decayed, though I loathed myself, I wanted her – I wanted her with all my soul. Suddenly I heard a voice. "That's right, old boy, have a good time." I looked up and there was Owen Griffiths. I tried to spring out of the chair, but that horrible woman wouldn't let me. "Don't you pay no attention to 'im," she said, "'e's only one of them nosy-parkers," "You go to it," he said. "I know Moll. She'll give you your money's worth all right." You know, I wasn't so much annoyed at his seeing me in the absurd situation as angry that he should address me as "old boy". I pushed the woman aside and stood up and faced him. "I don't know you and I don't want to know you," I said. "I know you all right," he said. "And my advice to you, Molly, is, see that you get your money, he'll bilk you if he can." There was a bottle of beer on the table close by. Without a word I seized it by the neck and hit him over the head with it as hard as I could. I made such a violent gesture that it woke me up.'

'A dream of that sort is not incomprehensible,' said Dr Audlin. 'It is the revenge nature takes on persons of unimpeachable character.'

'The story's idiotic. I haven't told it you for its own sake. I've told it you for what happened next day. I wanted to look up something in a hurry and I went into the library of the House. I got the book and began reading. I hadn't noticed when I sat down that Griffiths was sitting in a chair close by me. Another of the Labour Members came in and went up to him. "Hullo, Owen," he said to him, "you're looking pretty dicky today." "I've got an awful headache," he answered. "I feel as if I'd been cracked over the head with a bottle." '

Now Lord Mountdrago's face was grey with anguish.

'I knew then that the idea I'd had and dismissed as preposterous was true. I knew that Griffiths was dreaming my dreams and that he remembered them as well as I did.'

'It may also have been a coincidence.'

'When he spoke he didn't speak to his friend, he deliberately spoke to me. He looked at me with sullen resentment.'

'Can you offer any suggestion why this same man should come into your dreams?'

'None.'

Dr Audlin's eyes had not left his patient's face and he saw that he lied. He had a pencil in his hand and he drew a straggling line or two on his blotting-paper. It often took a long time to get people to tell the truth, and yet they knew that unless they told it he could do nothing for them.

'The dream you've just described to me took place just over three weeks ago. Have you had any since?'

'Every night.'

'And does this man Griffiths come into them all?'

'Yes.'

The doctor drew more lines on his blotting-paper. He

wanted the silence, the drabness, the dull light of that little room to have its effect on Lord Mountdrago's sensibility. Lord Mountdrago threw himself back in his chair and turned his head away so that he should not see the other's grave eyes.

'Dr Audlin, you must do something for me. I'm at the end of my tether. I shall go mad if this goes on. I'm afraid to go to sleep. Two or three nights I haven't. I've sat up reading and when I felt drowsy put on my coat and walked till I was exhausted. But I must have sleep. With all the work I have to do I must be at concert pitch; I must be in complete control of all my faculties. I need rest; sleep brings me none. I no sooner fall asleep than my dreams begin, and he's always there, that vulgar little cad, grinning at me, mocking me, despising me. It's a monstrous persecution. I tell you, doctor, I'm not the man of my dreams; it's not fair to judge me by them. Ask anyone you like. I'm an honest, upright, decent man. No one can say anything against my moral character either private or public. My whole ambition is to serve my country and maintain its greatness. I have money, I have rank, I'm not exposed to many of the temptations of lesser men, so that it's no credit to me to be incorruptible; but this I can claim, that no honour, no personal advantage, no thought of self would induce me to swerve by a hair's breadth from my duty. I've sacrificed everything to become the man I am. Greatness is my aim. Greatness is within my reach and I'm losing my nerve. I'm not that mean, despicable, cowardly, lewd creature that horrible little man sees. I've told you three of my dreams; they're nothing; that man has seen me do things that are so beastly, so horrible, so shameful, that even if my life depended on it I wouldn't tell them. And he remembers them. I can hardly meet the derision and disgust I see in his eyes and I even hestitate to speak because I know my words can seem to him nothing but utter humbug. He's seen me do things that no man with any self-respect would do, things for which men are driven out of the society of their fellows and sentenced to long terms of imprisonment; he's heard the foulness of my speech; he's seen me not only ridiculous, but revolting. He despises me and he no longer pretends to conceal it. I tell you that if you can't do something to help me I shall either kill myself or kill him.'

'I wouldn't kill him if I were you,' said Dr Audlin, coolly, in that soothing voice of his. 'In this country the consequences of killing a fellow-creature are awkward.'

'I shouldn't be hanged for it, if that's what you mean. Who would know that I'd killed him? That dream of mine has shown me how. I told you, the day after I'd hit him over the head with a beer-bottle he had such a headache that he couldn't see straight. He said so himself. That shows that he can feel with his waking body what happens to his body asleep. It's not with a bottle I shall hit him next time. One night, when I'm dreaming, I shall find myself with a knife in my hand or a revolver in my pocket, I must because I want to so intensely, and then I shall seize my opportunity. I'll stick him like a pig; I'll shoot him like a dog. In the heart. And then I shall be free of this fiendish persecution.'

Some people might have thought that Lord Mountdrago was mad; after all the years during which Dr Audlin had been treating the diseased souls of men he knew how thin a line divides those whom we call sane from those whom we call insane. He knew how often in men who to all appearance were healthy and normal, who were seemingly devoid of imagination, and who fulfilled the duties of common life with credit to themselves and with benefit to their fellows, when you gained their confidence, when you tore away the mask they wore to the world, you found not only hideous abnormality, but kinks so strange, mental extravagances so fantastic, that in that respect you could call them lunatic. If you put them in an asylum not all the asylums in the world would be large enough. Anyhow, a man was not certifiable because he had strange dreams and they had shattered his nerve. The case was singular, but it was only an exaggeration of others that had come under Dr Audlin's observation; he was doubtful, however, whether the methods of treatment that he had so often found efficacious would here avail.

'Have you consulted any other member of my profession?' he asked.

'Only Sir Augustus. I merely told him that I suffered from nightmares. He said I was overworked and recommended me to go for a cruise. That's absurd. I can't leave the Foreign Office just now when the international situation needs constant attention. I'm indispensable, and I know it. On my conduct at the present juncture my whole future depends. He gave me sedatives. They had no effect. He gave me tonics. They were worse than useless. He's an old fool.'

'Can you give any reason why it should be this particular man who persists in coming into your dreams?'

'You asked me that question before. I answered it.'

That was true. But Dr Audlin had not been satisfied with the answer.

'Just now you talked of persecution. Why should Owen Griffiths want to persecute you?'

'I don't know.'

Lord Mountdrago's eyes shifted a little. Dr Audlin was sure that he was not speaking the truth.

'Have you ever done him an injury?'

'Never.'

Lord Mountdrago made no movement, but Dr Audlin had a queer feeling that he shrank into his skin. He saw before him a large, proud man who gave the impression that the questions put to him were an insolence, and yet for all that, behind that façade, was something shifting and startled that made you think of a frightened animal in a trap. Dr Audlin leaned forward and by the power of his eyes forced Lord Mountdrago to meet them.

'Are you quite sure?'

'Quite sure. You don't seem to understand that our ways lead along different paths. I don't wish to harp on it, but I must remind you that I am a Minister of the Crown and

Griffiths is an obscure member of the Labour Party. Naturally there's no social connexion between us; he's a man of very humble origin, he's not the sort of person I should be likely to meet at any of the houses I go to; and politically our respective stations are so far separated that we could not possibly have anything in common.'

'I can do nothing for you unless you tell me the complete truth.'

Lord Mountdrago raised his eyebrows. His voice was rasping.

'I'm not accustomed to having my word doubted, Dr Audlin. If you're going to do that I think to take up any more of your time can only be a waste of mine. If you will kindly let my secretary know what your fee is he will see that a cheque is sent to you.'

For all the expression that was to be seen on Dr Audlin's face you might have thought that he simply had not heard what Lord Mountdrago said. He continued to look steadily into his eyes and his voice was grave and low.

'Have you done anything to this man that *he* might look upon as an injury?'

Lord Mountdrago hesitated. He looked away, and then, as though there were in Dr Audlin's eyes a compelling force that he could not resist, looked back. He answered sulkily:

'Only if he was a dirty, second-rate little cad.'

'But that is exactly what you've described him to be.'

Lord Mountdrago sighed. He was beaten. Dr Audlin knew that the sigh meant he was going at last to say what he had till then held back. Now he had no longer to insist. He dropped his eyes and began again drawing vague geometrical figures on his blotting-paper. The silence lasted two or three minutes.

'I'm anxious to tell you everything that can be of any use to you. If I didn't mention this before, it's only because it was so unimportant that I didn't see how it could possibly have anything to do with the case. Griffiths won a seat at the last election and he began to make a nuisance of himself almost at once. His father's a miner, and he worked in a mine himself when he was a boy; he's been a schoolmaster in the board schools and a journalist. He's that half-baked, conceited intellectual, with inadequate knowledge, ill-considered ideas, and impracticable plans, that compulsory education has brought forth from the working-classes. He's a scrawny, grey-faced man, who looks half-starved, and he's always very slovenly in appearance; heaven knows members nowadays don't bother much about their dress, but his clothes are an outrage to the dignity of the House. They're ostentatiously shabby, his collar's never clean and his tie's never tied properly; he looks as if he hadn't had a bath for a month and his hands are filthy. The Labour Party have two or three fellows on the Front Bench who've got a certain ability, but the rest of them don't amount to much. In the kingdom of the blind the one-eyed man is king: because Griffiths is glib and has a lot of superficial information on a number of subjects, the Whips on his side began to put him up to speak whenever there was a chance. It appeared that he fancied himself on foreign affairs, and he was continually asking me silly, tiresome questions. I don't mind telling you that I made a point of snubbing him as soundly as I thought he deserved. From the beginning I hated the way he talked, his whining voice and his vulgar accent; he had nervous mannerisms that intensely irritated me. He talked rather shyly, hesitatingly, as though it were torture to him to speak and yet he was forced on by some inner passion, and often he used to say some very disconcerting things. I'll admit that now and again he had a sort of tub-thumping eloquence. It had a certain influence over the ill-regulated minds of the members of his party. They were impressed by his earnestness and they weren't, as I was, nauseated by his sentimentality. A certain sentimentality is the common coin of political debate. Nations are governed by self-interest, but they prefer to believe that their aims are altruistic, and the politician is justified if with fair words and fine phrases he can persuade the electorate that the hard bargain he is driving for his country's advantage tends to the good of humanity. The mistake people like Griffiths make is to take these fair words and fine phrases at their face value. He's a crank, and a noxious crank. He calls himself an idealist. He has at his tongue's end all the tedious blather that the intelligentsia have been boring us with for years. Non-resistance. The brotherhood of man. You know the hopeless rubbish. The worst of it was that it impressed not only his own party, it even shook some of the sillier, more sloppy-minded members of ours. I heard rumours that Griffiths was likely to get office when a Labour Government came in; I even heard it suggested that he might get the Foreign Office. The notion was grotesque but not impossible. One day I had occasion to wind up a debate on foreign affairs which Griffiths had opened. He'd spoken for an hour. I thought it a very good opportunity to cook his goose, and by God, sir, I cooked it. I tore his speech to pieces. I pointed out the faultiness of his reasoning and emphasized the deficiency of his knowledge. In the House of Commons the most devastating weapon is ridicule: I mocked him; I bantered him; I was in good form that day and the House rocked with laughter. Their laughter excited me and I excelled myself. The Opposition sat glum and silent, but even some of them couldn't help laughing once or twice; it's not intolerable, you know, to see a colleague, perhaps a rival, made a fool of. And if ever a man was made a fool of I made a fool of Griffiths. He shrank down in a seat, I saw his face go white, and presently he buried it in his hands. When I sat down I'd killed him. I'd destroyed his prestige for ever; he had no more chance of getting office when a Labour Government came in than the policeman at the door. I heard afterwards that his father, the old miner, and his mother had come up from Wales, with various supporters of his in the constituency, to watch the triumph they expected him to have. They had seen only his utter humiliation. He'd won the constituency by the narrowest margin. An incident like that might very easily lose him his seat. But that was no business of mine.'

'Should I be putting it too strongly if I said you had ruined his career?' asked Dr Audlin.

'I don't suppose you would.'

'That is a very serious injury you've done him.'

'He brought it on himself.'

'Have you never felt any qualms about it?'

'I think perhaps if I'd known that his father and mother were there I might have let him down a little more gently.'

There was nothing further for Dr Audlin to say, and he set about treating his patient in such a manner as he thought might avail. He sought by suggestion to make him forget his dreams when he awoke; he sought to make him sleep so deeply that he would not dream. He found Lord Mountdrago's resistance impossible to break down. At the end of an hour he dismissed him. Since then he had seen Lord Mountdrago half a dozen times. He had done him no good. The frightful dreams continued every night to harass the unfortunate man, and it was clear that his general condition was growing rapidly worse. He was worn out. His irritability was uncontrollable. Lord Mountdrago was angry because he received no benefit from his treatment, and yet continued it, not only because it seemed his only hope, but because it was a relief to him to have someone with whom he could talk openly. Dr Audlin came to the conclusion at last that there was only one way in which Lord Mountdrago could achieve deliverance, but he knew him well enough to be assured that of his own free will he would never, never take it. If Lord Mountdrago was to be saved from the breakdown that was threatening he must be induced to take a step that must be abhorrent to his pride of birth and his self-complacency. Dr Audlin was convinced that to delay was impossible. He was treating his patient by suggestion, and after several visits found him more susceptible to it. At length he managed to get him into a condition of somnolence. With his low, soft, monotonous voice he soothed his tortured nerves. He repeated the same words over and over again. Lord Mountdrago lay quite still, his eyes closed; his breathing was regular, and his limbs were relaxed. Then Dr Audlin in the same quiet tone spoke the words he had prepared.

'You will go to Owen Griffiths and say that you are sorry that you caused him that great injury. You will say that you will do whatever lies in your power to undo the harm that you have done him.'

The words acted on Lord Mountdrago like the blow of a whip across his face. He shook himself out of his hypnotic state and sprang to his feet. His eyes blazed with passion and he poured forth upon Dr Audlin a stream of angry vituperation such as even he had never heard. He swore at him. He cursed him. He used language of such obscenity that Dr Audlin, who had heard every sort of foul word, sometimes from the lips of chaste and distinguished women, was surprised that he knew it.

'Apologize to that filthy little Welshman? I'd rather kill myself.'

'I believe it to be the only way in which you can regain your balance.'

Dr Audlin had not often seen a man presumably sane in such a condition of uncontrollable fury. He grew red in the face and his eyes bulged out of his head. He did really foam at the mouth. Dr Audlin watched him coolly, waiting for the storm to wear itself out, and presently he saw that Lord Mountdrago, weakened by the strain to which he had been subjected for so many weeks, was exhausted.

'Sit down,' he said then, sharply.

Lord Mountdrago crumpled up into a chair.

'Christ, I feel all in. I must rest a minute and then I'll go.'

For five minutes perhaps they sat in complete silence. Lord Mountdrago was a gross, blustering bully, but he was also a gentleman. When he broke the silence he had recovered his self-control.

'I'm afraid I've been very rude to you. I'm ashamed of the things I've said to you and I can only say you'd be justified if you refused to have anything more to do with me. I hope you won't do that. I feel that my visits to you do help me. I think you're my only chance.'

'You mustn't give another thought to what you said. It was of no consequence.'

'But there's one thing you mustn't ask me to do, and that is to make excuses to Griffiths.'

'I've thought a great deal about your case. I don't pretend to understand it, but I believe that your only chance of release is to do what I proposed. I have a notion that we're none of us one self, but many, and one of the selves in you has risen up against the injury you did Griffiths and has taken on the form of Griffiths in your mind and is punishing you for what you cruelly did. If I were a priest I should tell you that it is your conscience that has adopted the shape and lineaments of this man to scourge you to repentance and persuade you to reparation.'

'My conscience is clear. It's not my fault if I smashed the man's career. I crushed him like a slug in my garden. I regret nothing.'

It was on those words that Lord Mountdrago had left him. Reading through his notes, while he waited, Dr Audlin considered how best he could bring his patient to the state of mind that, now that his usual methods of treatment had failed, he thought alone could help him. He glanced at his clock. It was six. It was strange that Lord Mountdrago did not come. He knew he had intended to because a secretary had rung up that morning to say that he would be with him at the usual hour. He must have been detained by pressing work. This notion gave Dr Audlin something else to think of: Lord Mountdrago was quite unfit for work and in no condition to deal with important matters of state. Dr Audlin wondered whether it behoved him to get in touch with someone in authority, the Prime Minister or the Permanent Under-Secretary for Foreign Affairs, and impart to him his conviction that Lord Mountdrago's mind was so unbalanced that it was dangerous to leave affairs of moment in his hands. It was a ticklish thing to do. He might cause needless trouble and get roundly snubbed for his pains. He shrugged his shoulders.

'After all,' he reflected, 'the politicians have made such a mess of the world during the last five-and-twenty years, I don't suppose it makes much odds if they're mad or sane.'

He rang the bell.

'If Lord Mountdrago comes now will you tell him that I have another appointment at six-fifteen and so I'm afraid I can't see him.'

'Very good; sir,'

'Has the evening paper come yet?'

'I'll go and see.'

In a moment the servant brought it in. A huge headline ran across the front page: Tragic Death of Foreign Minister.

'My God!' cried Dr Audlin.

For once he was wrenched out of his wonted calm. He was shocked, horribly shocked, and yet he was not altogether surprised. The possibility that Lord Mountdrago might commit suicide had occurred to him several times, for that it was suicide he could not doubt. The paper said that Lord Mountdrago had been waiting in a Tube station, standing on the edge of the platform, and as the train came in was seen to fall on the rail. It was supposed that he had had a sudden attack of faintness. The paper went on to say that Lord Mountdrago had been suffering for some weeks from the effects of overwork, but had felt it impossible to absent himself while the foreign situation demanded his unremitting attention. Lord Mountdrago was another victim of the strain that modern politics placed upon those who played the more important parts in it. There was a neat little piece about the talents and industry, the patriotism and vision, of the deceased statesman, followed by various surmises upon the Prime Minister's choice of his successor. Dr Audlin read all this. He had not liked Lord Mountdrago. The chief emotion that his death caused in him was dissatisfaction with himself because he had been able to do nothing for him.

Perhaps he had done wrong in not getting into touch with Lord Mountdrago's doctor. He was discouraged, as always when failure frustrated his conscientious efforts, and repulsion seized him for the theory and practice of this empiric doctrine by which he earned his living. He was dealing with dark and mysterious forces that it was perhaps beyond the powers of the human mind to understand. He was like a man blindfold trying to feel his way to he knew not whither. Listlessly he turned the pages of the paper. Suddenly he gave a great start, and an exclamation once more was forced from his lips. His eyes had fallen on a small paragraph near the bottom of a column. Sudden Death of an M.P., he read. Mr Owen Griffiths, member of so-and-so, had been taken ill in Fleet Street that afternoon and when he was brought to Charing Cross Hospital life was found to be extinct. It was supposed that death was due to natural causes, but an inquest would be held. Dr Audlin could hardly believe his eyes. Was it possible that the night before Lord Mountdrago had at last in his dream found himself possessed of the weapon, knife or gun, that he had wanted, and had killed his tormentor, and had that ghostly murder, in the same way as the blow with the bottle had given him a racking headache on the following day, taken effect a certain number of hours later on the waking man? Or was it, more mysterious and more frightful, that when Lord Mountdrago sought relief in death, the enemy he had so cruelly wronged, unappeased, escaping from his own mortality, had pursued him to some other sphere there to torment him still? It was strange. The sensible thing was to look upon it merely as an odd coincidence. Dr Audlin rang the bell.

'Tell Mrs Milton that I'm sorry I can't see her this evening. I'm not well.'

It was true; he shivered as though of an ague. With some kind of spiritual sense he seemed to envisage a bleak, a horrible void. The dark night of the soul engulfed him, and he felt a strange, primeval terror of he knew not what.

The Colonel's Lady

ALL THIS HAPPENED two or three years before the outbreak of the war.

The Peregrines were having breakfast. Though they were alone and the table was long they sat at opposite ends of it. From the walls George Peregrine's ancestors, painted by the fashionable painters of the day, looked down upon them. The butler brought in the morning post. There were several letters for the colonel, business letters, *The Times*, and a small parcel for his wife Evie. He looked at his letters and then, opening *The Times*, began to read it. They finished breakfast and rose from the table. He noticed that his wife hadn't opened the parcel.

'What's that?' he asked.

'Only some books.'

'Shall I open it for you?'

'If you like.'

He hated to cut string and so with some difficulty untied the knots.

'But they're all the same,' he said when he had unwrapped the parcel. 'What on earth d'you want six copies of the same book for?' He opened one of them. 'Poetry.' Then he looked at the title page. *When Pyramids Decay*, he read, by E.K. Hamilton. Eva Katherine Hamilton: that was his wife's maiden name. He looked at her with smiling surprise. 'Have you written a book, Evie? You are a slyboots.'

'I didn't think it would interest you very much. Would you like a copy?'

'Well, you know poetry isn't much in my line, but – yes, I'd like a copy; I'll read it. I'll take it along to my study. I've got a lot to do this morning.'

He gathered up *The Times*, his letters, and the book, and went out. His study was a large and comfortable room, with a big desk, leather arm-chairs, and what he called 'trophies of the chase' on the walls. On the bookshelves were works of reference, books on farming, gardening, fishing, and shooting, and books on the last war, in which he had won an M.C. and a D.S.O. For before his marriage he had been in the Welsh Guards. At the end of the war he retired and settled down to the life of a country gentleman in the spacious house, some twenty miles from Sheffield, which one of his forebears had built in the reign of George III. George Peregrine had an estate of some fifteen hundred acres which he managed with ability; he was a Justice of the Peace and performed his duties conscientiously. During the season he rode to hounds two days a week. He was a good shot, a golfer, and though now a little over fifty could still play a hard game of tennis. He could describe himself with propriety as an all-round sportsman.

He had been putting on weight lately, but was still a fine figure of a man; tall, with grey curly hair, only just beginning to grow thin on the crown, frank blue eyes, good features, and a high colour. He was a public-spirited man, chairman of any number of local organizations and, as became his class and station, a loyal member of the Conservative Party. He looked upon it as his duty to see to the welfare of the people on his estate and it was a satisfaction to him to know that Evie could be trusted to tend the sick and succour the poor. He had built a cottage hospital on the outskirts of the village and paid the wages of a nurse out of his own pocket. All he asked of the recipients of his bounty was that at elections, county or general, they should vote for his candidate. He was a friendly man, affable to his inferiors, considerate with his tenants, and popular with the neighbouring gentry. He would have been pleased and at the same time slightly embarrassed if someone had told him he was a jolly good fellow. That was what he wanted to be. He desired no higher praise.

It was hard luck that he had no children. He would have been an excellent father, kindly but strict, and would have brought up his sons as gentlemen's sons should be brought up, sent them to Eton, you know, taught them to fish, shoot, and ride. As it was, his heir was a nephew, son of his brother killed in a motor accident, not a bad boy, but not a chip off the old block, no, sir, far from it; and would you believe it, his fool of a mother was sending him to a co-educational school. Evie had been a sad disappointment to him. Of course she was a lady, and she had a bit of money of her own; she managed the house uncommonly well and she was a good hostess. The village people adored her. She had been a pretty little thing when he married her, with a creamy skin, light brown hair, and a trim figure, healthy too, and not a bad tennis player; he couldn't understand why she'd had no children; of course she was faded now, she must be getting on for five and forty; her skin was drab, her hair had lost its sheen, and she was as thin as a rail. She was always neat and suitably dressed, but she didn't seem to bother how she looked, she wore no make-up and didn't even use lipstick; sometimes at night when she dolled herself up for a party you could tell that once she'd been quite attractive, but ordinarily she was – well, the sort of woman you simply didn't notice. A nice woman, of course, a good wife, and it wasn't her fault if she was barren, but it was tough on a fellow who wanted an heir of his own loins; she hadn't any vitality, that's what was the matter with her. He supposed he'd been in love with her when he asked her to marry him, at least sufficiently in love for a man who wanted to marry and settle down, but with time he discovered that they had nothing much in common. She didn't care about hunting, and fishing bored her. Naturally they'd drifted apart. He had to do her the justice to admit that she'd never bothered him. There'd been no scenes. They had no quarrels. She seemed to take it for granted that he should go his own way. When he went up to London now and then she never wanted to come with him. He had a girl there, well, she wasn't exactly a girl, she was thirty-five if she was a day, but she was blonde and luscious and he only had to wire ahead of time and they'd dine, do a show, and spend the night together. Well, a man, a healthy normal man had to have some fun in his life. The thought crossed his mind that if Evie hadn't been such a good woman she'd have been a better wife; but it was not the sort of thought that he welcomed and he put it away from him.

George Peregrine finished his *Times* and being a considerate fellow rang the bell and told the butler to take it to Evie. Then he looked at his watch. It was half past ten and at eleven he had an appointment with one of his tenants. He had half an hour to spare.

'I'd better have a look at Evie's book,' he said to himself.

He took it up with a smile. Evie had a lot of highbrow books in her sitting-room, not the sort of books that interested him, but if they amused her he had no objection to her reading them. He noticed that the volume he now held in his hand contained no more than ninety pages. That was all to the good. He shared Edgar Allan Poe's opinion that poems should be short. But as he turned the pages he noticed that several of Evie's had long lines of irregular length and didn't rhyme. He didn't like that. At his first school, when he was a little boy, he remembered learning a poem that began: *The boy stood on the burning deck*, and later, at Eton, one that started: *Ruin seize thee, ruthless king*; and then there was *Henry V*; they'd had to take that, one half. He stared at Evie's pages with consternation.

'That's not what I call poetry,' he said.

Fortunately it wasn't all like that. Interspersed with the pieces that looked so odd, lines of three or four words and then a line of ten or fifteen, there were little poems, quite short, that rhymed, thank God, with the lines all the same length. Several of the pages were just headed with the word *Sonnet*, and out of curiosity he counted the lines; there were fourteen of them. He read them. They seemed all right, but he didn't quite know what they were all about. He repeated to himself: *Ruin seize thee, ruthless king*.

'Poor Evie,' he sighed.

At that moment the farmer he was expecting was ushered into the study, and putting the book down he made him welcome. They embarked on their business.

'I read your book, Evie,' he said as they sat down to lunch. 'Jolly good. Did it cost you a packet to have it printed?'

'No, I was lucky. I sent it to a publisher and he took it.'

'Not much money in poetry, my dear,' he said in his good-natured, hearty way.

'No, I don't suppose there is. What did Bannock want to see you about this morning?'

Bannock was the tenant who had interrupted his reading of Evie's poems.

'He's asked me to advance the money for a pedigree bull he wants to buy. He's a good man and I've half a mind to do it.'

George Peregrine saw that Evie didn't want to talk about her book and he was not sorry to change the subject. He was glad she had used her maiden name on the title page; he didn't suppose anyone would ever hear about the book, but he was proud of his own unusual name and he wouldn't have liked it if some damned penny-a-liner had made fun of Evie's effort in one of the papers.

During the few weeks that followed he thought it tactful not to ask Evie any questions about her venture into verse, and she never referred to it. It might have been a discreditable incident that they had silently agreed not to mention. But then a strange thing happened. He had to go to London on business and he took Daphne out to dinner. That was the name of the girl with whom he was in the habit of passing a few agreeable hours whenever he went to town.

'Oh, George,' she said, 'is that your wife who's written a book they're all talking about?'

'What on earth d'you mean?'

'Well, there's a fellow I know who's a critic. He took me out to dinner the other night and he had a book with him. "Got anything for me to read?" I said. "What's that?" "Oh, I don't think that's your cup of tea," he said, "It's poetry. I've just been reviewing it." "No poetry for me," I said. "It's about the hottest stuff I ever read," he said. "Selling like hot cakes. And it's damned good." '

'Who's the book by?' asked George.

'A woman called Hamilton. My friend told me that wasn't her real name. He said her real name was Peregrine. "Funny," I said, "I know a fellow called Peregrine." "Colonel in the army," he said, "Lives near Sheffield." '

'I'd just as soon you didn't talk about me to your friends,' said George with a frown of vexation.

'Keep your shirt on, dearie. Who d'you take me for? I just said: "It's not the same one." ' Daphne giggled. 'My friend said: "They say he's a regular Colonel Blimp." '

George had a keen sense of humour.

'You could tell them better than that,' he laughed. 'If my wife had written a book I'd be the first to know about it, wouldn't I?'

'I suppose you would.'

Anyhow the matter didn't interest her and when the colonel began to talk of other things she forgot about it. He put it out of his mind too. There was nothing to it, he decided, and that silly fool of a critic had just been pulling Daphne's leg. He was amused at the thought of her tackling that book because she had been told it was hot stuff and then finding it just a lot of bosh cut up into unequal lines.

He was a member of several clubs and next day he thought he'd lunch at one in St James's Street. He was catching a train back to Sheffield early in the afternoon. He was sitting in a comfortable arm-chair having a glass of sherry before going into the dining-room when an old friend came up to him.

'Well, old boy, how's life?' he said. 'How d'you like being the husband of a celebrity?'

George Peregrine looked at his friend. He thought he saw an amused twinkle in his eyes.

'I don't know what you're talking about,' he answered.

'Come off it, George. Everyone knows E.K. Hamilton is your wife. Not often a book of verse has a success like that. Look here, Henry Dashwood is lunching with me. He'd like to meet you.'

'Who the devil is Henry Dashwood and why should he want to meet me?'

'Oh, my dear fellow, what do you do with yourself all the time in the country? Henry's about the best critic we've got. He wrote a wonderful review of Evie's book. D'you mean to say she didn't show it you?'

Before George could answer his friend had called a man over. A tall, thin man, with a high forehead, a beard, a long nose, and a stoop, just the sort of man whom George was prepared to dislike at first sight. Introductions were effected. Henry Dashwood sat down.

'Is Mrs Peregrine in London by any chance? I should very much like to meet her,' he said.

'No, my wife doesn't like London. She prefers the country,' said George stiffly.

'She wrote me a very nice letter about my review. I was pleased. You know, we critics get more kicks than halfpence. I was simply bowled over by her book. It's so fresh and original, very modern without being obscure. She seems to be as much at her ease in free verse as in the classical metres.' Then because he was a critic he thought he should criticize. 'Sometimes her ear is a trifle at fault, but you can say the same of Emily Dickinson. There are several of those short lyrics of hers that might have been written by Landor.'

All this was gibberish to George Peregrine. The man was nothing but a disgusting highbrow. But the colonel had good manners and he answered with proper civility; Henry Dashwood went on as though he hadn't spoken.

'But what makes the book so outstanding is the passion that throbs in every line. So many of these young poets are so anaemic, cold, bloodless, dully intellectual, but here you have real naked, earthy passion; of course deep, sincere emotion like that is tragic – ah, my dear Colonel, how right Heine was when he said that the poet makes little songs out of his great sorrows. You know, now and then, as I read and re-read those heart-rending pages I thought of Sappho.'

This was too much for George Peregrine and he got up.

'Well, it's jolly nice of you to say such nice things about my wife's little book. I'm sure she'll be delighted. But I must bolt, I've got to catch a train and I want to get a bite of lunch.'

'Damned fool,' he said irritably to himself as he walked upstairs to the dining-room.

He got home in time for dinner and after Evie had gone to bed he went into his study and looked for her book. He thought he'd just glance through it again to see for himself what they were making such a fuss about, but he couldn't find it. Evie must have taken it away.

'Silly,' he muttered.

He'd told her he thought it jolly good. What more could a fellow be expected to say? Well, it didn't matter. He lit his pipe and read the *Field* till he felt sleepy. But a week or so later it happened that he had to go into Sheffield for the day. He lunched there at his club. He had nearly finished when the Duke of Haverel came in. This was the great local magnate and of course the colonel knew him, but only to say how d'you do to; and he was surprised when the Duke stopped at his table.

'We're so sorry your wife couldn't come to us for the week-end,' he said, with a sort of shy cordiality. 'We're expecting rather a nice lot of people.'

George was taken aback. He guessed that the Haverels had asked him and Evie over for the week-end and Evie, without saying a word to him about it, had refused. He had the presence of mind to say he was sorry too.

'Better luck next time,' said the Duke pleasantly and moved on.

Colonel Pregrine was very angry and when he got home he said to his wife:

'Look here, what's this about our being asked over to Haverel? Why on earth did you say we couldn't go? We've never been asked before and it's the best shooting in the county.'

'I didn't think of that. I thought it would only bore you.'

'Damn it all, you might at least have asked me if I wanted to go.'

'I'm sorry.'

He looked at her closely. There was something in her expression that he didn't quite understand. He frowned.

'I suppose *I* was asked?' he barked.

Evie flushed a little.

'Well, in point of fact you weren't.'

'I call it damned rude of them to ask you without asking me.'

'I suppose they thought it wasn't your sort of party. The Duchess is rather fond of writers and people like that, you know. She's having Henry Dashwood, the critic, and for some reason he wants to meet me.'

'It was damned nice of you to refuse, Evie.'

'It's the least I could do,' she smiled. She hesitated a moment. 'George, my publishers want to give a little dinner party for me one day towards the end of the month and of course they want you to come too.'

'Oh, I don't think that's quite my mark. I'll come up to London with you if you like. I'll find someone to dine with.'

Daphne.

'I expect it'll be very dull, but they're making rather a point of it. And the day after, the American publisher who's taken my book is giving a cocktail party at Claridge's. I'd like you to come to that if you wouldn't mind.'

'Sounds like a crashing bore, but if you really want me to come I'll come.'

'It would be sweet of you.'

George Peregrine was dazed by the cocktail party. There were a lot of people. Some of them didn't look so bad, a few of the women were decently turned out, but the men seemed to him pretty awful. He was introduced to everyone as Colonel Peregrine, E.K. Hamilton's husband, you know. The men didn't seem to have anything to say to him, but the women gushed.

'You *must* be proud of your wife. Isn't it *wonderful*? You know,

I read it right through at a sitting, I simply couldn't put it down, and when I'd finished I started again at the beginning and read it right through a second time. I was simply *thrilled*.'

The English publisher said to him:

'We've not had a success like this with a book of verse for twenty years. I've never seen such reviews.'

The American publisher said to him:

'It's swell. It'll be a smash hit in America. You wait and see.'

The American publisher had sent Evie a great spray of orchids. Damned ridiculous, thought George. As they came in, people were taken up to Evie, and it was evident that they said flattering things to her, which she took with a pleasant smile and a word or two of thanks. She was a trifle flushed with the excitement, but seemed quite at her ease. Though he thought the whole thing a lot of stuff and nonsense George noted with approval that his wife was carrying it off in just the right way.

'Well, there's one thing,' he said to himself, 'you can see she's a lady and that's a damned sight more than you can say of anyone else here.'

He drank a good many cocktails. But there was one thing that bothered him. He had a notion that some of the people he was introduced to looked at him in rather a funny sort of way, he couldn't quite make out what it meant, and once when he strolled by two women who were sitting together on a sofa he had the impression that they were talking about him and after he passed he was almost certain they tittered. He was very glad when the party came to an end.

In the taxi on their way back to their hotel Evie said to him:

'You were wonderful, dear. You made quite a hit. The girls simply raved about you: they thought you so handsome.'

'Girls,' he said bitterly. 'Old hags.'

'Were you bored, dear?'

'Stiff.'

She pressed his hand in a gesture of sympathy.

'I hope you won't mind if we wait and go down by the afternoon train. I've got some things to do in the morning.'

'No, that's all right. Shopping?'

'I do want to buy one or two things, but I've got to go and be photographed. I hate the idea, but they think I ought to be. For America, you know.'

He said nothing. But he thought. He thought it would be a shock to the American public when they saw the portrait of the homely, desiccated little woman who was his wife. He'd always been under the impression that they liked glamour in America.

He went on thinking, and next morning when Evie had gone out he went to his club and up to the library. There he looked up recent numbers of *The Times Literary Supplement*, the *New Statesman*, and the *Spectator*. Presently he found reviews of Evie's book. He didn't read them very carefully, but enough to see that they were extremely favourable. Then he went to the bookseller's in Piccadilly where he occasionally bought books. He'd made up his mind that he had to read this damned thing of Evie's properly, but he didn't want to ask her what she'd done with the copy she'd given him. He'd buy one for himself. Before going in he looked in the window and the first thing he saw was a display of *When Pyramids Decay*. Damned silly title! He went in. A young man came forward and asked if he could help him.

'No, I'm just having a look round.' It embarrassed him to ask for Evie's book and he thought he'd find it for himself and then take it to the salesman. But he couldn't see it anywhere and at last, finding the young man near him, he said in a carefully casual tone: 'By the way, have you got a book called *When Pyramids Decay*?'

'The new edition came in this morning. I'll get a copy.'

In a moment the young man returned with it. He was a short, rather stout young man, with a shock of untidy carroty hair and spectacles. George Peregrine, tall, upstanding, very military, towered over him.

'Is this a new edition then?' he asked.

'Yes, sir. The fifth. It might be a novel the way it's selling.'

George Peregrine hesitated a moment.

'Why d'you suppose it's such a success? I've always been told no one reads poetry.'

'Well, it's good, you know. I've read it myself.' The young man, though obviously cultured, had a slight Cockney accent, and George quite instinctively adopted a patronizing attitude. 'It's the story they like. Sexy, you know, but tragic.'

George frowned a little. He was coming to the conclusion that the young man was rather impertinent. No one had told him anything about there being a story in the damned book and he had not gathered that from reading the reviews. The young man went on:

'Of course it's only a flash in the pan, if you know what I mean. The way I look at it, she was sort of inspired like by a personal experience, like Housman was with *The Shropshire Lad*. She'll never write anything else.'

'How much is the book?' said George coldly to stop his chatter. 'You needn't wrap it up. I'll just slip it into my pocket.'

The November morning was raw and he was wearing a greatcoat.

At the station he bought the evening papers and magazines and he and Evie settled themselves comfortably in opposite corners of a first-class carriage and read. At five o'clock they went along to the restaurant car to have tea and chatted a little. They arrived. They drove home in the car which was waiting for them. They bathed, dressed for dinner, and after dinner Evie, saying she was tired out, went to bed. She kissed him, as was her habit, on the forehead. Then he went into the hall, took Evie's book out of his greatcoat pocket and going into the study began to read it. He didn't read verse very easily and though he read with attention, every word of it, the impression he received was far from clear. Then he began at the beginning again and read it a second time. He read with increasing malaise, but he was not a stupid man and when he had finished he had a distinct understanding of what it was all about. Part of the book was in free verse, part in conventional metres, but the story it related was coherent and plain to the meanest intelligence. It was the story of a passionate love affair between an older woman, married, and a young man. George Peregrine made out the steps of it as easily as if he had been doing a sum in simple addition.

Written in the first person, it began with the tremulous surprise of the woman, past her youth, when it dawned upon her that the young man was in love with her. She hesitated to believe it. She thought she must be deceiving herself. And she was terrified when on a sudden she discovered that she was passionately in love with him. She told herself it was absurd; with the disparity of age between them nothing but unhappiness could come to her if she yielded to her emotion. She tried to prevent him from speaking but the day came when he told her that he loved her and forced her to tell him that she loved him too. He begged her to run away with him. She couldn't leave her husband, her home; and what life could they look forward to, she an ageing woman, he so young? How could she expect his love to last? She begged him to have mercy on her. But his love was impetuous. He wanted her, he wanted her with all his heart, and at last trembling, afraid, desirous, she yielded to him. Then there was a period of ecstatic happiness. The world, the dull, humdrum world of every day, blazed with glory. Love songs flowed from her pen. The woman worshipped the young, virile body of her lover. George flushed darkly when she praised his broad chest and slim flanks, the beauty of his legs and the flatness of his belly.

Hot stuff, Daphne's friend had said. It was that all right. Disgusting.

There were sad little pieces in which she lamented the emptiness of her life when as must happen he left her, but they ended with a cry that all she had to suffer would be worth it for the bliss that for a while had been hers. She wrote of the long, tremulous nights they passed together and the languor that lulled them to sleep in one another's arms. She wrote of the rapture of brief stolen moments when, braving all danger, their passion overwhelmed them and they surrendered to its call.

She thought it would be an affair of a few weeks, but miraculously it lasted. One of the poems referred to three years having gone by without lessening the love that filled their hearts. It looked as though he continued to press her to go away with him, far away, to a hill town in Italy, a Greek island, a walled city in Tunisia, so that they could be together always, for in another of the poems she besought him to let things be as they were. Their happiness was precarious. Perhaps it was owing to the difficulties they had to encounter and the rarity of their meetings that their love had retained for so long its first enchanting ardour. Then on a sudden the young man died. How, when or where George could not discover. There followed a long, heartbroken cry of bitter grief, grief she could not indulge in, grief that had to be hidden. She had to be cheerful, give dinner-parties and go out to dinner, behave as she had always behaved, though the light had gone out of her life and she was bowed down with anguish. The last poem of all was a set of four short stanzas in which the writer, sadly resigned to her loss, thanked the dark powers that rule man's destiny that she had been privileged at least for a while to enjoy the greatest happiness that we poor human beings can ever hope to know.

It was three o'clock in the morning when George Peregrine finally put the book down. It has seemed to him that he heard Evie's voice in every line, over and over again he came upon turns of phrase he had heard her use, there were details that were as familiar to him as to her: there was no doubt about it; it was her own story she had told, and it was as plain as anything could be that she had had a lover and her lover had died. It was not anger so much that he felt, nor horror or dismay, though he was dismayed and he was horrified, but amazement. It was as inconceivable that Evie should have had a love affair, and a widly passionate one at that, as that the trout in a glass case over the chimney piece in his study, the finest he had ever caught, should suddenly wag its tail. He understood now the meaning of the amused look he had seen in the eyes of that man he had spoken to at the club, he understood why Daphne when she was talking about the book had seemed to be enjoying a private joke, and why those two women at the cocktail party had tittered when he strolled past them.

He broke out into a sweat. Then on a sudden he was seized with fury and he jumped up to go and awake Evie and ask her sternly for an explanation. But he stopped at the door. After all, what proof had he? A book. He remembered that he'd told Evie he thought it jolly good. True, he hadn't read it, but he'd pretended he had. He would look a perfect fool if he had to admit that.

'I must watch my step,' he muttered.

He made up his mind to wait for two or three days and think it all over. Then he'd decide what to do. He went to bed, but he couldn't sleep for a long time.

'Evie,' he kept on saying to himself. 'Evie, of all people.'

They met at breakfast next morning as usual. Evie was as she always was, quiet, demure, and self-possessed, a middle-aged woman who made no effort to look younger than she was, a woman who had nothing of what he still called It. He looked at her as he hadn't looked at her for years. She had her usual placid serenity. Her pale blue eyes were untroubled. There was no sign of guilt on her candid brow. She made the same little casual remarks she always made.

'It's nice to get back to the country again after those two hectic days in London. What are you going to do this morning?'

It was incomprehensible.

Three days later he went to see his solicitor. Henry Blane was an old friend of George's as well as his lawyer. He had a place not far from Peregrine's and for years they had shot over one another's preserves. For two days a week he was a country gentleman and for the other five a busy lawyer in Sheffield. He was a tall, robust fellow, with a boisterous manner and a jovial laugh, which suggested that he liked to be looked upon essentially as a sportsman and a good fellow and only incidentally as a lawyer. But he was shrewd and wordly-wise.

'Well, George, what's brought you here today?' he boomed as the colonel was shown into his office. 'Have a good time in London? I'm taking my missus up for a few days next week. How's Evie?'

'It's about Evie I've come to see you,' said Peregrine, giving him a suspicious look. 'Have you read her book?'

His sensitivity had been sharpened during those last days of troubled thought and he was conscious of a faint change in the lawyer's expression. It was as though he were suddenly on his guard.

'Yes, I've read it. Great success, isn't it? Fancy Evie breaking out into poetry. Wonders will never cease.'

Geooge Peregrine was inclined to lose his temper.

'It's made me look a perfect damned fool.'

'Oh, what nonsense, George! There's no harm in Evie's writing a book. You ought to be jolly proud of her.'

'Don't talk such rot. It's her own story. You know it and everyone else knows it. I suppose I'm the only one who doesn't know who her lover was.'

'There is such a thing as imagination, old boy. There's no reason to suppose the whole thing isn't made up.'

'Look here, Henry, we've known one another all our lives. We've had all sorts of good times together. Be honest with me. Can you look me in the face and tell me you believe it's a made-up story?'

Harry Blane moved uneasily in his chair. He was disturbed by the distress in old George's voice.

'You're got no right to ask me a question like that. Ask Evie.'

'I daren't,' George answered after an anguished pause. 'I'm afraid she'd tell me the truth.'

There was an uncomfortable silence.

'Who was the chap?'

Harry Blane looked at him straight in the eye.

'I don't know, and if I did I wouldn't tell you.'

'You swine. Don't you see what a position I'm in? Do you think it's very pleasant to be made absolutely ridiculous?'

The lawyer lit a cigarette and for some moments silently puffed it.

'I don't see what I can do for you,' he said at last.

'You've got private detectives you employ, I suppose. I want you to put them on the job and let them find everything out.'

'It's not very pretty to put detectives on one's wife, old boy; and besides, taking for granted for a moment that Evie had an affair, it was a good many years ago and I don't suppose it would be possible to find out a thing. They seem to have covered their tracks pretty carefully.'

'I don't care. You put the detectives on. I want to know the truth.'

'I won't, George. If you're determined to do that you'd better consult someone else. And look here, even if you got evidence that Evie had been unfaithful to you what would you do with it? You'd look rather silly divorcing your wife because she'd committed adultery ten years ago.'

'At all events I could have it out with her.'

'You can do that now, but you know just as well as I do that if you do she'll leave you. D'you want her to do that?'

George gave him an unhappy look.

'I don't know. I always thought she'd been a damned good wife to me. She runs the house perfectly, we never have any servant trouble; she's done wonders with the garden and she's splendid with all the village people. But damn it, I have my self-respect to think of. How can I go on living with her when I know that she was grossly unfaithful to me?'

'Have you always been faithful to her?'

'More or less, you know. After all, we've been married for nearly twenty-four years and Evie was never much for bed.'

The solicitor slightly raised his eyebrows, but George was too intent on what he was saying to notice.

'I don't deny that I've had a bit of fun now and then. A man wants it. Women are different.'

'We only have men's word for that,' said Harry Blane, with a faint smile.

'Evie's absolutely the last woman I'd have suspected of kicking over the traces. In mean, she's a very fastidious, reticent woman. What on earth made her write the damned book?'

'I suppose it was a very poignant experience and perhaps it was a relief to her to get it off her chest like that.'

'Well, if she had to write it why the devil didn't she write it under an assumed name?'

'She used her maiden name. I suppose she thought that was enough, and it would have been if the book hadn't had this amazing boom.'

George Peregrine and the lawyer were sitting opposite one another with a desk between them. George, his elbow on the desk, his cheek on his hand, frowned at his thought.

'It's so rotten not to know what sort of a chap he was. One can't even tell if he was by way of being a gentleman. I mean, for all I know he may have been a farm-hand or a clerk in a lawyer's office.'

Harry Blane did not permit himself to smile and when he answered there was in his eyes a kindly, tolerant look.

'Knowing Evie so well I think the probabilities are that he was all right. Anyhow I'm sure he wasn't a clerk in my office.'

'It's been a shock to me,' the colonel sighed. 'I thought she was fond of me. She couldn't have written that book unless she hated me.'

'Oh, I don't believe that. I don't think she's capable of hatred.'

'You're not going to pretend that she loves me.'

'No.'

'Well, what does she feel for me?'

Harry Blane leaned back in his swivel chair and looked at George reflectively.

'Indifference, I should say.'

The colonel gave a little shudder and reddened.

'After all, you're not in love with her, are you?'

George Peregrine did not answer directly.

'It's been a great blow to me not to have any children, but I've never let her see that I think she's let me down. I've always been kind to her. Within reasonable limits I've tried to do my duty by her.'

The lawyer passed a large hand over his mouth to conceal the smile that trembled on his lips.

'It's been such an awful shock to me,' Peregrine went on. 'Damn it all, even ten years ago Evie was no chicken and God knows, she wasn't much to look at. It's so ugly.' He sighed deeply. 'What would *you* do in my place?'

'Nothing.'

George Peregrine drew himself bolt upright in his chair and he looked at Harry with the stern set face that he must have worn when he inspected his regiment.

'I can't overlook a thing like this. I've been made a laughing-stock. I can never hold up my head again.'

'Nonsense,' said the lawyer sharply, and then in a pleasant, kindly manner. 'Listen, old boy: the man's dead; it all happened a long while back. Forget it. Talk to people about Evie's book, rave about it, tell 'em how proud you are of her. Behave as though you had so much confidence in her, you *knew* she could never have been unfaithful to you. The world moves so quickly and people's memories are so short. They'll forget.'

'I shan't forget.'

'You're both middle-aged people. She probably does a great deal more for you than you think and you'd be awfully lonely without her. I don't think it matters if you don't forget. It'll be all to the good if you can get it into that thick head of yours that there's a lot more in Evie than you ever had the gumption to see.'

'Damn it all, you talk as if I was to blame.'

'No, I don't think you were to blame, but I'm not to sure that Evie was either. I don't suppose she wanted to fall in love with this boy. D'you remember those verses right at the end? The impression they gave me was that though she was shattered by his death in a strange sort of way she welcomed it. All through she'd been aware of the fragility of the tie that bound them. He died in the full flush of his first love and had never known that love so seldom endures; he'd only known its bliss and beauty. In her own bitter grief she found solace in the thought that he'd been spared all sorrow.'

'All that's a bit above my head, old boy. I see more or less what you mean.'

George Peregrine stared unhappily at the inkstand on the desk. He was silent and the lawyer looked at him with curious, yet sympathetic, eyes.

'Do you realize what courage she must have had never by a sign to show how dreadfully unhappy she was?' he said gently.

Colonel Peregrine sighed.

'I'm broken. I suppose you're right; it's no good crying over spilt milk and it would only make things worse if I made a fuss.'

'Well?'

George Peregrine gave a pitiful little smile.

'I'll take your advice. I'll do nothing. Let them think me a damned fool and to hell with them. The truth is, I don't know what I'd do without Evie. But I'll tell you what, there's one thing I shall never understand till my dying day: What in the name of heaven did the fellow ever see in her?'

Red

THE SKIPPER THRUST his hand into one of his trouser pockets and with difficulty, for they were not at the sides but in front and he was a portly man, pulled out a large silver watch. He looked at it and then looked again at the declining sun. The Kanaka at the wheel gave him a glance, but did not speak. The skipper's eyes rested on the island they were approaching. A white line of foam marked the reef. He knew there was an opening large enough to get his ship through, and when they came a little nearer he counted on seeing it. They had nearly an hour of daylight still before them. In the lagoon the water was deep and they could anchor comfortably. The chief of the village which he could already see among the coconut trees was a friend of the mate's, and it would be pleasant to go ashore for the night. The mate came forward at that minute and the skipper turned to him.

'We'll take a bottle of booze along with us and get some girls in to dance,' he said.

'I don't see the opening,' said the mate.

He was a Kanaka, a handsome, swarthy fellow, with somewhat the look of a later Roman emperor, inclined to stoutness; but his face was fine and clean-cut.

'I'm dead sure there's one right here,' said the captain, looking through his glasses. 'I can't understand why I can't pick it up. Send one of the boys up the mast to have a look.'

The mate called one of the crew and gave him the order. The captain watched the Kanaka climb and waited for him to speak. But the Kanaka shouted down that he could see nothing but the unbroken line of foam. The captain spoke Samoan like a native, and he cursed him freely.

'Shall he stay up there?' asked the mate.

'What the hell good does that do?' answered the captain.

'The blame fool can't see worth a cent. You bet your sweet life I'd find the opening if I was up there.'

He looked at the slender mast with anger. It was all very well for a native who had been used to climbing up coconut trees all his life. He was fat and heavy.

'Come down,' he shouted. 'You're no more use than a dead dog. We'll just have to go along the reef till we find the opening.'

It was a seventy-ton schooner with paraffin auxiliary, and it ran, when there was no head wind, between four and five knots an hour. It was a bedraggled object; it had been painted white a very long time ago, but it was now dirty, dingy, and mottled. It smelt strongly of paraffin, and of the copra which was its usual cargo. They were within a hundred feet of the reef now and the captain told the steersman to run along it till they came to the opening. But when they had gone a couple of miles he realized that they had missed it. He went about and slowly worked back again. The white foam of the reef continued without interruption and now the sun was setting. With a curse at the stupidity of the crew the skipper resigned himself to waiting till next morning.

'Put her about,' he said. 'I can't anchor here.'

They went out to sea a little and presently it was quite dark. They anchored. When the sail was furled the ship began to roll a good deal. They said in Apia that one day she would roll right over; and the owner, a German-American who managed one of the largest stores, said that no money was big enough to induce him to go out in her. The cook, a Chinese in white trousers, very dirty and ragged, and a thin white tunic, came to say that supper was ready, and when the skipper went into the cabin he found the engineer already seated at table. The engineer was a long, lean man with a scraggy neck. He was dressed in blue overalls and a sleeveless jersey which showed his thin arms tattooed from elbow to wrist.

'Hell, having to spend the night outside,' said the skipper.

The engineer did not answer, and they ate their supper in

silence. The cabin was lit by a dim oil-lamp. When they had eaten the canned apricots with which the meal finished the Chink brought them a cup of tea. The skipper lit a cigar and went on the upper deck. The island now was only a darker mass against the night. The stars were very bright. The only sound was the ceaseless breaking of the surf. The skipper sank into a deck-chair and smoked idly. Presently three or four members of the crew came up and sat down. One of them had a banjo and another a concertina. They began to play, and one of them sang. The native song sounded strange on these instruments. Then to the singing a couple began to dance. It was a barbaric dance, savage and primeval, rapid, with quick movements of the hands and feet and contortions of the body; it was sensual, sexual even, but sexual without passion. It was very animal, direct, weird without mystery, natural in short, and one might almost say childlike. At last they grew tired. They stretched themselves on the deck and slept, and all was silent. The skipper lifted himself heavily out of his chair and clambered down the companion. He went into his cabin and got out of his clothes. He climbed into his bunk and lay there. He panted a little in the heat of the night.

But next morning, when the dawn crept over the tranquil sea, the opening in the reef which had eluded them the night before was seen a little to the east of where they lay. The schooner entered the lagoon. There was not a ripple on the surface of the water. Deep down among the coral rocks you saw little coloured fish swim. When he had anchored his ship the skipper ate his breakfast and went on deck. The sun shone from an unclouded sky, but in the early morning the air was grateful and cool. It was Sunday, and there was a feeling of quietness, a silence as though nature were at rest, which gave him a peculiar sense of comfort. He sat, looking at the wooded coast, and felt lazy and well at ease. Presently a slow smile moved his lips and he threw the stump of his cigar into the water.

'I guess I'll go ashore,' he said. 'Get the boat out.'

He climbed stiffly down the ladder and was rowed to a little cove. The coconut trees came down to the water's edge, not in rows, but spaced out with an ordered formality. They were like a ballet of spinsters, elderly but flippant, standing in affected attitudes with the simpering graces of a bygone age. He sauntered idly through them, along a path that could be just seen winding its tortuous way, and it led him presently to a broad creek. There was a bridge across it, but a bridge constructed of single trunks of coconut trees, a dozen of them, placed end to end and supported where they met by a forked branch driven into the bed of the creek. You walked on a smooth, round surface, narrow and slippery, and there was no support for the hand. To cross such a bridge required sure feet and a stout heart. The skipper hesitated. But he saw on the other side, nestling among the trees, a white man's house; he made up his mind and, rather gingerly, began to walk. He watched his feet carefully, and where one trunk joined on to the next and there was a difference of level, he tottered a little. It was with a gasp of relief that he reached the last tree and finally set his feet on the firm ground of the other side. He had been so intent on the difficult crossing that he never noticed anyone was watching him, and it was with surprise that he heard himself spoken to.

'It takes a bit of nerve to cross these bridges when you're not used to them.'

He looked up and saw a man standing in front of him. He had evidently come out of the house which he had seen.

'I saw you hesitate,' the man continued, with a smile on his lips, 'and I was watching to see you fall in.'

'Not on your life,' said the captain, who had now recovered his confidence.

'I've fallen in myself before now. I remember, one evening I came back from shooting, and I fell in, gun and all. Now I get a boy to carry my gun for me.'

He was a man no longer young, with a small beard, now somewhat grey, and a thin face. He was dressed in a singlet, without arms, and a pair of duck trousers. He wore neither shoes nor socks. He spoke English with a slight accent.

'Are you Neilson?' asked the skipper.

'I am.'

'I've heard about you. I thought you lived somewheres round here.'

The skipper followed his host into the little bungalow and sat down heavily in the chair which the other motioned him to take. While Neilson went out to fetch whisky and glasses he took a look round the room. It filled him with amazement. He had never seen so many books. The shelves reached from floor to ceiling on all four walls, and they were closely packed. There was a grand piano littered with music, and a large table on which books and magazines lay in disorder. The room made him feel embarrassed. He remembered that Neilson was a queer fellow. No one knew very much about him, although he had been in the islands for so many years, but those who knew him agreed that he was queer. He was a Swede.

'You've got one big heap of books here,' he said, when Neilson returned.

'They do no harm,' answered Neilson with a smile.

'Have you read them all?' asked the skipper.

'Most of them.'

'I'm a bit of a reader myself. I have the *Saturday Evening Post* sent me regler.'

Neilson poured his visitor a good stiff glass of whisky and gave him a cigar. The skipper volunteered a little information.

'I got in last night, but I couldn't find the opening, so I had to anchor outside. I never been this run before, but my people had some stuff they wanted to bring over here. Gray, d'you know him?'

'Yes, he's got a store a little way along.'

'Well, there was a lot of canned stuff that he wanted over, an' he's got some copra. They thought I might just as well come over as lie idle at Apia. I run between Apia and Pago-

Pago mostly, but they've got smallpox there just now, and there's nothing stirring.'

He took a drink of his whisky and lit a cigar. He was a taciturn man, but there was something in Neilson that made him nervous, and his nervousness made him talk. The Swede was looking at him with large dark eyes in which there was an expression of faint amusement.

'This is a tidy little place you've got here.'

'I've done my best with it.'

'You must do pretty well with your trees. They look fine. With copra at the price it is now. I had a bit of a plantation myself once, in Upolu it was, but I had to sell it.'

He looked round the room again, where all those books gave him a feeling of something incomprehensible and hostile.

'I guess you must find it a bit lonesome here though,' he said.

'I've got used to it. I've been here for twenty-five years.'

Now the captain could think of nothing more to say, and he smoked in silence. Neilson had apparently no wish to break it. He looked at his guest with a meditative eye. He was a tall man, more than six feet high, and very stout. His face was red and blotchy, with a network of little purple veins on the cheeks, and his features were sunk into its fatness. His eyes were bloodshot. His neck was buried in rolls of fat. But for a fringe of long curly hair, nearly white, at the back of his head, he was quite bald; and that immense, shiny surface of forehead, which might have given him a false look of intelligence, on the contrary gave him one of peculiar imbecility. He wore a blue flannel shirt, open at the neck and showing his fat chest covered with a mat of reddish hair , and a very old pair of blue serge trousers. He sat in his chair in a heavy ungainly attitude, his great belly thrust forward and his fat legs uncrossed. All elasticity had gone from his limbs. Neilson wondered idly what sort of man he had been in his youth. It was almost impossible to imagine that this creature of vast bulk had ever been a boy who ran about. The skipper finished his whisky, and Neilson pushed the bottle towards him.

'Help yourself.'

The skipper leaned forward and with his great hand seized it.

'And how come you in these parts anyways?' he said.

'Oh, I came out to the islands for my health. My lungs were bad and they said I hadn't a year to live. You see they were wrong.'

'I meant, how come you to settle down right here?'

'I am a sentimentalist.'

'Oh!'

Neilson knew that the skipper had not an idea what he meant, and he looked at him with an ironical twinkle in his dark eyes. Perhaps just because the skipper was so gross and dull a man the whim seized him to talk further.

'You were too busy keeping your balance to notice, when you crossed the bridge, but this spot is generally considered rather pretty.'

'It's a cute little house you've got here.'

'Ah, that wasn't here when I first came. There was a native hut, with its beehive roof and its pillars, overshadowed by a great tree with red flowers; and the croton bushes, their leaves yellow and red and golden, made a pied fence around it. And then all about were the coconut trees, as fanciful as women, and as vain. They stood at the water's edge and spent all day looking at their reflections. I was a young man then – good heavens, it's a quarter of a century ago – and I wanted to enjoy all the loveliness of the world in the short time allotted to me before I passed into the darkness. I thought it was the most beautiful spot I had ever seen. The first time I saw it I had a catch at my heart, and I was afraid I was going to cry. I wasn't more than twenty-five, and though I put the best face I could on it, I didn't want to die. And somehow it seemed to me that the very beauty of this place made it easier for me to accept my fate. I felt when I came here that all my past life had fallen away, Stockholm and its University, and then Bonn: it all seemed the life of somebody else, as though now at last I had achieved the reality which our doctors of philosophy – I am one myself, you know – had discussed so much. "A year," I cried to myself. "I have a year. I will spend it here and then I am content to die."

'We are foolish and sentimental and melodramatic at twenty-five, but if we weren't perhaps we should be less wise at fifty.

'Now drink, my friend. Don't let the nonsense I talk interfere with you.'

He waved his thin hand towards the bottle, and the skipper finished what remained in his glass.

'You ain't drinking nothin',' he said, reaching for the whisky.

'I am of sober habit,' smiled the Swede. 'I intoxicate myself in ways which I fancy are more subtle. But perhaps that is only vanity. Anyhow, the effects are more lasting and the results less deleterious.'

'They say there's a deal of cocaine taken in the States now,' said the captain.

Neilson chuckled.

'But I do not see a white man often,' he continued, 'and for once I don't think a drop of whisky can do me any harm.'

He poured himself out a little, added some soda, and took a sip.

'And presently I found out why the spot had such an unearthly loveliness. Here love had tarried for a moment like a migrant bird that happens on a ship in mid-ocean and for a little while folds its tired wings. The fragrance of a beautiful passion hovered over it like the fragrance of hawthorn in May in the meadows of my home. It seems to me that the places where men have loved or suffered keep about them always some faint aroma of something that has not wholly died. It is as though they had acquired a spiritual significance which mysteriously affects those who pass. I wish I could make myself clear.' He smiled a little. 'Though I cannot imagine that if I did you would understand.'

He paused.

'I think this place was beautiful because here for a period the ecstasy of love had invested it with beauty.' And now he shrugged his shoulders. 'But perhaps it is only that my aesthetic sense is gratified by the happy conjunction of young love and a suitable setting.'

Even a man less thick-witted than the skipper might have been forgiven if he were bewildered by Neilson's words. For he seemed faintly to laugh at what he said. It was as though he spoke from emotion which his intellect found ridiculous. He had said himself that he was a sentimentalist, and when sentimentality is joined with scepticism there is often the devil to pay.

He was silent for an instant and looked at the captain with eyes in which there was a sudden perplexity.

'You know, I can't help thinking that I've seen you before somewhere or other,' he said.

'I couldn't say as I remember you,' returned the skipper.

'I have a curious feeling as though your face were familiar to me. It's been puzzling me for some time. But I can't situate my recollection in any place or at any time.'

The skipper massively shrugged his heavy shoulders.

'It's thirty years since I first come to the islands. A man can't figure on remembering all the folk he meets in a while like that.'

The Swede shook his head.

'You know how one sometimes has the feeling that a place one has never been to before is strangely familiar. That's how I seem to see you.' He gave a whimsical smile. 'Perhaps I knew you in some past existence. Perhaps, perhaps you were the master of a galley in ancient Rome and I was a slave at the oar. Thirty years have you been here?'

'Every bit of thirty years.'

'I wonder if you knew a man called Red?'

'Red?'

'That is the only name I've ever known him by. I never knew him personally. I never even set eyes on him. And yet I seem to see him more clearly than many men, my brothers, for instance, with whom I passed my daily life for many years. He lives in my imagination with the distinctness of a Paolo Malatesta or a Romeo. But I dare say you have never read Dante or Shakespeare?'

'I can't say as I have,' said the captain.

Neilson, smoking a cigar, leaned back in his chair and looked vacantly at the ring of smoke which floated in the still air. A smile played on his lips, but his eyes were grave. Then he looked at the captain. There was in his gross obesity something extraordinarily repellent. He had the plethoric self-satisfaction of the very fat. It was an outrage. It set Neilson's nerves on edge. But the contrast between the man before him and the man he had in mind was pleasant.

'It appears that Red was the most comely thing you ever saw. I've talked to quite a number of people who knew him in those days, white men, and they all agree that the first time you saw him his beauty just took your breath away. They called him Red on account of his flaming hair. It had a natural wave and he wore it long. It must have been of that wonderful colour that the pre-Raphaelites raved over. I don't think he was vain of it, he was much too ingenuous for that, but no one could have blamed him if he had been. He was tall, six feet and an inch or two – in the native house that used to stand here was the mark of his height cut with a knife on the central trunk that supported the roof – and he was made like a Greek god, broad in the shoulders and thin in the flanks; he was like Apollo, with just that soft roundness which Praxiteles gave him, and that suave, feminine grace which has in it something troubling and mysterious. His skin was dazzling white, milky, like satin; his skin was like a woman's.'

'I had kind of a white skin myself when I was a kiddie,' said the skipper, with a twinkle in his bloodshot eyes.

But Neilson paid no attention to him. He was telling his story now and interruption made him impatient.

'And his face was just as beautiful as his body. He had large blue eyes, very dark, so that some say they were black, and unlike most red-haired people he had dark eyebrows and long dark lashes. His features were perfectly regular and his mouth was like a scarlet wound. He was twenty.'

On these words the Swede stopped with a certain sense of the dramatic. He took a sip of whisky.

'He was unique. There never was anyone more beautiful. There was no more reason for him than for a wonderful blossom to flower on a wild plant. He was a happy accident of nature.

'One day he landed at that cove into which you must have put this morning. He was an American sailor and he had deserted from a man-of-war in Apia. He had induced some good-humoured native to give him a passage on a cutter that happened to be sailing from Apia to Safoto, and he had been put ashore here in a dug-out. I do not know why he deserted. Perhaps life on a man-of-war with its restrictions irked him, perhaps he was in trouble, and perhaps it was the South Seas and these romantic islands that got into his bones. Every now and then they take a man strangely, and he finds himself like a fly in a spider's web. It may be that there was a softness of fibre in him, and these green hills with their soft airs, this blue sea, took the northern strength from him as Delilah took the Nazarite's. Anyhow, he wanted to hide himself, and he thought he would be safe in this secluded nook till his ship had sailed from Samoa.

'There was a native hut at the cove and as he stood there, wondering where exactly he should turn his steps, a young girl came out and invited him to enter. He knew scarcely two words of the native tongue and she as little English. But he understood well enough what her smiles meant, and her pretty gestures, and he followed her. He sat down on a mat and she gave him slices of pineapple to eat. I can speak of Red only from hearsay, but I saw the girl three years after he first met her, and she was scarcely nineteen then. You cannot imagine how exquisite she was. She had the passionate grace of the hibiscus and the rich colour. She was rather tall, slim, with the delicate features of her race, and large eyes like pools of still water under the palm trees; her hair, black and curling, fell down her back, and she wore a wreath of scented flowers. Her hands were lovely. They were so small, so exquisitely formed, they gave your heart-strings a wrench. And in those days she laughed easily. Her smile was so delightful that it made your knees shake. Her skin was like a field of ripe corn on a summer day. Good heavens, how can I describe her? She was too beautiful to be real.

'And these two young things, she was sixteen and he was twenty, fell in love with one another at first sight. That is the real love, not the love that comes from sympathy, common interests, of intellectual community, but love pure and simple. That is the love that Adam felt for Eve when he awoke and found her in the garden gazing at him with dewy eyes. That is the love that draws the beasts to one another, and the Gods. That is the love that makes the world a miracle. That is the love which gives life its pregnant meaning. You have never heard of the wise, cynical French duke who said that with two lovers there is always one who loves and one who lets himself be loved; it is bitter truth to which most of us have to resign ourselves; but now and then there are two who love and two who let themselves be loved. Then one might fancy that the sun stands still as it stood when Joshua prayed to the God of Isreal.

'And even now after all these years, when I think of these two, so young, so fair, so simple, and of their love, I feel a pang. It tears my heart just as my heart is torn when on certain nights I watch the full moon shining on the lagoon from an unclouded sky. There is always pain in the contemplation of perfect beauty.

'They were children. She was good and sweet and kind. I know nothing of him, and I like to think that then at all events he was ingenuous and frank. I like to think that his soul was as comely as his body. But I dare say he had no more soul than the creatures of the woods and forests who made pipes from reeds and bathed in the mountain streams when the world was young, and you might catch sight of little fawns galloping through the glade on the back of a bearded centaur. A soul is a troublesome possession and when man developed it he lost the Garden of Eden.

'Well, when Red came to the island it had recently been visited by one of those epidemics which the white man brought to the South Seas, and one third of the inhabitants had died. It seems that the girl had lost all her near kin and she lived now in the house of distant cousins. The household consisted of two ancient crones, bowed and wrinkled, two younger women, and a man and a boy. For a few days he stayed there. But perhaps he felt himself too near the shore, with the possibility that he might fall in with white men who would reveal his hiding-place; perhaps the lovers could not bear that the company of others should rob them for an instant of the delight of being together. One morning they set out, the pair of them, with the few things that belonged to the girl, and walked along a grassy path under the coconuts, till they came to the creek you see. They had to cross the bridge you crossed, and the girl laughed gleefully because he was afraid. She held his hand till they came to the end of the first tree, and then his courage failed him and he had to go back. He was obliged to take off all his clothes before he could risk it, and she carried them over for him on her head. They settled down in the empty but that stood there. Whether she had any rights over it (land tenure is a complicated business in the islands), or whether the owner had died during the epidemics, I do not know, but anyhow no one questioned them, and they took possession. Their furniture consisted of a couple of grass mats on which they slept, a fragment of looking-glass, and a bowl or two. In this pleasant land that is enough to start housekeeping on.

'They say that happy people have no history, and certainly

a happy love had none. They did nothing all day long and yet the days seemed all too short. The girl had a native name, but Red called her Sally. He picked up the easy language very quickly, and he used to lie on the mat for hours while she chattered gaily to him. He was a silent fellow, and perhaps his mind was lethargic. He smoked incessantly the cigarettes which she made him out of the native tobacco and pandanus leaf, and he watched her while with deft fingers she made grass mats. Often natives would come in and tell long stories of the old days when the island was disturbed by tribal wars. Sometimes he would go fishing on the reef, and bring home a basket full of coloured fish. Sometimes at night he would go out with a lantern to catch lobster. There were plantains round the hut and Sally would roast them for their frugal meal. She knew how to make delicious messes from coconuts, and the breadfruit tree by the side of the creek gave them its fruit. On feast-days they killed a little pig and cooked it on hot stones. They bathed together in the creek; and in the evening they went down to the lagoon and paddled about in a dug-out, with its great outrigger. The sea was deep blue, wine-coloured at sundown, like the sea of Homeric Greece; but in the lagoon the colour had an infinite variety, aquamarine and amethyst and emerald; and the setting sun turned it for a short moment to liquid gold. Then there was the colour of the coral, brown, white, pink, red, purple; and the shapes it took were marvellous. It was like a magic garden, and the hurrying fish were like butterflies. It strangely lacked reality. Among the coral were pools with a floor of white sand and here, where the water was dazzling clear, it was very good to bathe. Then, cool and happy, they wandered back in the gloaming over the soft grass road to the creek, walking hand in hand, and now the mynah birds filled the coconut trees with their clamour. And then the night, with that great sky shining with gold, that seemed to stretch more widely than the skies of Europe, and the soft airs that blew gently through the open hut, the long night again was all too short. She was sixteen and he was barely twenty. The dawn crept in among the wooden pillars of the hut and looked at those lovely children sleeping in one another's arms. The sun hid behind the great tattered leaves of the plantains so that it might not disturb them, and then, with playful malice, shot a golden ray, like the outstretched paw of a Persian cat, on their faces. They opened their sleepy eyes and they smiled to welcome another day. The weeks lengthened into months, and a year passed. They seemed to love one another as – I hesitate to say passionately, for passion has in it always a shade of sadness, a touch of bitterness or anguish, but as wholeheartedly, as simply and naturally as on that first day on which, meeting, they had recognized that a god was in them.

'If you had asked them I have no doubt that they would have thought it impossible to suppose their love could ever cease. Do we not know that the essential element of love is a belief in its own eternity? And yet perhaps in Red there was already a very little seed, unknown to himself and unsuspected by the girl which would in time have grown to weariness. For one day one of the natives of the cove told them that some way down the coast at the anchorage was a British whaling-ship.

'"Gee," he said, "I wonder if I could make a trade of some nuts and plantains for a pound or two of tobacco."

'The pandanus cigarettes that Sally made him with untiring hands were strong and pleasant enough to smoke, but they left him unsatisfied; and he yearned on a sudden for real tobacco, hard, rank, and pungent. He had not smoked a pipe for many months. His mouth watered at the thought of it. One would have thought some premonition of harm would have made Sally seek to dissuade him, but love possessed her so completely that it never occurred to her any power on earth could take him from her. They went up into the hills together and gathered a great basket of wild oranges, green, but sweet and juicy; and they picked plantains from around the hut, and coconuts from their trees, and breadfruit and mangoes; and they carried them down to the cove. They loaded the unstable canoe with them, and Red and the native boy who had brought them the news of the ship paddled along outside the reef.

'It was the last time she ever saw him.

'Next day the boy came back alone. He was all in tears. This is the story he told. When after their long paddle they reached the ship and Red hailed it, a white man looked over the side and told them to come on board. They took the fruit they had brought with them and Red piled it up on the deck. The white man and he began to talk, and they seemed to come to some agreement. One of them went below and brought up tobacco. Red took some at once and lit a pipe. The boy imitated the zest with which he blew a great cloud of smoke from his mouth. Then they said something to him and he went into the cabin. Through the open door the boy, watching curiously, saw a bottle brought out and glasses. Red drank and smoked. They seemed to ask him something, for he shook his head and laughed. The man, the first man who had spoken to them, laughed too, and he filled Red's glass once more. They went on talking and drinking, and presently, growing tired of watching a sight that meant nothing to him, the boy curled himself up on the deck and slept. He was awakened by a kick; and jumping to his feet, he saw that the ship was slowly sailing out of the lagoon. He caught sight of Red seated at the table, with his head resting heavily on his arms, fast asleep. He made a movement towards him, intending to wake him, but a rough hand seized his arm, and a man, with a scowl and words which he did not understand, pointed to the side. He shouted to Red, but in a moment he was seized and flung overboard. Helpless, he swam round to his canoe, which was drifting a little way off, and pushed it on to the reef. He climbed in and, sobbing all the way, paddled back to shore.

'What had happened was obvious enough. The whaler, by desertion or sickness, was short of hands, and the captain when Red came aboard had asked him to sign on; on his refusal he had made him drunk and kidnapped him.

'Sally was beside herself with grief. For three days she screamed and cried. The natives did what they could to comfort her, but she would not be comforted. She would not eat. And then, exhausted, she sank into a sullen apathy. She spent long days at the cove, watching the lagoon, in the vain hope that Red somehow or other would manage to escape. She sat on the white sand, hour after hour, with the tears running down her cheeks, and at night dragged herself wearily back across the creek to the little hut where she had been happy. The people with whom she had lived before Red came to the island wished her to return to them, but she would not; she was convinced that Red would come back, and she wanted him to find her where he had left her. Four months later she was delivered of a still-born child, and the old woman who had come to help her through her confinement remained with her in the hut. All joy was taken from her life. If her anguish with time became less intolerable it was replaced by a settled melancholy. You would not have thought that among these people, whose emotions, though so violent, are very transient, a woman could be found capable of so enduring a passion. She never lost the profound conviction that sooner or later Red would come back. She watched for him, and every time someone crossed this slender little bridge of coconut trees she looked. It might at last be he.'

Neilson stopped talking and gave a faint sigh.

'And what happened to her in the end?' asked the skipper.

Neilson smiled bitterly.

'Oh, three years afterwards she took up with another white man.'

The skipper gave a fat, cynical chuckle.

'That's generally what happens to them,' he said.

The Swede shot him a look of hatred. He did not know why that gross, obese man excited in him so violent a repulsion. But his thoughts wandered and he found his mind filled with memories of the past. He went back five-and-twenty years. It was when he first came to the island, weary of Apia, with its heavy drinking, its gambling and coarse sensuality, a sick man, trying to resign himself to the loss of the career which had fired his imagination with ambitious thought. He set behind him resolutely all his hopes of making a great name for himself and strove to content himself with the few poor months of careful life which was all that he could count on. He was boarding with a half-caste trader who had a store a couple of miles along the coast at the edge of a native village; and one day, wandering aimlessly along the grassy paths of the coconut groves, he had come upon the hut in which Sally lived. The beauty of the spot had filled him with a rapture so great that it was almost painful, and then he had seen Sally. She was the loveliest creature he had ever seen, and the sadness in those dark, magnificent eyes of hers affected him strangely. The Kanakas were a handsome race, and beauty was not rare among them, but it was the beauty of shapely animals. It was empty. But those tragic eyes were dark with mystery, and you felt in them the bitter complexity of the groping, human soul. The trader told him the story and it moved him.

'Do you think he'll ever come back?' asked Neilson.

'No fear. Why, it'll be a couple of years before the ship is paid off, and by then he'll have forgotten all about her. I bet he was pretty mad when he woke up and found he'd been shanghaied, and I shouldn't wonder but he wanted to fight somebody. But he'd got to grin and bear it, and I guess in a month he was thinking it the best thing that had ever happened to him that he got away from the island.'

But Neilson could not get the story out of his head. Perhaps because he was sick and weakly, the radiant health of Red appealed to his imagination. Himself an ugly man, insignificant of appearance, he prized very highly comeliness in others. He had never been passionately in love, and certainly he had never been passionately loved. The mutual attraction of those two young things gave him a singular delight. It had the ineffable beauty of the Absolute. He went again to the little hut by the creek. He had a gift for languages and an energetic mind, accustomed to work, and he had already given much time to the study of the local tongue. Old habit was strong in him and he was gathering together material for a paper on the Samoan speech. The old crone who shared the hut with Sally invited him to come in and sit down. She gave him *kava* to drink and cigarettes to smoke. She was glad to have someone to chat with and while she talked he looked at Sally. She reminded him of the Psyche in the museum at Naples. Her features had the same clear purity of line, and though she had borne a child she had still a virginal aspect.

It was not till he had seen her two or three times that he induced her to speak. Then it was only to ask him if he had seen in Apia a man called Red. Two years had passed since his disappearance, but it was plain that she still thought of him incessantly.

It did not take Neilson long to discover that he was in love with her. It was only by an effort of will now that he prevented himself from going every day to the creek, and when he was not with Sally his thoughts were. At first, looking upon himself as a dying man, he asked only to look at her, and occasionally hear her speak, and his love gave him a wonderful happiness. He exulted in its purity. He wanted nothing from her but the opportunity to weave around her graceful person a web of beautiful fancies. But the open air, the equable temperature, the rest, the simple fare, began to have an unexpected effect on his health. His temperature did not soar at night to such alarming heights, he coughed less and began to put on weight; six months passed without his having a haemorrhage; and on a sudden he saw the possibility that he might live. He had studied his disease carefully, and the hope dawned upon him that with great care he might arrest its course. It exhilarated him to look forward once more to the future. He made plans. It was evident that any active life was out of the question, but he could live on the islands, and the small income he had, insufficient elsewhere, would be ample to keep him. He could grow coconuts; that would give him an occupation; and he would send for his books and a piano; but his quick mind saw that in all this he was merely trying to conceal from himself the desire which obsessed him.

He wanted Sally. He loved not only her beauty, but that dim soul which he divined behind her suffering eyes. He would intoxicate her with his passion. In the end he would make her forget. And in an ecstasy of surrender he fancied himself giving her too the happiness which he had thought never to know again, but had now so miraculously achieved.

He asked her to live with him. She refused. He had expected that and did not let it depress him, for he was sure that sooner or later she would yield. His love was irresistible. He told the old woman of his wishes, and found somewhat to his surprise that she and the neighbours, long aware of them, were strongly urging Sally to accept his offer. After all, every native was glad to keep house for a white man, and Neilson according to the standards of the island was a rich one. The trader with whom he boarded went to her and told her not to be a fool; such an opportunity would not come again, and after so long she could not still believe that Red would ever return. The girl's resistance only increased Neilson's desire, and what had been a very pure love now became an agonizing passion. He was determined that nothing should stand in his way. He gave Sally no peace. At last, worn out by his persistence and the persuasions, by turns pleading and angry, of everyone around her, she consented. But the day after, when exultant he went to see her he found that in the night she had burnt down the hut in which she and Red had lived together. The old crone ran towards him full of angry abuse of Sally, but he waved her aside; it did not matter; they would build a bungalow on the place where the hut had stood. A European house would really be more convenient if he wanted to bring out a piano and a vast number of books.

And so the little wooden house was built in which he had now lived for many years, and Sally became his wife. But after the first few weeks of rapture, during which he was satisfied with what she gave him, he had known little happiness. She had yielded to him, through weariness, but she had only yielded what she set no store on. The soul which he had dimly glimpsed escaped him. He knew that she cared nothing for him. She still loved Red, and all the time she was waiting for his return. At a sign from him, Neilson knew that, notwithstanding his love, his tenderness, his sympathy, his generosity, she would leave him without a moment's hesitation. She would never give a thought to his distress. Anguish seized him and he battered at that impenetrable self of hers which sullenly resisted him. His love became bitter. He tried to melt her heart with kindness, but it remained as hard as before; he feigned indifference, but she did not notice it. Sometimes he lost his temper and abused her, and then she wept silently. Sometimes he thought she was nothing but a fraud, and that soul simply an invention of his own, and that he could not get into the sanctuary of her heart because there was no sanctuary there. His love became a prison from which he longed to escape, but he had not the strength merely to open the door – that was all it needed – and walk out into the open air. It was torture and at last he became numb and hopeless. In the end the fire burnt itself out and, when he saw her eyes rest for an instant on the slender bridge, it was no longer rage that filled his heart but impatience. For many years now they had lived together bound by the ties of habit and convenience, and it was with a smile that he looked back on his old passion. She was an old woman, for the women on the islands age quickly, and if he had no love for her any more he had tolerance. She left him alone. He was contented with his piano and his books.

His thoughts led him to a desire for words.

'When I look back now and reflect on that brief passionate love of Red and Sally, I think that perhaps they should thank the ruthless fate that separated them when their love seemed still to be at its height. They suffered, but they suffered in beauty. They were spared the real tragedy of love.'

'I don't know exactly as I get you,' said the skipper.

'The tragedy of love is not death or separation. How long do you think it would have been before one or other of them ceased to care? Oh, it is dreadfully bitter to look at a woman whom you have loved with all your heart and soul, so that you felt you could not bear to let her out of your sight, and realize that you would not mind if you never saw her again. The tragedy of love is indifference.'

But while he was speaking a very extraordinary thing happened. Though he had been addressing the skipper he had not been talking to him, he had been putting his thoughts into words for himself, and with his eyes fixed on the man in front of him he had not seen him. But now an image presented itself to them, an image not of the man he saw, but of another man. It was as though he were looking into one of those distorting mirrors that make you extraordinarily squat or outrageously elongate, but here exactly the opposite took place, and in the obese, ugly old man he caught the shadowy glimpse of a stripling. He gave him now a quick, searching scrutiny. Why had a haphazard stroll brought him just to this place? A sudden tremor of his heart made him slightly breathless. An absurd suspicion seized him. What had occurred to him was impossible and yet it might be a fact.

'What is your name?' he asked abruptly.

The skipper's face puckered and he gave a cunning chuckle. He looked then malicious and horribly vulgar.

'It's such a damned long time since I heard it that I almost forget it myself. But for thirty years now in the islands they've always called me Red.'

His huge form shook as he gave a low, almost silent laugh. It was obscene. Neilson shuddered. Red was hugely amused, and from his bloodshot eyes tears ran down his cheeks.

Neilson gave a gasp, for at that moment a woman came in. She was a native, a woman of somewhat commanding presence, stout without being corpulent, dark, for the natives grow darker with age, with very grey hair. She wore a black Mother Hubbard, and its thinness showed her heavy breasts. The moment had come.

She made an observation to Neilson about some household matter and he answered. He wondered if his voice sounded as unnatural to her as it did to himself. She gave the man who was sitting in the chair by the window an indifferent glance, and went out of the room. The moment had come and gone.

Neilson for a moment could not speak. He was strangely shaken. Then he said:

'I'd be very glad if you'd stay and have a bit of dinner with me. Pot luck.'

'I don't think I will,' said Red. 'I must go after this fellow Gray. I'll give him his stuff and then I'll get away. I want to be back in Apia tomorrow.'

'I'll send a boy along with you to show you the way.'

'That'll be fine.'

Red heaved himself out of his chair, while the Swede called one of the boys who worked on the plantation. He told him where the skipper wanted to go, and the boy stepped along the bridge. Red prepared to follow him.

'Don't fall in,' said Neilson.

'Not on your life.'

Neilson watched him make his way across and when he had disappeared among the coconuts he looked still. Then he sank heavily in his chair. Was that the man who had prevented him from being happy? Was that the man whom Sally had loved all these years and for whom she had waited so desperately? It was grotesque. A sudden fury seized him so that he had an instinct to spring up and smash everything around him. He had been cheated. They had seen each other at last and had not known it. He began to laugh, mirthlessly, and his laughter grew till it became hysterical. The Gods had played him a cruel trick. And he was old now.

At last Sally came in to tell him dinner was ready. He sat down in front of her and tried to eat. He wondered what she would say if he told her now that the fat old man sitting in the chair was the lover whom she remembered still with the passionate abandonment of her youth. Years ago, when he hated her because she made him so unhappy, he would have been glad to tell her. He wanted to hurt her then as she hurt him, because his hatred was only love. But now he did not care. He shrugged his shoulders listlessly.

'What did that man want?' she asked presently.

He did not answer at once. She was too old, a fat old native woman. He wondered why he had ever loved her so madly. He had laid at her feet all the treasures of his soul, and she had cared nothing for them. Waste, what waste! And now, when he looked at her, he felt only contempt. His patience was at last exhausted. He answered her question.

'He's the captain of a schooner. He's come from Apia.'

'Yes.'

'He brought me news from home. My eldest brother is very ill and I must go back.'

'Will you be gone long?'

He shrugged his shoulders.

The Lotus Eater

MOST PEOPLE, the vast majority in fact, lead the lives that circumstances have thrust upon them, and though some repine, looking upon themselves as round pegs in square holes, and think that if things had been different they might have made a much better showing, the greater part accept their lot, if not with serenity, at all events with resignation. They are like tramcars travelling for ever on the selfsame rails. They go backwards and forwards, backwards and forwards, inevitably, till they can go no longer and then are sold as scrap-iron. It is not often that you find a man who has boldly taken the course of his life into his own hands. When you do, it is worth while having a good look at him.

That was why I was curious to meet Thomas Wilson. It was an interesting and a bold thing he had done. Of course the end was not yet and until the experiment was concluded it was impossible to call it successful. But from what I had heard it seemed he must be an odd sort of fellow and I thought I should like to know him. I had been told he was reserved, but I had a notion that with patience and tact I could persuade him to confide in me. I wanted to hear the facts from his own lips. People exaggerate, they love to romanticize, and I was quite prepared to discover that his story was not nearly so singular as I had been led to believe.

And this impression was confirmed when at last I made his acquaintance. It was on the Piazza in Capri, where I was spending the month of August at a friend's villa, and a little before sunset, when most of the inhabitants, native and foreign, gather together to chat with their friends in the cool of the evening. There is a terrace that overlooks the Bay of Naples, and when the sun sinks slowly into the sea the island of Ischia is silhouetted against a blaze of splendour. It is one of the most lovely sights in the world. I was standing there with my friend and host watching it, when suddenly he said:

'Look, there's Wilson.'

'Where?'

'The man sitting on the parapet, with his back to us. He's got a blue shirt on.'

I saw an undistinguished back and a small head of grey hair, short and rather thin.

'I wish he'd turn round,' I said.

'He will presently.'

'Ask him to come and have a drink with us at Morgano's.'

'All right.'

The instant of overwhelming beauty had passed and the sun, like the top of an orange, was dipping into a wine-red sea. We turned round and leaning our backs against the parapet looked at the people who were sauntering to and fro. They were all talking their heads off and the cheerful noise was exhilarating. Then the church bell, rather cracked, but with a fine resonant note, began to ring. The Piazza at Capri, with its clock tower over the footpath that leads up from the harbour, with the church up a flight of steps, is a perfect setting for an opera by Donizetti, and you felt that the voluble crowd might at any moment break out into a rattling chorus. It was charming and unreal.

I was so intent on the scene that I had not noticed Wilson get off the parapet and come towards us. As he passed us my friend stopped him.

'Hullo, Wilson, I haven't seen you bathing the last few days.'

'I've been bathing on the other side for a change.'

My friend then introduced me. Wilson shook hands with me politely, but with indifference; a great many strangers come to Capri for a few days, or a few weeks, and I had no doubt he was constantly meeting people who came and went; and then my friend asked him to come along and have a drink with us.

'I was just going back to supper,' he said.

'Can't it wait?' I asked.

'I suppose it can,' he smiled.

Though his teeth were not very good his smile was attractive. It was gentle and kindly. He was dressed in a blue cotton shirt and a pair of grey trousers, much creased and none too clean, of a thin canvas, and on his feet he wore a pair of very old espadrilles. The get-up was picturesque, and very suitable to the place and the weather, but it did not at all go with his face. It was a lined, long face, deeply sunburned, thin-lipped, with small grey eyes rather close together and tight, neat features. The grey hair was carefully brushed. It was not a plain face, indeed in his youth Wilson might have been good-looking, but a prim one. He wore the blue shirt, open at the neck, and the grey canvas trousers, not as though they belonged to him, but as though, shipwrecked in his pyjamas, he had been fitted out with odd garments by compassionate strangers. Notwithstanding this careless attire he looked like the manager of a branch office in an insurance company, who should by rights be wearing a black coat with pepper-and-salt trousers, a white collar, and an unobjectionable tie. I could very well see myself going to him to claim the insurance money when I had lost a watch, and being rather disconcerted while I answered the questions he put to me by his obvious impression, for all his politeness, that people who made such claims were either fools or knaves.

Moving off, we strolled across the Piazza and down the street till we came to Morgano's. We sat in the garden. Around us people were talking in Russian, German, Italian, and English. We ordered drinks. Donna Lucia, the host's wife, waddled up and in her low, sweet voice passed the time of day with us. Though middle-aged now and portly, she had still traces of the wonderful beauty that thirty years before had driven artists to paint so many bad portraits of her. Her eyes, large and liquid, were the eyes of Hera and her smile was affectionate and gracious. We three gossiped for a while, for there is always a scandal of one sort or another in Capri to make a topic of conversation, but nothing was said of particular interest and in a little while Wilson got up and left us. Soon afterwards we strolled up to my friend's villa to dine. On the way he asked me what I had thought of Wilson.

'Nothing,' I said. 'I don't believe there's a word of truth in your story.'

'Why not?'

'He isn't the sort of man to do that sort of thing.'

'How does anyone know what anyone is capable of?'

'I should put him down as an absolutely normal man of business who's retired on a comfortable income from gilt-edged securities. I think your story's just the ordinary Capri tittle-tattle.'

'Have it your own way,' said my friend.

We were in the habit of bathing at a beach called the Baths of Tiberius. We took a fly down the road to a certain point and then wandered through lemon groves and vineyards, noisy with cicadas and heavy with the hot smell of the sun, till we came to the top of the cliff down which a steep winding path led to the sea. A day or two later, just before we got down my friend said:

'Oh, there's Wilson back again.'

We scrunched over the beach, the only drawback to the bathing-place being that it was shingle and not sand, and as we came along Wilson saw us and waved. He was standing up, a pipe in his mouth, and he wore nothing but a pair of trunks. His body was dark brown, thin but not emaciated, and, considering his wrinkled face and grey hair, youthful. Hot from our walk, we undressed quickly and plunged at once into the water. Six feet from the shore it was thirty feet deep, but so clear that you could see the bottom. It was warm, yet invigorating.

When I got out Wilson was lying on his belly, with a towel under him reading a book. I lit a cigarette and went and sat down beside him.

'Had a nice swim?' he asked.

He put his pipe inside his book to mark the place and closing it put it down on the pebbles beside him. He was evidently willing to talk.

'Lovely,' I said. 'It's the best bathing in the world.'

'Of course people think those were the Baths of Tiberius.' He waved his hand towards a shapeless mass of masonry that stood half in the water and half out. 'But that's all rot. It was just one of his villas, you know.'

I did. But it is just as well to let people tell you things when they want to. It disposes them kindly towards you if you suffer them to impart information. Wilson gave a chuckle.

'Funny old fellow, Tiberius. Pity they're saying now there's not a word of truth in all those stories about him.'

He began to tell me all about Tiberius. Well, I had read my Suetonius too and I had read histories of the Early Roman Empire, so there was nothing very new to me in what he said. But I observed that he was not ill-read. I remarked on it.

'Oh, well, when I settled down here I was naturally interested, and I have plenty of time for reading. When you live in a place like this, with all its associations, it seems to make history so actual. You might almost be living in historical times yourself.'

I should remark here that this was in 1913. The world was an easy, comfortable place and no one could have imagined that anything might happen seriously to disturb the serenity of existence.

'How long have you been here?' I asked.

'Fifteen years.' He gave the blue and placid sea a glance, and a strangely tender smile hovered on his thin lips. 'I fell in love with the place at first sight. You've heard, I dare say, of the mythical German who came here on the Naples boat just for lunch and a look at the Blue Grotto and stayed forty years; well, I can't say I exactly did that, but it's come to the same thing in the end. Only it won't be forty years in my case. Twenty-five. Still, that's better than a poke in the eye with a sharp stick.'

I waited for him to go on. For what he had just said looked indeed as though there might be something after all in the singular story I had heard. But at that moment my friend came dripping out of the water very proud of himself because he had swum a mile, and the conversation turned to other things.

After that I met Wilson several times, either in the Piazza or on the beach. He was amiable and polite. He was always pleased to have a talk and I found out that he not only knew every inch of the island but also the adjacent mainland. He had read a great deal on all sorts of subjects, but his speciality was the history of Rome and on this he was very well informed. He seemed to have little imagination and to be of no more than average intelligence. He laughed a good deal, but with restraint, and his sense of humour was tickled by simple jokes. A commonplace man. I did not forget the odd remark he had made during the first short chat we had had by ourselves, but he never so much as approached the topic again. One day on our return from the beach, dismissing the cab at the Piazza, my friend and I told the driver to be ready to take us up to Anacapri at five. We were going to climb Monte Solaro, dine at a tavern we favoured, and walk down in the moonlight. For it was full moon and the views by night were lovely. Wilson was standing by while we gave the cabman instructions, for we had given him a lift to save him the hot dusty walk, and more from politeness than for any other reason I asked him if he would care to join us.

'It's my party,' I said.

'I'll come with pleasure,' he answered.

But when the time came to set out my friend was not feeling well, he thought he had stayed too long in the water, and would not face the long and tiring walk. So I went alone with Wilson. We climbed the mountain, admired the spacious view, and got back to the inn as night was falling, hot, hungry, and thirsty. We had ordered our dinner beforehand. The food was good, for Antonio was an excellent cook, and the wine came from his own vineyard. It was so light that you felt you could drink it like water and we finished the first bottle with our macaroni. By the time we had finished the second we felt that there was nothing much wrong with life. We sat in a little garden under a great vine laden with grapes. The air was exquisitely soft. The night was still and we were alone. The maid brought us *bel paese* cheese and a plate of figs. I ordered coffee and strega, which is the best liqueur they make in Italy. Wilson would not have a cigar, but lit his pipe.

'We've got plenty of time before we need start,' he said, 'the moon won't be over the hill for another hour.'

'Moon or no moon,' I said briskly, 'of course we've got plenty of time. That's one of the delights of Capri, that there's never any hurry.'

'Leisure,' he said. 'If people only knew! It's the most priceless thing a man can have and they're such fools they don't even know it's something to aim at. Work? They work for work's sake. They haven't got the brains to realize that the only object of work is to obtain leisure.'

Wine has the effect on some people of making them indulge in general reflections. These remarks were true, but no one could have claimed that they were original. I did not say anything, but struck a match to light my cigar.

'It was full moon the first time I came to Capri,' he went on reflectively. 'It might be the same moon as tonight.'

'It was, you know,' I smiled.

He grinned. The only light in the garden was what came from an oil lamp that hung over our heads. It had been scanty to eat by, but it was good now for confidences.

'I didn't mean that. I mean, it might be yesterday. Fifteen years it is, and when I look back it seems like a month. I'd never been to Italy before. I came for my summer holiday. I went to Naples by boat from Marseilles and I had a look round, Pompeii, you know, and Paestum and one or two places like that; then I came here for a week. I liked the look of the place right away, from the sea, I mean, as I watched it come closer; and then when we got into the little boats from the steamer and landed at the quay, with all that crowd of jabbering people who wanted to take your luggage, and the hotel touts, and the tumbledown houses on the Marina and the walk up to the hotel, and dining on the terrace – well, it just got me. That's the truth. I didn't know if I was standing on my head or my heels. I'd never drunk Capri wine before, but I'd heard of it; I think I must have got a bit tight. I sat on that terrace after they'd all gone to bed and watched the moon over the sea, and there was Vesuvius with a great red plume of smoke rising up from it. Of course I know now that wine I drank was ink, Capri wine my eye, but I thought it all right then. But it wasn't the wine that made me drunk, it was the shape of the island and those jabbering people, the moon and the sea and the oleander in the hotel garden. I'd never seen an oleander before.'

It was a long speech and it had made him thirsty. He took up his glass, but it was empty. I asked him if he would have another strega.

'It's sickly stuff. Let's have a bottle of wine. That's sound, that is, pure juice of the grape and can't hurt anyone.'

I ordered more wine, and when it came filled the glasses. He took a long drink and after a sigh of pleasure went on.

'Next day I found my way to the bathing-place we go to. Not bad bathing, I thought. Then I wandered about the island. As luck would have it, there was a *festa* up at the Punta di Timberio and I ran straight into the middle of it. An image of the Virgin and priests, acolytes swinging censers, and a whole crowd of jolly, laughing, excited people, a lot of them all dressed up. I ran across an Englishman there and asked him what it was all about. "Oh, it's the feast of the Assumption," he said, "at least that's what the Catholic Church says it is, but that's just their hanky-panky. It's the festival of Venus. Pagan, you know. Aphrodite rising from the sea and all that." It gave me quite a funny feeling to hear him. It seemed to take one a long way back, if you know what I mean. After that I went down one night to have a look at the Faraglioni by moonlight. If the fates had wanted me to go on being a bank manager they oughtn't to have let me take that walk.'

'You were a bank manager, were you?' I asked.

I had been wrong about him, but not far wrong.

'Yes. I was manager of the Crawford Street branch of the York and City. It was convenient for me because I lived up Hendon way. I could get from door to door in thirty-seven minutes.'

He puffed at his pipe and relit it.

'That was my last night, that was. I'd got to be back at the bank on Monday morning. When I looked at those two great rocks sticking out of the water, with the moon above them, and all the little lights of the fishermen in their boats catching cuttle-fish, all so peaceful and beautiful, I said to myself, well, after all, why should I go back? It wasn't as if I had anyone dependent on me. My wife had died of bronchial pneumonia four years before and the kid went to live with her grandmother, my wife's mother. She was an old fool, she didn't look after the kid properly and she got blood-poisoning, they amputated her leg, but they couldn't save her and she died, poor little thing.'

'How terrible,' I said.

'Yes, I was cut up at the time, though of course not so much as if the kid had been living with me, but I dare say it was a mercy. Not much chance for a girl with only one leg. I was sorry about my wife too. We got on very well together. Though I don't know if it would have continued. She was the sort of woman who was always bothering about what other people'd think. She didn't like travelling. Eastbourne was her idea of a holiday. D'you know, I'd never crossed the Channel till after her death.'

'But I suppose you've got other relations, haven't you?'

'None. I was an only child. My father had a brother, but he went to Australia before I was born. I don't think anyone could easily be more alone in the world than I am. There wasn't any reason I could see why I shouldn't do exactly what I wanted. I was thirty-four at that time.'

He had told me he had been on the island for fifteen years. That would make him forty-nine. Just about the age I should have given him.

'I'd been working since I was seventeen. All I had to look forward to was doing the same old thing day after day till I retired on my pension. I said to myself, is it worth it? What's wrong with chucking it all up and spending the rest of my life down here? It was the most beautiful place I'd ever seen. But I'd had a business training, I was cautious by nature. "No," I said, "I won't be carried away like this, I'll go tomorrow like I said I would and think it over. Perhaps when I get back to London I'll think quite differently," Damned fool, wasn't I? I lost a whole year that way.'

'You didn't change your mind, then?'

'You bet I didn't. All the time I was working I kept thinking of the bathing here and the vineyards and the walks over the hills and the moon and the sea, and the Piazza in the evening when everyone walks about for a bit of a chat after the day's work is over. There was only one thing that bothered me: I wasn't sure if I was justified in not working like everybody else did. Then I read a sort of history book, by a man called Marion Crawford it was, and there was a story about Sybaris and Crotona. There were two cities; and in Sybaris they just enjoyed life and had a good time, and in Crotona they were hardy and industrious and all that. And one day the men of Crotona came over and wiped Sybaris out, and then after a while a lot of other fellows came over from somewhere else and wiped Crotona out. Nothing remains of Sybaris, not a stone, and all that's left of Crotona is just one column. That settled the matter for me.'

'Oh?'

'It came to the same in the end, didn't it? And when you look back now, who were the mugs?'

I did not reply and he went on.

'The money was rather a bother. The bank didn't pension one off till after thirty years' service, but if you retired before that they gave you a gratuity. With that and what I'd got for the sale of my house and the little I'd managed to save, I just hadn't enough to buy an annuity to last the rest of my life. It would have been silly to sacrifice everything so as to lead a pleasant life and not have a sufficient income to make it pleasant. I wanted to have a little place of my own, a servant to look after me, enough to buy tobacco, decent food, books now and then, and something over for emergencies. I knew pretty well how much I needed. I found I had just enough to buy an annuity for twenty-five years.'

'You were thirty-five at the time?'

'Yes. It would carry me on till I was sixty. After all, no one can be certain of living longer than that, a lot of men die in their fifties, and by the time a man's sixty he's had the best of life.'

'On the other hand no one can be sure of dying at sixty,' I said.

'Well, I don't know. It depends on himself, doesn't it?'

'In your place I should have stayed on at the bank till I was entitled to my pension.'

'I should have been forty-seven then. I shouldn't have been too old to enjoy my life here, I'm older than that now and I enjoy it as much as I ever did, but I should have been too old to experience the particular pleasure of a young man. You know, you can have just as good a time at fifty as you can at thirty, but it's not the same sort of good time. I wanted to live the perfect life while I still had the energy and the spirit to make the most of it. Twenty-five years seemed a long time to me, and twenty-five years of happiness seemed worth paying something pretty substantial for. I'd made up my mind to wait a year and I waited a year. Then I sent in my resignation and as soon as they paid me my gratuity I bought the annuity and came on here.'

'An annuity for twenty-five years?'

'That's right.'

'Have you never regretted?'

'Never. I've had my money's worth already. And I've got ten years more. Don't you think after twenty-five years of perfect happiness one ought to be satisfied to call it a day?'

'Perhaps.'

He did not say in so many words what he would do then, but his intention was clear. It was pretty much the story my friend had told me, but it sounded different when I heard it from his own lips. I stole a glance at him. There was nothing about him that was not ordinary. No one, looking at that neat, prim face, could have thought him capable of an unconventional action. I did not blame him. It was his own life that he had arranged in this strange manner, and I did not see why he should not do what he liked with it. Still, I could not prevent the little shiver that ran down my spine.

'Getting chilly?' he smiled. 'We might as well start walking down. The moon'll be up by now.'

Before we parted Wilson asked me if I would like to go and see his house one day; and two or three days later, finding out where he lived, I strolled up to see him. It was a peasant's cottage, well away from the town, in a vineyard, with a view of the sea. By the side of the door grew a great oleander in full flower. There were only two small rooms, a tiny kitchen, and a lean-to in which firewood could be kept. The bedroom was furnished like a monk's cell, but the sitting-room, smelling agreeably of tobacco, was comfortable enough, with two large arm-chairs that he had brought from England, a large roll-top desk, a cottage piano, and crowded bookshelves. On the walls were framed engravings of pictures by G. F. Watts and Lord Leighton. Wilson told me that the house belonged to the owner of the vineyard who lived in another cottage higher up the hill, and his wife came in every day to do the rooms and the cooking. He had found the place on his first visit to Capri, and taking it on his return for good had been there ever since. Seeing the piano and music open on it, I asked him if he would play.

'I'm no good, you know, but I've always been fond of music and I get a lot of fun out of strumming.'

He sat down at the piano and played one of the movements from a Beethoven sonata. He did not play very well. I looked at his music, Schumann and Schubert, Beethoven, Bach, and Chopin. On the table on which he had his meals was a greasy pack of cards. I asked him if he played patience.

'A lot.'

From what I saw of him then and from what I heard from other people I made for myself what I think must have been a fairly accurate picture of the life he had led for the last fifteen years. It was certainly a very harmless one. He bathed; he walked a great deal, and he seemed never to lose his sense of the beauty of the island which he knew so intimately; he played the piano and he played patience; he read. When he was asked to a party he went and, though a trifle dull, was agreeable. He was not affronted if he was neglected. He liked people, but with an aloofness that prevented intimacy. He lived thriftily, but with sufficient comfort. He never owed a penny. I imagine he had never been a man whom sex had greatly troubled, and if in his younger days he had had now and then a passing affair with a visitor to the island whose head was turned by the atmosphere, his emotion, while it lasted, remained, I am pretty sure, well under his control. I think he was determined that nothing should interfere with his independence of spirit. His only passion was for the beauty of nature, and he sought felicity in the simple and natural things that life offers to everyone. You may say that it was a grossly selfish existence. It was. He was of no use to anybody, but on the other hand he did nobody any harm. His only object was his own happiness, and it looked as though he had attained it. Very few people know where to look for happiness; fewer still find it. I don't know whether he was a fool or a wise man. He was certainly a man who knew his own mind. The odd thing about him to me was that he was so immensely commonplace. I should never have given him a second thought but for what I knew, that on a certain day, ten years from then, unless a chance illness cut the thread before, he must deliberately take leave of the world he loved so well.

I wondered whether it was the thought of this, never quite absent from his mind, that gave him the peculiar zest with which he enjoyed every moment of the day.

I should do him an injustice if I omitted to state that he was not at all in the habit of talking about himself. I think the friend I was staying with was the only person in whom he had confided. I believe he only told me the story because he suspected I already knew it, and on the evening on which he told it me he had drunk a good deal of wine.

My visit drew to a close and I left the island. The year after, war broke out. A number of things happened to me, so that the course of my life was greatly altered, and it was thirteen years before I went to Capri again. My friend had been back some time, but he was no longer so well off, and had moved into a house that had no room for me; so I was putting up at the hotel. He came to meet me at the boat and we dined together. During dinner I asked him where exactly his house was.

'You know it,' he answered. 'It's the little place Wilson had. I've built on a room and made it quite nice.'

With so many other things to occupy my mind I had not given Wilson a thought for years; but now, with a little shock, I remembered. The ten years he had before him when I made his acquaintance must have elapsed long ago.

'Did he commit suicide as he said he would?'

'It's rather a grim story.'

Wilson's plan was all right. There was only one flaw in it and this, I suppose, he could not have foreseen. It had never occurred to him that after twenty-five years of complete happiness, in this quiet backwater, with nothing in the world to disturb his serenity, his character would gradually lose its strength. The will needs obstacles in order to exercise its power; when it is never thwarted, when no effort is needed to achieve one's desires, because one has placed one's desires only in the things that can be obtained by stretching out one's hand, the will grows impotent. If you walk on a level all the time the muscles you need to climb a mountain will atrophy. These observations are trite, but there they are. When Wilson's annuity expired he had no longer the resolution to make the end which was the price he had agreed to pay for that long period of happy tranquillity. I do not think, as far as I could gather, both from what my friend told me and afterwards from others, that he wanted courage. It was just that he couldn't make up his mind. He put it off from day to day.

He had lived on the island for so long and had always settled his accounts so punctually that it was easy for him to get credit; never having borrowed money before, he found a number of people who were willing to lend him small sums when now he asked for them. He had paid his rent regularly for so many years that his landlord, whose wife Assunta still acted as his servant, was content to let things slide for several months. Everyone believed him when he said that a relative had died and that he was temporarily embarrassed because owing to legal formalities he could not for some time get the money that was due to him. He managed to hang on after this fashion for something over a year. Then he could get no more credit from the local tradesmen, and there was no one to lend him any more money. His landlord gave him notice to leave the house unless he paid up the arrears of rent before a certain date.

The day before this he went into his tiny bedroom, closed the door and the window, drew the curtain, and lit a brazier of charcoal. Next morning when Assunta came to make his breakfast she found him insensible but still alive. The room was draughty, and though he had done this and that to keep out the fresh air he had not done it very thoroughly. It almost looked as though at the last moment, and desperate though his situation was, he had suffered from a certain infirmity of purpose. Wilson was taken to the hospital, and though very ill for some time he at last recovered. But as a result either of the charcoal poisoning or of the shock he was no longer in complete possession of his faculties. He was not insane, at all events not insane enough to be put in an asylum, but he was quite obviously no longer in his right mind.

'I went to see him,' said my friend. 'I tried to get him to talk, but he kept looking at me in a funny sort of way, as though he couldn't quite make out where he'd seen me before. He looked rather awful lying there in bed, with a week's growth of grey beard on his chin; but except for that funny look in his eyes he seemed quite normal.'

'What funny look in his eyes?'

'I don't know exactly how to describe it. Puzzled. It's an absurd comparison, but suppose you threw a stone up into the air and it didn't come down but just stayed there . . .'

'It would be rather bewildering,' I smiled.

'Well, that's the sort of look he had.'

It was difficult to know what to do with him. He had no money and no means of getting any. His effects were sold, but for too little to pay what he owed. He was English, and the Italian authorities did not wish to make themselves responsible for him. The British Consul in Naples had no funds to deal with the case. He could of course be sent back to England, but no one seemed to know what could be done with him when he got there. Then Assunta, the servant, said that he had been a good master and a good tenant, and as long as he had the money had paid his way; he could sleep in the woodshed in the cottage in which she and her husband lived, and he could share their meals. This was suggested to him. It was difficult to know whether he understood or not. When Assunta came to take him from the hospital he went with her without remark. He seemed to have no longer a will of his own. She had been keeping him now for two years.

'It's not very comfortable, you know,' said my friend. 'They've rigged him up a ramshackle bed and given him a couple of blankets, but there's no window, and it's icy cold in winter and like an oven in summer. And the food's pretty rough. You know how these peasants eat: macaroni on Sundays and meat once in a blue moon.'

'What does he do with himself all the time?'

'He wanders about the hills. I've tried to see him two or

three times, but it's no good; when he sees you coming he runs like a hare. Assunta comes down to have a chat with me now and then and I give her a bit of money so that she can buy him tobacco, but God knows if he ever gets it.'

'Do they treat him all right?' I asked.

'I'm sure Assunta's kind enough. She treats him like a child. I'm afraid her husband's not very nice to him. He grudges the cost of his keep. I don't believe he's cruel or anything like that, but I think he's a bit sharp with him. He makes him fetch water and clean the cow-shed and that sort of thing.'

'It sounds pretty rotten,' I said.

'He brought it on himself. After all, he's only got what he deserved.'

'I think on the whole we all get what we deserve,' I said. 'But that doesn't prevent its being rather horrible.'

Two or three days later my friend and I were taking a walk. We were strolling along a narrow path through an olive grove.

'There's Wilson,' said my friend suddenly. 'Don't look, you'll only frighten him. Go straight on.'

I walked with my eyes on the path, but out of the corners of them I saw a man hiding behind an olive tree. He did not move as we approached, but I felt that he was watching us. As soon as we had passed I heard a scamper. Wilson, like a hunted animal, had made for safety. That was the last I ever saw of him.

He died last year. He had endured that life for six years. He was found one morning on the mountainside lying quite peacefully as though he had died in his sleep. From where he lay he had been able to see those two great rocks called the Faraglioni which stand out of the sea. It was full moon and he must have gone to see them by moonlight. Perhaps he died of the beauty of that sight.

An Official Position

HE WAS A sturdy broad-shouldered fellow, of the middle height; though his bones were well covered as became his age, which was fifty, he was not fat; he had a ruddy complexion which neither the heat of the sun nor the unwholesomeness of the climate had affected. It was good rich blood that ran through his veins. His hair was brown and thick, and only at the temples touched with grey; he was very proud of his fair, handsome moustache and he kept it carefully brushed. There was a pleasant twinkle in his blue eyes. You would have said that this was a man whom life had treated well. There was in his appearance an air of good nature and in his vigour a glow of health that gave you confidence. He reminded you of one of those well-fed, rubicund burghers in an old Dutch picture, with their pink-cheeked wives, who made money and enjoyed the good things with which their industry provided them. He was, however, a widower. His name was Louis Remire, and his number 68763. He was serving a twelve-year sentence at St Laurent de Maroni, the great penal settlement of French Guiana, for killing his wife, but partly because he had served in the police force at Lyons, his native town, and partly on account of his good character, he had been given an official position. He had been chosen among nearly two hundred applicants to be the public executioner.

That was why he was allowed to sport the handsome moustache of which he took so much care. He was the only convict who wore one. It was in a manner of speaking his badge of office. That also was why he was allowed to wear his own clothes. The convicts wear pyjamas in pink and white stripes, round straw hats, and clumsy boots with wooden soles and leather tops. Louis Remire wore espadrilles on his bare feet, blue cotton trousers, and a khaki shirt the open neck of which exposed to view his hairy and virile chest. When you saw him strolling about the public garden, with a kindly eye looking at the children, black or half-caste, who played there, you would have taken him for a respectable shopkeeper who was enjoying an hour's leisure. He had his own house. That was not only one of the perquisites of his office, but it was a necessity, since if he had lodged in the prison camp the convicts would have made short work of him. One morning he would have been found with his belly ripped open. It was true that the house was small, it was just a wooden shack of one room, with a lean-to that served as a kitchen; but it was surrounded by a tiny garden, within a palisade, and in the garden grew bananas, papaias, and such vegetables as the climate allowed him to raise. The garden faced the sea and was surrounded by a coconut grove. The situation was charming. It was only a quarter of a mile from the prison, which was convenient for his rations. They were fetched by his assistant, who lived with him. The assistant, a tall, gawky, ungainly fellow, with deep-set, staring eyes and cavernous jaws, was serving a life sentence for rape and murder; he was not very intelligent, but in civil life he had been a cook and it was wonderful what, with the help of the vegetables they grew and such condiments as Louis Remire could afford to buy at the Chinese grocer's, he managed to do with the soup, potatoes and cabbage, and eternal beef, beef for three hundred and sixty-five days of the year, which the prison kitchens provided. It was on this account that Louis Remire had pressed his claim on the commandant when it had been found necessary to get a new assistant. The last one's nerves had given way and, absurdly enough, thought Louis Remire with a good-natured laugh, he had developed scruples about capital punishment; now, suffering from neurasthenia, he was on the Ile St Joseph, where the insane were confined.

His present assistant happened to be ill. He had high fever, and looked very much as if he were going to die. It had been necessary to send him to hospital. Louis Remire was sorry; he would not easily find so good a cook again. It was bad luck that this should have happened just now, for next day there was a job of work to be done. Six men were to be executed. Two were Algerians, one was a Pole, another a Spaniard from the mainland, and only two were French. They had escaped from prison in a band and gone up the river. For nearly twelve months, stealing, raping, and killing they had spread terror through the colony. People scarcely dared move from their homesteads. Recaptured at last, they had all been sentenced to death, but the sentence had to be confirmed by the Minister of the Colonies, and the confirmation had only just arrived. Louis Remire could not manage without help, and besides there was a lot to arrange beforehand; it was particularly unfortunate that on this occasion of all others he should have to depend on an inexperienced man. The commandant had assigned to him one of the turnkeys. The turnkeys are convicts like the others, but they have been given their places for good behaviour and they live in separate quarters. They are on the side of the authorities and so are disliked by the other prisoners. Louis Remire was a conscientious fellow, and he was anxious that everything next day should go without a hitch. He arranged that his temporary assistant should come that afternoon to the place where the guillotine was kept so that he might explain to him thoroughly how it worked and show him exactly what he would have to do.

The guillotine, when not in use, stood in a small room which was part of the prison building, but which was entered by a separate door from the outside. When he sauntered along there at the appointed hour he found the man already waiting. He was a large-limbed, coarse-faced fellow. He was dressed in the pink and white stripes of the prison garb, but as turnkey he wore a felt hat instead of the straw of common convicts.

'What are you here for?'

The man shrugged his shoulders.

'I killed a farmer and his wife.'

'H'm. How long have you got?'

'Life.'

He looked a brute, but you could never be sure of people.

He had himself seen a warder, a big, powerful man, faint dead away at an execution. He did not want his assistant to have an attack of nerves at the wrong moment. He gave him a friendly smile, and with his thumb pointed to the closed door behind which stood the guillotine.

'This is another sort of job,' he said. 'There are six of them, you know. They're a bad lot. The sooner they're out of the way the better.'

'Oh, that's all right. After what I've seen in this place I'm scared of nothing. It means no more to me than cutting the head off a chicken.'

Louis Remire unlocked the door and walked in. His assistant followed him. The guillotine in that small room, hardly larger than a cell, seemed to take up a great deal of space. It stood grim and sinister. Louis Remire heard a slight gasp and turning round saw that the turnkey was staring at the instrument with terrified eyes. His face was sallow and drawn from the fever and the hookworm from which all the convicts intermittently suffered, but now its pallor was ghastly. The executioner smiled good-naturedly.

'Gives you a turn, does it? Have you never seen it before?'

'Never.'

Louis Remire gave a little throaty chuckle.

'If you had, I suppose you wouldn't have survived to tell the tale. How did you escape it?'

'I was starving when I did my job. I'd asked for something to eat and they set the dogs on me. I was condemned to death. My lawyer went to Paris and he got the President to reprieve me.'

'It's better to be alive than dead, there's no denying that,' said Louis Remire, with that agreeable twinkle in his eyes.

He always kept his guillotine in perfect order. The wood, a dark hard native wood somewhat like mahogany, was highly polished; but there was a certain amount of brass, and it was Louis Remire's pride that this should be as bright and clean as the brass-work on a yacht. The knife shone as though it had just come out of the workshop. It was necessary not only to see that everything functioned properly, but to show his assistant how it functioned. It was part of the assistant's duty to refix the rope when the knife had dropped, and to do this he had to climb a short ladder.

It was with the satisfaction of a competent workman who knows his job from A to Z that Remire entered upon the necessary explanations. It gave him a certain quiet pleasure to point out the ingenuity of the apparatus. The condemned man was strapped to the bascule, a sort of shelf, and this by a simple mechanism was precipitated down and forwards so that the man's neck was conveniently under the knife. The conscientious fellow had brought with him a banana stem, about five feet long, and the turnkey wondered why. He was now to learn. The stem was of about the same circumference and consistency as the human neck, so that it afforded a very good way, not only of showing a novice how the apparatus worked, but of making sure beforehand that it was in perfect order. Louis Remire placed the banana stem in position. He released the knife. It fell with incredible speed and with a great bang. From the time the man was attached to the bascule to the time his head was off only thirty seconds elapsed. The head fell in the basket. The executioner took it up by the ears and exhibited it to those whose duty it was to watch the execution. He uttered the solemn words:

'*Au nom du peuple français justice est faite.* In the name of the French people justice is done.'

Then he dropped the head into the basket. Tomorrow, with six to be dispatched, the trunk would have to be unstrapped from the bascule and placed with the head on a stretcher, and the next man brought forward. They were taken in order of their guilt. The least guilty, executed first, were spared the horror of seeing the death of their mates.

'We shall have to be careful that the right head goes with the right body,' said Louis Remire, in that rather jovial manner of his, 'or there may be no end of confusion at the Resurrection.'

He let down the knife two or three times in order to make quite sure that the assistant understood how to fix it, and then getting his cleaning-materials from the shelf on which he kept them set him to work on the brass. Though it was spotless he thought that a final polish would do no harm. He leaned against the wall and idly smoked cigarettes.

Finally everything was in order and Louis Remire dismissed the assistant till midnight. At midnight they were moving the guillotine from the room in which it stood to the prison yard. It was always a bit of a job to set it up again, but it had to be in place an hour before dawn, at which time the execution took place. Louis Remire strolled slowly home to his shack. The afternoon was drawing to its close, and as he walked along he passed a working party who were returning to the prison. They spoke to one another in undertones and he guessed that they spoke of him; some looked down, two or three threw him a glance of hatred and one spat on the ground. Louis Remire, the end of a cigarette sticking to his lip, looked at them with irony. He was indifferent to the loathing, mingled with fear, with which they regarded him. It did not matter to him that not one of them would speak to him, and it only amused him to think that there was hardly one who would not gladly have thrust a knife into his guts. He had a supreme contempt for them all. He could take care of himself. He could use a knife as well as any of them, and he had confidence in his strength. The convicts knew that men were to be executed next day, and as always before an execution they were depressed and nervous. They went about their work in sullen silence, and the warders had to be more than usually on the alert.

'They'll settle down when it's all over,' said Louis Remire as he let himself into his little compound.

The dogs barked as he came along, and brave though he was, he listened to their uproar with satisfaction. With his own assistant ill, so that he was alone in the house, he was not sorry that he had the protection of those two savage mongrels. They prowled about the coconut grove outside his compound all night and they would give him good warning if anyone lurked there. They could be relied on to spring at the throat of any stranger who ventured too near. If his predecessor had had these dogs he wouldn't have come to his end.

The man who had been executioner before Louis Remire had only held the job a couple of years when one day he disappeared. The authorities thought he had run away; he was known to have a bit of money, and it was very probable that he had managed to make arrangements with the captain of a schooner to take him to Brazil. His nerves had given way. He had gone two or three times to the governor of the prison and told him that he feared for his life. He was convinced that the convicts were out to kill him. The governor felt prety sure that his fears were groundless and paid no attention, but when the man was nowhere to be found he concluded that his terror had got the better of him and he had preferred to run the danger of escape, and the danger of being recaptured and put back into prison, rather than face the risk of an avenging convict's knife. About three weeks later the warder in charge of a working party in the jungle noticed a great flock of vultures clustered round a tree. These vultures, called urubus, are large black birds, of a horrible aspect, and they fly about the market-place of St Laurent, picking up the offal that is left there by the starving liberated convicts, and flit heavily from tree to tree in the neat, well-kept streets of the town. They fly in the prison yard to remind the convicts that if they attempt an escape into the jungle their end, ten to one, will be to have their bones picked clean by these loathsome creatures. They were fighting and screaming in such a mass round the tree that the warder thought there was something strange there. He reported it and the commandant sent a party to see. They found a man hanging by the neck from one of the branches, and when they cut him down discovered that he was the executioner. It was given out that he had committed suicide, but there was a knife-thrust in his back, and the convicts knew that he had been stabbed and then, still alive, taken to the jungle and hanged.

Louis Remire had no fear that anything of that sort would happen to him. He knew how his predecessor had been caught. The job had not been done by the convicts. By the French law when a man is sentenced to hard labour for a certain number of years he has at the expiration of his sentence to remain in the colony for the same number of years. He is free, but he may not stir from the spot that is assigned to him as a residence. In certain circumstances he can get a concession and if he works hard he manages to scrape a bare living from it, but after a long term of penal servitude, during which he has lost all power of initiative, what with the debilitating effect of fever, hookworm, and so on, he is unfit for heavy and continuous labour, and so most of the liberated men subsist on begging, larceny, smuggling tobacco or money to the prisoners, and loading and unloading cargoes when two or three times a month a steamer comes into the harbour. It was the wife of one of these freed men that had been the means of the undoing of Louis Remire's predecessor. She was a coloured woman, young and pretty, with a neat little figure and mischievous eyes. The plot was well-considered. The executioner was a burly, sanguine man, of ardent passions. She had thrown herself in his way, and when she caught his approving glance, had cast him a saucy look. He saw her a day or two later in the public garden. He did not venture to speak to her (no one, man, woman, or child, would be seen speaking to him), but when he winked at her she smiled. One evening he met her walking through the coconut grove that surrounded his compound. No one was about. He got into conversation with her. They only exchanged a few words, for she was evidently terrified of being seen with him. But she came again to the coconut grove. She played him carefully till his suspicions were allayed; she teased his desires; she made him give her little presents, and at last on the promise of what was for both of them quite a sum of money she agreed to come one dark night to the compound. A ship had just come in and her husband would be working till dawn. It was when he opened the door for her and she hesitated to come in as though at the last moment she could not make up her mind, that he stepped outside to draw her in, and fell to the ground with the violence of the knife-thrust in his back.

'The fool,' muttered Louis Remire. 'He only got what he deserved. He should have smelt a rat. The eternal vanity of man.'

For his part he was through with women. It was on account of women that he found himself in the situation he was in now, at least on account of one woman; and besides, at his time of life, his passions were assuaged. There were other things in life and after a certain age a man, if he was sensible, turned his attention to them. He had always been a great fisherman. In the old days, at home in France before he had had his misfortune, as soon as he came off duty, he took his rod and line and went down to the Rhône. He got a lot of fishing now. Every morning, till the sun grew hot, he sat on his favourite rock and generally managed to get enough for the prison governor's table. The governor's wife knew the value of things and beat him down on the price he asked, but he did not blame her for that; she knew that he had to take what she was prepared to give and it would have been stupid of her to pay a penny more than she had to. In any case it brought in a little money useful for tobacco and rum and other odds and ends. But this evening he was going to fish for himself. He got his bait from the lean-to, and his rod, and settled down on his rock. No fish was so good as the fish you caught yourself, and by now he knew which were those that were good to eat and which were so tough and flavourless that you could only throw them back into the sea. There was one sort that, fried in real olive oil, was as good as mullet. He had not been sitting there five minutes when his float gave a sudden jerk, and when he pulled up his line, there, like an answer to prayer, was one of those very fish wriggling on the hook. He took it off, banged its head on the rock, and putting it down, replaced his bait. Four of them would make a good supper, the best a man could have, and with a night's hard work before him he needed a hearty meal. He would not have time to fish tomorrow morning. First of all the scaffold would have to be taken down and the pieces brought back to the room in which it was kept, and there would be a lot of cleaning to do. It was a bloody business; last time he had had his pants so soaked that he had been able to do nothing with them and had had to throw them away. The brass would have to be polished, the knife would have to be honed. He was not a man to leave a job half finished, and by the time it was through he would be pretty peckish. It would be worth while to catch a few more fish and put them in a cool place so that he could have a substantial breakfast. A cup of coffee, a couple of eggs, and a bit of fried fish; he could do with that. Then he would have a good sleep; after a night on his feet, the anxiety of an inexperienced assistant, and the clearing away of all the mess, God knew he would deserve it.

In front of him was spread the bay in a noble sweep, and in the distance was a little island green with trees. The afternoon was exquisitely still. Peace descended on the fisherman's soul. He watched his float idly. When you came to think of it, he reflected, he might be a great deal worse off; some of them, the convicts he meant, the convicts who swarmed in the prison a few hundred yards away from him, some of them had such a nostalgia for France that they went mad with melancholy; but he was a bit of a philosopher, so long as he could fish he was content; and did it really matter if he watched his float on the southern sea or in the Rhône? His thoughts wandered back to the past. His wife was an intolerable woman and he did not regret that he had killed her. He had never meant to marry her. She was a dressmaker, and he had taken a fancy to her because she was always neatly and smartly dressed. She seemed respectable and ladylike. He would not have been surprised if she had looked upon herself as a cut above a policeman. But he had a way with him. She soon gave him to understand that she was no snob, and when he made the customary advances he discovered to his relief, for he was not a man who considered that resistance added a flavour to conquest, that she was no prude. He liked to be seen with her when he took her out to dinner. She talked intelligently, and she was economical. She knew where they could dine well at the cheapest price. His situation was enviable. It added to his satisfaction that he could gratify the sexual desires natural to his healthy temperament at so moderate an expense. When she came to him and said she was going to have a baby it seemed natural enough that they should get married. He was earning good wages, and it was time that he should settle down. He often grew tired of eating, *en pension*, at a restaurant, and he looked forward to having his own home and home cooking. Well, it turned out that it had been a mistake about the baby, but Louis Remire was a good-natured fellow, and he didn't hold it up against Adèle. But he found, as many men have found before, that the wife was a very different woman from the mistress. She was jealous and possessive. She seemed to think that on a Sunday afternoon he ought to take her for a walk instead of going fishing, and she made it a grievance that, on coming off duty, he would go to the café. There was one café he frequented where other fishermen went and where he met men with whom he had a lot in common. He found it much pleasanter to spend his free evenings there over a glass or two of beer, whiling away the time with a game of cards, than to sit at home with his wife. She began to make scenes. Though sociable and jovial by nature he had a quick temper. There was a rough crowd at Lyons, and sometimes you could not manage them unless you were prepared to show a certain amount of firmness. When his wife began to make a nuisance of herself it never occurred to him that there was any other way of dealing with her than that he adopted. He let her know the strength of his hand. If she had been a sensible woman she would have learnt her lesson, but she was not a sensible woman. He found occasion more and more often to apply a necessary correction; she revenged herself by screaming the place down and by telling the neighbours – they lived in a two-roomed apartment on the fifth floor of a big house – what a brute he was. She told them that she was sure he would kill her one day. And yet never was there a more good-natured man than Louis Remire; she blamed him for the money he spent at the café, she accused him of wasting it on other women; well, in his position he had opportunities now and then, and as any man would he took them, and he was easy with his money, he never minded paying a round of drinks for his friends, and when a girl who had been nice to him wanted a new hat or a pair of silk stockings he wasn't the man to say no. His wife looked upon money that he did not spend on her as money stolen from her; she tried to make him account for every penny he spent, and when in his jovial way he told her he had thrown it out of the window, she was infuriated. Her tongue grew bitter and her voice was rasping. She was in a sullen rage with him all the time. She could not speak without saying something disagreeable. They led a cat-and-dog life. Louis Remire used to tell his friends what a harridan she was, he used to tell them that he wished ten times a day that he had never married her, and sometimes he would add that if an epidemic of influenza did not carry her off he would really have to kill her.

It was these remarks, made merely in jest, and the fact that she had so often told the neighbours that she knew he would murder her, that had sent him to St Laurent de Maroni with a twelve-year sentence. Otherwise he might very well have got off with three or four years in a French prison. The end had come one hot summer's day. He was, which was rare for him, in a bad temper. There was a strike in progress and the strikers had been violent. The police had had to make a good many arrests and the men had not submitted to this peaceably. Louis Remire had got a nasty blow on the jaw and he had had to make free use of his truncheon. To get the arrested men to the station had been a hot and tiring job. On coming off duty he had gone home to get out of his uniform and was intending to go to the café and have a glass of beer and a pleasant game of cards. His jaw was hurting him. His wife chose that moment to ask him for money and when he told her that he had none to give her she made a scene. He had plenty of money to go to the café, but none for her to buy a scrap of food with, she could starve for all he cared. He told her to shut up, and then the row began. She got in front of the door and swore that he should not pass till he gave her money. He told her to get out of the way, and took a step towards her. She whipped out his service revolver which he had taken off when he removed his uniform and threatened that she would shoot him if he moved a step. He was used to dealing with dangerous criminals, and the words were hardly out of her mouth before he had sprung upon her and snatched the revolver out of her hand. She screamed and hit him in the face. She hit him exactly where his jaw most hurt him. Blind with rage and mad with pain, he fired, he fired twice and she fell to the floor. For a moment he stood and stared at her. He was dazed. She looked as if she were dead. His first feeling was one of indescribable relief. He listened. No one seemed to have heard the sound of the shot. The neighbours must be out. That was a bit of luck, for it gave him time to do what he had to do in his own way. He changed back into his uniform, went out, locking the door behind him and putting the key in his pocket; he stopped for five minutes at his familiar café to have a glass of beer and then returned to the police-station he had lately left. On account of the day's disturbances the chief inspector was still there. Louis Remire went to his room and told him what had happened. He spent the night in a cell adjoining those of the strikers he had so recently himself arrested. Even at that tragic moment he was struck by the irony of the situation.

Louis Remire had on frequent occasions appeared as a police witness in criminal cases and he knew how eager are a man's companions to give any information that may damage him when he gets into trouble. It had caused him a certain grim amusement to realize how often it happened that a conviction was obtained only by the testimony of a prisoner's best friends.

But notwithstanding his experience he was amazed, when his own case came up for trial, to listen to the evidence given by the proprietor of the little café he had so much frequented, and to that of the men who for years had fished with him, played cards with him, and drunk with him. They seemed to have treasured every careless word he had ever uttered, the complaints he had made about his wife and the joking threats he had from time to time made that he would get even with her. He knew that at the time they had taken them no more seriously than he meant them. If he was able to do them a small service, and a man in the force often has it in his power to do one, he never hesitated. He had never been ungenerous with his money. You would have thought as you listened to them in the witness-box that it gave them the most intense satisfaction to disclose every trivial detail that could damage him.

From what appeared at the trial you would have thought that he was a bad man, dissolute, of violent temper, extravagant, idle, and corrupt. He knew that he was nothing of the kind. He was just an ordinary, good-natured, easy-going fellow, who was willing to let you go your way if you would let him go his. It was true that he liked his game of cards and his glass of beer, it was true that he liked a pretty girl, but what of it? When he looked at the jury he wondered how many of them would come out of it any better than he if all their errors, all their rash words, all their follies were thus laid bare. He did not resent the long term of penal servitude to which he was sentenced. He was an officer of the law; he had committed a crime and it was right that he should be punished. But he was not a criminal; he was the victim of an unfortunate accident.

At St Laurent de Maroni, in the prison camp, wearing the pink and white stripe of the prison garb and the ugly straw hat, he remembered still that he had been a policeman and that the convicts with whom he must now consort had always been his natural enemies. He despised and disliked them. He had as little to do with them as he could. And he was not frightened of them. He knew them too well. Like all the rest he had a knife and he showed that he was prepared to use it. He did not want to interfere with anybody, but he was not going to allow anyone to interfere with him.

The chief of the Lyons police had liked him, his character while in the force had been exemplary, and the *fiche* which accompanied every prisoner spoke well of him. He knew that what officials like is a prisoner who gives no trouble, who accepts his position with cheerfulness, and who is willing. He got a soft job; very soon he got a cell of his own and so escaped the horrible promiscuity of the dormitories; he got on well with the warders, they were decent chaps, most of them, and knowing that he had formerly been in the police they treated him more as a comrade than as a convict. The commandant of the prison trusted him. Presently he got the job of servant to one of the prison officials. He slept in the prison, but otherwise enjoyed complete freedom. He took the children of his master to school every day and fetched them at the end of their school hours. He made toys for them. He accompanied his mistress to market and carried back the provisions she bought. He spent long hours gossiping with her. The family liked him. They liked his chaffing manner and his good-natured smile. He was industrious and trustworthy. Life once more was tolerable.

But after three years his master was transferred to Cayenne. It was a blow. But it happened just then that the post of executioner fell free and he obtained it. Now once more he was in the service of the state. He was an official. However humble his residence it was his own. He need no longer wear the prison uniform. He could grow his hair and his moustache. He cared little if the convicts looked upon him with horror and contempt. That was how he looked upon them. Scum. When he took the bleeding head of an executed man from the basket and holding it by the ears pronounced those solemn words: *Au nom du peuple français justice est faite*, he felt that he did represent the Republic. He stood for law and order. He was the protector of society against that vast horde of ruthless criminals.

He got a hundred francs for each execution. That and what

the governor's wife paid him for his fish provided him with many a pleasant comfort and not a few luxuries. And now as he sat on his rock in the peace of eventide he considered what he would do with the money he would earn next day. Occasionally he got a bite, now and then a fish; he drew it out of the water, took it off the hook, and put on fresh bait; but he did this mechanically, and it did not disturb the current of his thoughts. Six hundred francs. It was a respectable sum. He scarcely knew what to do with it. He had everything he wanted in his little house, he had a good store of groceries, and plenty of rum for one who was as little of a drinker as he was; he needed no fishing tackle; his clothes were good enough. The only thing was to put it aside. He already had a tidy little sum hidden in the ground at the root of a papaia tree. He chuckled when he thought how Adèle would have stared had she known that he was actually saving. It would have been balm to her avaricious soul. He was saving up gradually for when he was released. That was the difficult moment for the convicts. So long as they were in prison they had a roof over their heads and food to eat, but when they were released, with the obligation of staying for so many years more in the colony, they had to shift for themselves. They all said the same thing: it was at the expiration of their term that their real punishment began. They could not get work. Employers mistrusted them. Contractors would not engage them because the prison authorities hired out convict labour at a price that defied competition. They slept in the open, in the market-place, and for food were often glad to go to the Salvation Army. But the Salvation Army made them work hard for what they gave and besides forced them to listen to their services. Sometimes they committed a violent crime merely to get back to the safety of prison. Louis Remire was not going to take any risks. He meant to amass a sufficient capital to start in business. He ought to be able to get permission to settle in Cayenne, and there he might open a bar. People might hesitate to come at first because he had been the executioner, but if he provided good liquor they would get over their prejudice, and with his jovial manner, with his experience in keeping order, he ought to be able to make a go of it. Visitors came to Cayenne now and then and they would come out of curiosity. It would be something interesting to tell their friends when they got home that the best rum punch they had had in Cayenne was at the executioner's. But he had a good many years to go yet, and if there really was something he needed there was no reason why he shouldn't get it. He racked his brains. No, there wasn't a thing in the world he wanted. He was surprised. He allowed his eyes to wander from his float. The sea was wonderfully calm and now it was rich with all the colour of the setting sun. In the sky already a solitary star twinkled. A thought came to him that filled him with an extraordinary sensation.

'But if there's nothing in the world you want, surely that's happiness.' He stroked his handsome moustache and his blue eyes shone softly. 'There are no two ways about it, I'm a happy man and till this moment I never knew it.'

The notion was so unexpected that he did not know what to make of it. It was certainly a very odd one. But there it was, as obvious to anyone with a logical mind as a proposition of Euclid.

'Happy, that's what I am. How many men can say the same? In St Laurent de Maroni of all places, and for the first time in my life.'

The sun was setting. He had caught enough fish for his supper and enough for his breakfast. He drew in his line, gathered up his fish, and went back to his house. It stood but a few yards from the sea. It did not take him long to light his fire and in a little while he had four little fish cheerfully frizzling in a pan. He was always very particular about the oil he used. The best olive oil was expensive, but it was worth the money. The prison bread was good, and after he had fried his fish, he fried a couple of pieces of bread in the rest of the oil. He sniffed the savoury smell with satisfaction. He lit a lamp, washed a lettuce grown in his own garden, and mixed himself a salad. He had a notion that no one in the world could mix a salad better than he. He drank a glass of rum and ate his supper with appetite. He gave a few odds and ends to the two mongrel dogs who were lying at his feet, and then, having washed up, for he was by nature a tidy man and when he came in to breakfast next morning did not want to find things in a mess, let the dogs out of the compound to wander about the coconut grove. He took the lamp into the house, made himself comfortable in his deck-chair, and smoking a cigar smuggled in from the neighbouring Dutch Colony settled down to read one of the French papers that had arrived by the last mail. Replete, his mind at ease, he could not but feel that life, with all its disadvantages, was good to live. He was still affected by the amused surprise that had overcome him when it suddenly occurred to him that he was a happy man. When you considered that men spent their lives seeking for happiness, it seemed hardly believable that he had found it. Yet the fact stared him in the face. A man who has everything he wants is happy, he had everything he wanted; therefore he was happy. He chuckled as a new thought crossed his mind.

'There's no denying it, I owe it to Adèle.'

Old Adèle. What a foul woman!

Presently he decided that he had better have a nap; he set his alarm clock for a quarter to twelve and lying down on his bed in a few minutes was fast asleep. He slept soundly and no dreams troubled him. He woke with a start when the alarm sounded, but in a moment remembered why he had set it. He yawned and stretched himself lazily.

'Ah, well, I suppose I must get to work. Every job has its inconveniences.'

He slipped from under his mosquito-net and relit his lamp. To freshen himself he washed his hands and face, and then as a protection against the night air drank a glass of rum. He thought for a moment of his inexperienced assistant and wondered whether it would be wise to take some rum in a flask with him.

'It would be a pretty business if his nerves went back on him.'

It was unfortunate that so many as six men had to be executed. If there had been only one, it wouldn't have mattered so much his assistant being new to the game; but with five others waiting there, it would be awkward if there were a hitch. He shrugged his shoulders. They would just have to do the best they could. He passed a comb through his tousled hair and carefully brushed his handsome moustache. He lit a cigarette. He walked through his compound, unlocked the door in the stout palisade that surrounded it, and locked it again behind him. There was no moon. He whistled for his dogs. He was surprised that they did not come. He whistled again. The brutes. They'd probably caught a rat and were fighting over it. He'd give them a good hiding for that; he'd teach them not to come when he whistled. He set out to walk in the direction of the prison. It was dark under the coconut trees and he would just as soon have had the dogs with him. Still there were only fifty yards to go and then he would be out in the open. There were lights in the governor's house, and it gave him confidence to see them. He smiled, for he guessed what those lights at that late hour meant: the governor, with the execution before him at dawn, was finding it hard to sleep. The anxiety, the malaise, that affected convicts and ex-convicts alike on the eve of an execution, had got on his nerves. It was true that there was always the chance of an outbreak then, and the warders went around with their eyes skinned and their hands ready to draw their guns at a suspicious movement.

Louis Remire whistled for his dogs once more, but they did not come. He could not understand it. It was a trifle disquieting. He was a man who habitually walked slowly, strolling along with a sort of roll, but now he hastened his pace. He spat the cigarette out of his mouth. It had struck him that it was prudent not to betray his whereabouts by the light it gave. Suddenly he stumbled against something. He stopped dead. He was a brave man, with nerves of steel, but on a sudden he felt sick with terror. It was something soft and rather large that he had stumbled against, and he was pretty sure what it was. He wore espadrilles, and with one foot he cautiously felt the object on the ground before him. Yes, he was right. It was one of his dogs. It was dead. He took a step backwards and drew his knife. He knew it was no good to shout. The only house in the neighbourhood was the prison governor's, it faced the clearing just beyond the coconut grove; but they would not hear him, or if they did would not stir. St Laurent de Maroni was not a place where you went out in the dead of night when you heard a man calling for help. If next day one of the freed convicts was found lying dead, well, it was no great loss. Louis Remire saw in a flash what had happened.

He thought rapidly. They had killed his dogs while he was sleeping. They must have got them when he had put them out of his compound after supper. They must have thrown them some poisoned meat and the brutes had snatched at it. If the one he had stumbled over was near his house it was because it tried to crawl home to die. Louis Remire strained his eyes. He could see nothing. The night was pitch black. He could hardly see the trunks of the coconut trees a yard away from him. His first thought was to make a rush for his shack. If he got back to the safety of that he could wait till the prison people, wondering why he did not come, sent to fetch him. But he knew he could never get back. He knew they were there in the darkness, the men who had killed his dogs; he would have to fumble with the key to find the lock and before he found it he would have a knife plunged in his back. He listened intently. There was not a sound. And yet he felt that there were men there, lurking behind the trees, and they were there to kill him. They would kill him as they had killed his dogs. And he would die like a dog. There was more than one certainly. He knew them, there were three or four of them at least, there might be more, convicts in service in private houses who were not obliged to get back to the camp till a late hour, or desperate and starving freed men who had nothing to lose. For a moment he hesitated what to do. He dared not make a run for it, they might easily have put a rope across the pathway that led from his house to the open, and if he tripped he was done for. The coconut trees were loosely planted and among them his enemies would see him as little as he saw them. He stepped over the dead dog and plunged into the grove. He stood with his back to a tree to decide how he should proceed. The silence was terrifying. Suddenly he heard a whisper and the horror of it was frightful. Again a dead silence. He felt he must move on, but his feet seemed rooted to the ground. He felt that they were peering at him out of the darkness and it seemed to him that he was as visible to them as though he stood in the broad light of day. Then from the other side was a little cough. It came as such a shock that Louis Remire nearly screamed. He was conscious now that they were all round him. He could expect no mercy from those robbers and murderers. He remembered the other executioner, his predecessor, whom they had carried still alive into the jungle, whose eyes they had gouged out, and whom they had left hanging for the vultures to devour. His knees began to tremble. What a fool he had been to take on the job! There were soft jobs he could have found in which you ran no risk. It was too late to think of that. He pulled himself together. He had no chance of getting out of the coconut grove alive, he knew that; he wanted to be sure that he would be dead. He tightened his grip on his knife. The awful part was that he could hear no one, he could see no one, and yet he knew that they were lurking there waiting to strike. For one moment he had a mad idea, he would throw his knife away and shout out to them that he was unarmed and they could come and kill him in safety. But he knew them; they would never be satisfied merely to kill him. Rage seized him. He was not the man to surrender tamely to a pack of criminals. He was an honest man and an official of the state; it was his duty to defend himself. He could not stay there all night. It was better to get it over quickly. Yet that tree at his back seemed to offer a sort of security, he could not bring himself to move. He stared at the trunk of a tree in front of him and suddenly it moved and he realized with horror that it was a man. That made up his mind for him and with a huge effort he stepped forwards. He advanced slowly and cautiously. He could hear nothing, he could see nothing. But he knew that as he advanced they advanced too. It was as though he were accompanied by an invisible bodyguard. He thought he could hear the sound of their naked feet on the ground. His fear had left him. He walked on, keeping as close to the trees as he could, so that they should have less chance of attacking him from behind; a wild hope sprang up in his breast that they would be afraid to strike, they knew him, they all knew him, and whoever struck the first blow would be lucky if he escaped a knife in his own guts; he had only another thirty yards to go, and once in the open, able to see, he could make a fight for it. A few yards more and then he would run for his life. Suddenly something happened that made him start out of his skin, and he stopped dead. A light was flashed and in that heavy darkness the sudden glare was terrifying. It was an electric torch. Instinctively he sprang to a tree and stood with his back to it. He could not see who held the light. He was blinded by it. He did not speak. He held his knife low, he knew that when they struck it was in the belly, and if someone flung himself at him he was prepared to strike back. He was going to sell his life dearly. For half a minute perhaps the light shone on his face, but it seemed to him an eternity. He thought now that he discerned dimly the faces of men. Then a word broke the horrible silence.

'Throw.'

At the same instant a knife came flying through the air and struck him on the breast-bone. He threw up his hands and as he did so someone sprang at him and with a great sweep of the knife ripped up his belly. The light was switched off. Louis Remire sank to the ground with a groan, a terrible groan of pain. Five, six men gathered out of the gloom and stood over him. With his fall the knife that had stuck in his breast-bone was dislodged. It lay on the ground. A quick flash of the torch showed where it was. One of the men took it and with a single, swift motion cut Remire's throat from ear to ear.

'*Au nom du peuple français justice est faite*,' he said.

They vanished into the darkness and in the coconut grove was the immense silence of death.

The Luncheon

I CAUGHT SIGHT of her at the play and in answer to her beckoning I went over during the interval and sat down beside her. It was long since I had last seen her and if someone had not mentioned her name I hardly think I would have recognized her. She addressed me brightly.

'Well, it's many years since we first met. How time does fly! We're none of us getting any younger. Do you remember the first time I saw you? You asked me to luncheon.'

Did I remember?

It was twenty years ago and I was living in Paris. I had a tiny apartment in the Latin Quarter overlooking a cemetery and I was earning barely enough money to keep body and soul together. She had read a book of mine and had written to me about it. I answered, thanking her, and presently I received from her another letter saying that she was passing through Paris and would like to have a chat with me; but her time was limited and the only free moment she had was on the following Thursday; she was spending the morning at the Luxembourg and would I give her a little luncheon at Foyot's afterwards? Foyot's is a restaurant at which the French senators eat and it was so far beyond my means that I had never even thought of going there. But I was flattered and I was too young to have learned to say no to a woman. (Few men, I may add, learn this until they are too old to make it of any consequence to a woman what they say.) I had eighty francs (gold francs) to last me the rest of the month and a modest luncheon should not cost more than fifteen. If I cut out coffee for the next two weeks I could manage well enough.

I answered that I would meet my friend – by correspondence – at Foyot's on Thursday at half past twelve. She was not so young as I expected and in appearance imposing rather than attractive. She was in fact a woman of forty (a charming age, but not one that excites a sudden and devastating passion at first sight), and she gave me the impression of having more teeth, white and large and even, than were necessary for any practical purpose. She was talkative, but since she seemed inclined to talk about me I was prepared to be an attentive listener.

I was startled when the bill of fare was brought, for the prices were a great deal higher than I had anticipated. But she reassured me.

'I never eat anything for luncheon,' she said.

'Oh, don't say that!' I answered generously.

'I never eat more than one thing. I think people eat far too much nowadays. A little fish, perhaps. I wonder if they have any salmon.'

Well, it was early in the year for salmon and it was not on the bill of fare, but I asked the waiter if there was any. Yes, a beautiful salmon had just come in, it was the first they had had. I ordered it for my guest. The waiter asked her if she would have something while it was being cooked.

'No,' she answered, 'I never eat more than one thing. Unless you had a little caviare. I never mind caviare.'

My heart sank a little. I knew I could not afford caviare, but I could not very well tell her that. I told the waiter by all means to bring caviare. For myself I chose the cheapest dish on the menu and that was a mutton chop.

'I think you're unwise to eat meat,' she said. 'I don't know how you can expect to work after eating heavy things like chops. I don't believe in overloading my stomach.'

Then came the question of drink.

'I never drink anything for luncheon,' she said.

'Neither do I,' I answered promptly.

'Except white wine,' she proceeded as though I had not spoken. 'These French white wines are so light. They're wonderful for the digestion.'

'What would you like?' I asked, hospitable still, but not exactly effusive.

She gave me a bright and amicable flash of her white teeth.

'My doctor won't let me drink anything but champagne.'

I fancy I turned a trifle pale. I ordered half a bottle. I mentioned casually that my doctor had absolutely forbidden me to drink champagne.

'What are you going to drink, then?'

'Water.'

She ate the caviare and she ate the salmon. She talked gaily of art and literature and music. But I wondered what the bill would come to. When my mutton chop arrived she took me quite seriously to task.

'I see that you're in the habit of eating a heavy luncheon. I'm sure it's a mistake. Why don't you follow my example and just eat one thing? I'm sure you'd feel ever so much better for it.'

'I *am* only going to eat one thing,' I said, as the waiter came again with the bill of fare.

She waved him aside with an airy gesture.

'No, no, I never eat anything for luncheon. Just a bite, I never want more than that, and I eat that more as an excuse for conversation than anything else. I couldn't possibly eat anything more – unless they had some of those giant asparagus. I should be sorry to leave Paris without having some of them.'

My heart sank. I had seen them in the shops and I knew that they were horribly expensive. My mouth had often watered at the sight of them.

'Madame wants to know if you have any of those giant asparagus,' I asked the waiter.

I tried with all my might to will him to say no. A happy smile spread over his broad, priest-like face, and he assured me that they had some so large, so splendid, so tender, that it was a marvel.

'I'm not in the least hungry,' my guest sighed, 'but if you insist I don't mind having some asparagus.'

I ordered them.

'Aren't you going to have any?'

'No, I never eat asparagus.'

'I know there are people who don't like them. The fact is, you ruin your palate by all the meat you eat.'

We waited for the asparagus to be cooked. Panic seized me. It was not a question now how much money I should have left over for the rest of the month, but whether I had enough to pay the bill. It would be mortifying to find myself ten francs short and be obliged to borrow from my guest. I could not bring myself to do that. I knew exactly how much I had and if the bill came to more I made up my mind that I would put my hand in my pocket and with a dramatic cry start up and say it had been picked. Of course it would be awkward if she had not money enough either to pay the bill. Then the only thing would be to leave my watch and say I would come back and pay later.

The asparagus appeared. They were enormous, succulent, and appetizing. The smell of the melted butter tickled my nostrils as the nostrils of Jehovah were tickled by the burned offerings of the virtuous Semites. I watched the abandoned woman thrust them down her throat in large voluptuous mouthfuls and in my polite way I discoursed on the condition of the drama in the Balkans. At last she finished.

'Coffee?' I said.

'Yes, just an ice-cream and coffee,' she answered.

I was past caring now, so I ordered coffee for myself and an ice-cream and coffee for her.

'You know, there's one thing I thoroughly believe in,' she said, as she ate the ice-cream. 'One should always get up from a meal feeling one could eat a little more.'

'Are you still hungry?' I asked faintly.

'Oh, no, I'm not hungry; you see, I don't eat luncheon. I have a cup of coffee in the morning and then dinner, but I never eat more than one thing for luncheon. I was speaking for you.'

'Oh, I see!'

Then a terrible thing happened. While we were waiting for

the coffee, the head waiter, with an ingratiating smile on his false face, came up to us bearing a large basket full of huge peaches. They had the blush of an innocent girl; they had the rich tone of an Italian landscape. But surely peaches were not in season then? Lord knew what they cost. I knew too – a little later, for my guest, going on with her conversation, absent-mindedly took one.

'You see, you've filled your stomach with a lot of meat' – my one miserable little chop – 'and you can't eat any more. But I've just had a snack and I shall enjoy a peach.'

The bill came and when I paid it I found that I had only enough for a quite inadequate tip. Her eyes rested for an instant on the three francs I left for the waiter and I knew that she thought me mean. But when I walked out of the restaurant I had the whole month before me and not a penny in my pocket.

'Follow my example,' she said as we shook hands, 'and never eat more than one thing for luncheon.'

'I'll do better than that,' I retorted. 'I'll eat nothing for dinner tonight.'

'Humorist!' she cried gaily, jumping into a cab. 'You're quite a humorist!'

But I have had my revenge at last. I do not believe that I am a vindictive man, but when the immortal gods take a hand in the matter it is pardonable to observe the result with complacency. Today she weighs twenty-one stone.

The Mother

TWO OR THREE people, hearing sounds of a quarrel in the patio, came out of their rooms and listened.

'It's the new lodger,' said a woman. 'She's having a row with the porter who brought her things.'

It was a tenement house of two storeys, built round a patio, in a back street of La Macarena, which is the roughest quarter in Seville. The rooms were let to working men and the small functionaries with whom Spain is overrun, postmen, policemen, or tram-conductors, and the place swarmed with children. There were twenty families there. They squabbled and made it up; they chattered their heads off; they helped one another when help was needed; for the Andalusians are good-natured people, and on the whole they got on well enough together. One room had been for some time unlet. A woman had taken it that morning, and an hour later had brought her bits and pieces, carrying as much as she could herself, a *gallego* – the Galicians are the general porters of Spain – laden with the rest.

But the quarrel was growing more violent, and the two women above, on the first floor, anxious not to miss a word, leant over the balcony.

They heard the newcomer's shrill voice raised in a torrent of abuse and the man's sullen interjections. The two women nudged one another.

'I shan't go till you pay me,' he kept on saying.

'But I've paid you already. You said you'd do it for three *reales*.'

'Never! You promised me four.'

They were haggling over rather less than twopence halfpenny.

'Four *reales* for moving those few things? You're crazy.'

She tried to push him away.

'I shan't go till you pay me,' he repeated.

'I'll give you a penny more.'

'I won't take it.'

The dispute grew more and more noisy. The woman screamed at the porter and cursed him. She shook her fist in his face. At last he lost patience.

'Oh, all right, give me the penny and I'll go. I'm not going to waste time on a slut like you.'

She paid him, and the man, throwing down her mattress, left her. She flung a filthy word at him as he went. She came out of the room to drag the things in, and the two women in the balcony saw her face.

'*Carai*, what an evil face! She looks like a murderess.'

A girl came up the stairs at that moment, and her mother called out: 'Did you see her, Rosalia?'

'I asked the *gallego* where she came from, he says he brought the things from Triana. She promised him four *reales* and then wouldn't pay.'

'Did he tell you her name?'

'He didn't know. But in Triana they called her La Cachirra.'

The vixen appeared again to fetch a bundle she had forgotten. She glanced at the women in the balcony watching her unconcernedly, but said nothing. Rosalia shuddered.

'She frightens me.'

La Cachirra was forty, haggard and very thin, with bony hands and fingers like a vulture's claws. Her cheeks were sunken and her skin wrinkled and yellow. When she opened her mouth, with its pale, heavy lips, she showed teeth that were pointed like those of a beast of prey. Her hair was black and coarse; she wore it in a clumsy knot, which seemed on the point of falling over her shoulders, and in front of each ear fell a straight wisp. Her eyes, deep-set in their sockets, large and black, shone fiercely. Her face bore an expression of such ferocity that no one dared come near to speak with her. She kept entirely to herself. The curiosity of the neighbours was aroused. They knew she was very poor, for her clothes were wretched.

She went out every morning at six and did not return till night; but they could not even find out how she earned her living. They urged a policeman who lived in the house to make inquiries.

'As long as she doesn't break the peace, I have nothing to do with her,' said he.

But in Seville scandal travels quickly and in a few days a mason who lived in an upper room brought the news that a friend in Triana knew her story. La Cachirra had only come out of prison one month before, and she had spent seven years there – for murder. She had lodged in a house in Triana, but the children, finding out what had happened, threw stones at her and called her names; and she, turning upon them with foul words and with blows, had filled the whole place with such tumult that the landlord gave her notice. Cursing him and all who had turned her out, La Cachirra one morning suddenly disappeared.

'And whom did she murder?' asked Rosalia.

'They say it was her lover,' replied the mason.

'She can never have had one,' said Rosalia, with a laugh of scorn.

'*Santa Maria!*' cried Pilar, her mother, 'I hope she won't kill any of us. I said she looked like a murderess!'

Rosalia, shivering, crossed herself. At that moment La Cachirra came in from her day's work and a sudden oppression fell upon the talkers. They made a movement as if to huddle together and looked nervously at the wild-eyed woman. She seemed to see something ominous in their silence and gave them a rapid, suspicious glance. The policeman, to make conversation, bade her good evening.

'*Buena sera*,' she replied, with a scowl, and, passing quickly into her room, slammed the door.

They heard her lock it. The evil, sullen eyes had cast a gloom over them and they talked in whispers as if under a mischievous spell.

'She has the devil in her,' said Rosalia.

'I'm glad you're here to protect us, Manuel,' added her mother to the policeman.

But La Cachirra seemed indisposed to give trouble. She went her way, unbending, never addressing so much as a word to anyone, and brusquely cut short every attempt at friendliness. She felt that the neighbours had discovered her secret, the homicide and the long years of imprisonment; and the lines in her face grew sterner, the expression of her deep-set eyes more inhuman. But gradually the anxiety she had caused was dispelled. Even the garrulous Pilar ceased to pay attention to the silent gaunt figure who occasionally passed through the group sitting in the patio.

'I dare say the prison has sent her mad, they say it often does.'

But one day an event occurred to revive the gossip. A youth came to the *reja* – the wrought-iron gate that serves as front door to the Sevillan house – and asked for Antonia Sánchez. Pilar, who was mending a skirt in the patio, looked up at her daughter and shrugged her shoulders.

'No one of that name lives here,' she said.

'Yes, she does,' the young man answered; then, after a pause: 'They call her La Cachirra.'

'Ah!' Rosalia opened the gate and pointed to the door. 'She's in there.'

'Thank you.'

The youth gave her a smile. She was a pretty girl, with a high colour and fine bold eyes. A red carnation threw up the glossy blackness of her hair. Her breasts were full and the nipples were prominent under her blouse.

'Blessed be the mother that bore you,' he said, using a hackneyed phrase.

'*Vaya Usted con Dios*, go you with God,' answered Pilar.

He passed on and knocked at the door. The two women looked after him curiously.

'Who can he be?' asked Pilar. 'La Cachirra's never had a visitor before.'

There was no reply to his knocking, and he knocked again. They heard La Cachirra's rasping voice ask who was there.

'*Madre*!' he cried. 'Mother.'

There was a shriek. The door was burst open.

'Currito!'

The woman threw her arms round his neck and kissed him passionately. She fondled him and with a loving gesture stroked his face with both her hands. The girl and her mother who watched would never have thought her capable of such tenderness. At last, with little sobs of joy, she dragged him into her room.

'He's her son,' said Rosalia, with surprise. 'Who'd have thought it! And a fine fellow like that.'

Currito had a lean face and white, even teeth; his hair was cut very close, shaved on the temples, and set on the scalp with a truly Andalusian perfection. The shadow of his precocious beard showed blue beneath his brown skin. And of course he was a dandy. He had the national love of fine clothes, and his trousers were skin-tight; his short jacket and his frilled shirt were as new as new could be. He wore a broad-brimmed hat.

At last the door of La Cachirra's room was opened and she appeared, hanging on her son's arm.

'You'll come again next Sunday?' she asked.

'If nothing stops me.'

He glanced at Rosalia and, having bidden his mother good night, nodded to her also.

'*Vaya Usted con Dios!*' said she.

She gave him a smile and a flash of her dark eyes. La Cachirra intercepted the look; and the sullenness which her intense joy had driven away suddenly darkened her face like a thunder-cloud. She scowled fiercely at the handsome girl.

'Is that your son?' asked Pilar, when the youth was gone.

'Yes, he's my son,' answered La Cachirra gruffly, going back to her room.

Nothing could soften her, and even when her heart was brimming over with happiness she repelled the overtures of friendship.

'He's a good-looking fellow,' said Rosalia; and she thought of him more than once during the next few days.

It was a terrible love that La Cachirra had for her son. He was all she had in the world and she adored him with a fiery, jealous passion that demanded in return impossible devotion. She wished to be all in all to him. On account of his work they could not live together and it tortured her to imagine what he did when he was away from her. She could not bear him to look at a woman and she writhed at the bare idea that he might pay court to some girl. No amusement is more common in Seville than the long flirtation in which the maid sits at her window half the night long, guarded by iron bars, or stands at the gate, while her lover in the street pours his rapture into her willing ear. La Cachirra asked the boy if he had a *novia*, a sweetheart, aware that so attractive a youth must enjoy the smiles of women, and she knew he lied when he swore he spent his evenings at work. But his denials gave her a fierce delight.

When she saw Rosalia's provoking glance and Currito's answering smile, rage leapt to her throat. She had hated her neighbours before, because they were happy and she was wretched, because they knew her terrible secret; but now she hated them more, already fancying, half crazily, that they were conspiring to rob her of her son. On the following Sunday, in the afternoon, La Cachirra came out of her room, crossed the patio and stood at the gate. This was a proceeding so unusual that the neighbours commented upon it.

'Don't you know why she's there?' said Rosalia, with a stifled laugh. 'Her precious son is coming, and she doesn't want us to see him.'

'Does she think we'll eat him?'

Currito arrived and his mother took him quickly to her room.

'She's as jealous of him as if he was her lover,' said Pilar.

Rosalia looked at the closed door, laughing again, and her shining eyes were filled with mischief. It occurred to her that it would be very amusing to have a word with Currito. Rosalia's white teeth gleamed at the thought of La Cachirra's anger. She stationed herself at the gate, so that the pair, when they came out, could not help crossing her; but La Cachirra, seeing the girl, moved to the other side of her son so that not even a glance should pass between them. Rosalia shrugged her shoulders.

'You won't beat me so easily as that,' she thought.

The Sunday after, when La Cachirra took up her place at the gate, Rosalia went out into the street and strolled along in the direction from which she guessed he would come. In a minute she saw Currito, and walked on, elaborately ignoring him.

'*Hola!*' said he, stopping.

'Is it you? I thought you were afraid to speak to me.'

'I'm afraid of nothing,' he answered boastingly.

'Except mamma!'

She walked on, as if she wanted him to leave her; but she knew very well he would do no such thing.

'Where are you going?' he asked.

'What has that to do with you, Currito? Go to your mother, my son, or she'll beat you. You're afraid to look at me when she's with you.'

'What nonsense.'

'Well, *vaya Usted con Dios!* I have commissions.'

He went off rather sheepishly, and Rosalia laughed to herself. She was in the courtyard once more when he passed through with La Cachirra on his way out; and this time, shamed into courage, he stopped and said good night. La Cachirra turned red with anger.

'Come, Currito,' she cried, with a rasping voice, 'what are you waiting for?'

He went away, and the woman stopped a moment in front

of Rosalia as if she were going to speak, but, with a visible effort, she restrained herself, and went back to her dark, silent room.

A few days later was the feast of San Isidoro, the patron saint of Seville, and to celebrate the holiday the mason and one or two others had put a string of Chinese lanterns in the patio. They glowed warmly in the clear summer night. The sky was soft against the shining stars. The people of the house were gathered in the middle of the patio, sitting on chairs; and the women, some with babies at their breasts, fanned themselves with little paper fans, interrupting their ceaseless chattering to fling a word of abuse at some older child who was making a nuisance of himself. The cool air was very pleasant after the day's breathless heat. Those who had been to the bull-fight were telling the less fortunate all about it. They described with precise detail a wonderful feat that Belmonte, the famous matador, had performed. With their vivid imaginations, the particulars gained every minute in variety and colour, so that it appeared that never in the history of Seville had there been a more excellent *corrida*. Everyone was present but La Cachirra, and in her room they saw the light of a solitary candle.

'And her son?'

'He's in there,' answered Pilar. 'I saw him pass an hour ago.'

'He must be amusing himself,' said Rosalia, with a laugh.

'Oh, don't bother about La Cachirra,' said another. 'Give us a dance, Rosalia.'

'Yes, yes,' they cried. 'Go on, my girl. You dance.'

In Spain they love dancing and they love to look at dancing. Years and years ago it was said that there was never a Spanish woman that was not born to dance.

The chairs were quickly set in a ring. The mason and the tram conductor fetched their guitars. Rosalia got her castanets, and stepping forward with another girl, began.

Currito, in the poky room, pricked up his ears when he heard the music.

'They're dancing,' he said, and an itching shot down his limbs.

He looked through the curtain and saw the group in the mellow light of the Chinese lanterns. He saw the two girls dancing. Rosalia wore her Sunday clothes, and, as is customary, she was heavily powdered. A splendid carnation gleamed in her hair. Currito's heart beat quickly. Love in Spain grows fast, and he had thought often of the handsome girl since that day on which he first spoke to her. He moved towards the door.

'What are you doing?' asked La Cachirra.

'I'm going to look at them dance. You never wish me to amuse myself.'

'It's Rosalia you want to see.'

He pushed her away as she tried to stop him, and joined the group that watched the dancers. La Cachirra followed a step or two, and then stood, half hidden by the gloom, with fury gnawing at her heart. Rosalia saw him.

'Aren't you frightened to look at me?' she whispered, as she passed him.

The dancing had made her light-headed and she felt no fear of La Cachirra. When the measure ended and her partner sank into a chair, Rosalia marched up to Currito and stood in front of him, upright, with her head thrown back and her breast heaving with the rapid motion.

'Of course, you don't know how to dance,' she said.

'Yes, I do.'

'Well, come then.'

She smiled provokingly, but he hesitated. He looked over his shoulder at his mother, whom he divined, rather than saw, in the darkness. Rosalia caught the glance and its meaning.

'Are you afraid?'

'What should I be afraid of?' he asked with a shrug of the shoulders.

He stepped into the ring. The guitarists strummed away and the onlookers rhythmically clapped their hands, punctuating the time with an occasional cry of *Olé*. A girl gave Currito a pair of castanets and the pair began to dance. They heard a little hiss, as of a serpent in the darkness, and Rosalia, quite reckless now, looked with a laugh at the face, ghastly white, that gleamed from the shadows. La Cachirra did not move. She watched the movements of the dance, the swaying of the bodies, the intricate steps; she saw Rosalia lean back with a graceful gesture and smile in Currito's face as he wound about her, clapping his castanets. Her eyes glowed like coals of fire and she felt them burning in the sockets; but no one noticed her, and she gave a groan of rage. The dance came to an end, and Rosalia, smiling with pleasure at the applause, told Currito she did not know he could dance so well.

La Cachirra flung herself into her room and bolted the door. She gave no answer when Currito came and bade her open.

'Well, I shall go home,' he said.

Her heart bled with pain, but she would not speak. He was all she had, all she loved in the world; and yet she hated him. She could not sleep that night, but lay thinking, half-madly, that they were robbing her of her son. In the morning she did not go to work, but lay in wait for Rosalia. The girl came out at last, rather bedraggled after the night's festivities, and she started when La Cachirra suddenly faced her.

'What do you want with my son?'

'What do you mean?' replied Rosalia, assuming an expression of surprise.

La Cachirra quivered with passion and she bit her hand to keep herself quiet.

'Oh, you know what I mean. You're stealing him from me.'

'Do you think I want your son? Keep him away from me. I can't help it if he runs after me wherever I go.'

'That's a lie!'

'Ask him!' And now Rosalia's voice was so scornful that La Cachirra could hardly contain herself. 'He waits an hour in the street to see me. Why don't you keep him to yourself?'

'You lie, you lie! You throw yourself in his way.'

'If I wanted lovers I could get them without asking. I don't want the son of a murderess.'

Then everything grew confused to La Cachirra; the blood leaped to her head and choked her eyes. She sprang at Rosalia and tore her hair. The girl gave a shrill cry and sought to defend herself, but immediately a passer-by wrenched them apart.

'If you don't leave Currito alone, I'll kill you!' cried La Cachirra.

'Do you think I'm frightened? Keep him from me if you can. You fool, don't you see that he loves me better than his eyes?'

'Now then, go away,' said the man. 'Don't answer her, Rosalia.'

La Cachirra gave a little roar of passion, like a wild beast baulked of its prey, and pushed past into the street.

But the dance had left Currito madly in love with Rosalia, and all next day he thought of her red lips; the light of her eyes shone in his heart and filled him with enchantment. He passionately desired her. At nightfall he wandered towards the Macarena and presently found himself at her house. He waited in the darkness of the porch till he saw her in the patio. At the other end burned his mother's lonely light.

'Rosalia,' he called in a low voice.

She turned, stifling a cry of surprise.

'Why are you here today,' she whispered, going towards him.

'I couldn't keep away from you.'

'Why?' she smiled.

'Because I love you.'

'Do you know your mother nearly killed me this morning?'

And with the embellishments necessary to the Andalusian temperament, she related the occurrence, omitting, however, the final taunt which had enraged La Cachirra beyond endurance.

'She's got the temper of the devil,' said Currito; and then, with bravado: 'I shall tell her that you're my sweetheart.'

'She will be pleased,' said Rosalia ironically.

'Will you come to the *reja* tomorrow?'

'Perhaps,' she answered.

He gave a little chuckle, for he knew by her tone that she would. He swaggered even more than usual when he walked through the Sierpes on his way home. She was waiting for him when he came next day and, as is the way with lovers in Seville, they talked for hours under their breath, with the iron gate between them, and it never even occurred to Currito that it was a needless impediment. When he asked Rosalia if she loved him she answered with a little amorous sigh. They tried to see the passion that burnt hotly in one another's eyes. Then he went every night.

But fearing that his mother knew of his visits, Currito did not go to see her on the following Sunday. The wretched woman waited for him with an aching heart. She was ready to fall on her knees and beg him to forgive her, but then, when he did not come, she hated him; she would have liked to see him dead at her feet. Her heart sank when she thought that another week must pass before she could even hope to see him.

The week passed and still he did not come. She could not bear it. Anguish, anguish! She loved him as no sweetheart could ever love him. She told herself that this was Rosalia's doing and when she thought of her, rage filled her heart. At last Currito plucked up his courage and went to see his mother; but she had waited too long. It seemed as though her love was dead. She pushed him away when he wanted to kiss her.

'Why haven't you come before?'

'You locked the door on me. I thought you didn't want me!'

'Was it only that? Had you no other reason?'

'I've been busy,' he said, shrugging his shoulders.

'Busy? An idle loafer like you. What have you been doing? You wouldn't have been too busy to come and see Rosalia.'

'Why did you hit her?'

'How do you know I hit her? Have you seen her?' La Cachirra strode up to her son; her eyes flashed. 'She called me a murderess.'

'Well, what of it?'

'What of it?' she screamed, so that they heard her in the patio. 'And if I am a murderess – it was for you. Yes, I killed Pepe Santi; but it was because he was beating you. It was for your sake that I lay in prison for seven years – for seven years. Oh, you fool, you think she cares for you, and every night she spends hours at the gate.'

'I know,' Currito answered with a grin.

La Cachirra started violently. She shot a puzzled look at him and then she understood. She gasped with pain and wrath; she clutched at her heart as though the agony were too intense to bear.

'You're been coming every night to the *reja* and you never came near me? Oh, how cruel! I've done everything in the world for you. Do you think I loved Pepe Santi? I endured his blows so that I could give you bread; and I killed him when he beat you. Oh, God, I only lived for you. But for the thought of you I would have died rather than suffer those years of prison.'

'Come, woman, be reasonable. I'm twenty. What d'you expect? If it wasn't Rosalia it would be another.'

'You beast. I hate you. Get out.'

She pushed him violently to the door. Currito shrugged his shoulders.

'You needn't think I want to stay.'

He walked jauntily through the patio and slammed the iron gate behind him. La Cachirra stalked to and fro in her tiny room. The hours passed slowly. For a long while she remained at the window, watching with the horrible steadfastness of a savage beast ready to spring. She stood motionless, repressing the convulsive restlessness that tore at her heart-strings. There was a clapping of hands at the *reja* as a signal that someone was without, and she peered forward with panting mouth, her fiery eyes almost starting from her head. But it was only the mason. She waited longer, and Pilar, Rosalia's mother, came in and walked slowly up the stairs to her room. La Cachirra clutched at her throat to relieve the intolerable oppression of her breath. Still she waited. Now and then an extraordinary quiver travelled through all her limbs.

At last! There was a clap of light hands at the gate, and a voice above called out: 'Who is it?'

'Peace!'

La Cachirra recognized Rosalia's voice. She gave a gasp of triumph. The door was opened from above, and Rosalia, entering, crossed the courtyard with a buoyant and easy step. The joy of life was in her every motion. She was about to put her foot on the stair when La Cachirra sprang forward and stopped her. She caught hold of her arm and the girl could not shake herself free.

'What do you want?' said Rosalia. 'Let me pass.'

'What have you been doing with my son?'

'Let me pass, or I shall call out.'

'Is it true that you meet at the *reja* every night?'

'Mother, help! Antonio!' Rosalia cried out shrilly.

'Answer me.'

'Well, if you want the truth, you can have it. He's going to marry me. He loves me, and I – I love him with all my heart.' She turned on La Cachirra, trying to free herself from the vicious grip. 'D'you think you can prevent us? D'you think he's frightened of you? He hates you, he told me so. He wishes you'd never come out of prison.'

'He told you that?'

La Cachirra shrank back. Rosalia pursued the advantage.

'Yes, he told me that; and he told me much more. He told me that you murdered Pepe Santi; and that you were in prison for seven years; and he wished you were dead.'

Rosalia hissed the words venomously, laughing with a shrill voice when she saw the wretched woman shrink as though struck by palpable blows.

'And you ought to be proud that I don't refuse to marry the son of a murderess.'

Then, giving La Cachirra a push, she leapt to the stairs; but the movement revived the woman, stunned by the horrible taunts, and with a cry of brutal rage she sprang upon Rosalia and caught her by the shoulders and dragged her down. Rosalia turned and hit her in the face. La Cachirra drew a knife from her bosom, and with an oath buried it in the girl's neck. Rosalia shrieked.

'Mother, she's killed me.'

She fell to the bottom of the stairs and lay huddled up on the stones. Blood made a little pool on the ground.

Half a dozen doors were flung open at the despairing cry, and people rushed to seize La Cachirra; but she backed against the wall and faced them, with an expression of such ferocity on her face that no one dared approach her. The hesitation was momentary, but Pilar ran from the balcony shrieking, and the common attention for an instant was distracted. La Cachirra saw the the opportunity and ran forward. She reached her room and locked and bolted the door behind her.

Suddenly the court was filled with people. Pilar with loud dreadful cries flung herself down on her daughter and would not let herself be dragged away. Someone rushed for a doctor and someone else went for the police. The crowd surged in from the street and collected round the door. The doctor hurried in with a black bag in his hand. When the police came a dozen people at once excitedly explained what had happened. They pointed to the door of La Cachirra's room, and the police broke in. There was a scuffle and they came out with La Cachirra handcuffed. The mob rushed forward, but the police surrounded her and with their scabbards beat the people off; but they shook their fists and hurled curses at her. She looked at them scornfully. She deigned to make no answer. Her eyes shone with triumph. The policemen led her through the patio and they passed by the body of Rosalia.

'Is she dead?' asked La Cachirra.

'Yes,' the doctor answered gravely.

'Thanks be to God!' she said.

Notes

The notes in this edition are intended to serve the needs of overseas students as well as those of British-born users.

The Facts of Life

2 *club*: a building in which elected fee-paying members go to meet or dine.
grave error: serious mistake.
considerable heat: almost to lose one's temper.
broker: a person who makes a commission from selling securities and shares in public companies.
suckers: people who are easily swindled.

3 *Monte*: Monte Carlo in the South of France.
baize: a woollen material used on card tables to avoid cards slipping over a shiny surface.
rubber: series of games in the card game bridge.
denied a suit: indicated that he did not have one of the four card suits of clubs, diamonds, hearts and spades.

4 *K.C.*: King's Counsel, a barrister.
chaffing: light-hearted teasing.

5 *virtuous*: high moral standing.
discerned: recognised.
reconciled: allowed him to accept gracefully.
Davis Cup: the international tennis competition.
plaudits of the multitude: applause and praise from the spectators.
assiduous: regular, with sincere interest.

6 *Austin and von Cramm*: two leading tennis players.
smaller fry: less experienced players, unimportant.

7 *first flight*: top group of players.
precedent: an example used to justify future actions.
crack: outstandingly good.

8 *Provost*: the Head of the college.
work like blazes: work very hard.
9 *allowed*: agreed.
chips: counters used to represent money.
10 *trente et quarante*: card game; French, literally: thirty and forty.
baccara: gambling card game.
Syndicate: a group possessing great capital organised for a specific project, in this case to make money by gambling.
13 *cocotte*: prostitute.
17 *Cheri*: French for 'darling'.
18 *infuriated*: angered.
19 *Bon voyage*: French for 'have a safe journey'.
as pleased as Punch: delighted. Punch is one of the two main characters in the traditional children's puppet show Punch and Judy.
21 *a cat swallowing a canary*: everyday saying meaning great pleasure in accomplishment.

The Unconquered

26 *decadent*: in a state of decay or decline; corrupt.
matriculating: attaining a high enough standard in his studies to be accepted at a college or university.
28 *C'est le premier pas qui coûte*: French for 'It is the beginning which is hard.'
Arc de Triomphe: a famous, public monument containing the tomb of the unknown soldier.
billeted: housed.
29 *bump of locality*: sense of direction and memory for a place.
undulating: making a pattern like waves.
Cochon: French for 'pig'.
invincible: unbeatable.

Maginot line: a fortified line built by France on its borders to keep the Germans out. It proved ineffective.

30 *Boches*: a slang word for German soldiers or Germans generally.

31 *Au revoir, mademoiselle*: French for 'goodbye, young woman'.

Bonjour, la compagnie: French for 'Good day everyone'.

33 *elated*: filled with high spirits, very happy.

tantalized: frustrated, worried; he could not explain it.

34 *amicably*: in a friendly manner.

mobilized: called up into the armed forces.

35 *vicinity*: nearby area.

ingratiate: make himself popular.

wiles: tricks.

derision: scorn.

cordial: friendly.

arable: land capable of being tilled for crops.

convulsion: violent disturbance.

36 *pathetic*: pitiable, deserving pity.

37 *resignation*: as a matter of fact, a fact of life.

38 *irregular*: not having a (monthly) menstrual period regularly.

he was a devout Catholic and would not help them: Annette wanted to have an abortion, but firm Catholics, amongst others, are against the practice.

Il faut souffrir: French for 'one must suffer' and put up with the problem.

freemason: member of a secret society.

39 *Paris-Soir*: a French newspaper.

it was the circumstances: 'The Unconquered' first appeared in a collection entitled *Creatures of Circumstance*.

40 *demobilized*: discharged from one of the armed services.

41 *commune*: community; a small administrative unit having its own leaders and council.

42 *uncultivated*: not used for growing crops.

proposition: suggestion, plan.

reparation: make amends, try to repair damage done.
anguish: extreme pain or misery.
44 *lashed*: hurtful use of words.
C.O.: Commanding Officer.
Revolution was imminent: the Germans mistakenly believed – or were informed by propaganda – that the British people would rebel and thus seek peace to end the Second World War.
45 *hostile*: unfriendly, as to an enemy.
approaching maternity: nearing motherhood.
exultation: great joy.
the Ritz: a leading luxurious London hotel.
46 *I've seen it .... the cards*: fortune-telling, as with tea-leaves.
Reich: Third Reich; the Nazi dictatorship from 1933 to 1945.
plutocrats: members of the wealthy class who rule by virtue of their wealth.
49 *the last straw*: the final and most severe of a series of difficulties.
by-blow: a bastard, a child born to an unmarried mother.
51 *Balkans*: the countries of Yugoslavia, Romania, Bulgaria, Greece.
Ukraine: an area in the south east of the Soviet Union.
52 *dismal squalor*: a disgustingly filthy and depressing appearance.

Mr Know-All

56 *monogram*: initials.
57 *Prohibition*: the period in the United States (1920–1933) when the manufacture and sale of alcoholic liquor were forbidden by law.
58 *sweeps*: lotteries.
quoit: a game involving the throwing of rings.
intolerable: difficult to put up with.

59 *loquacious*: talkative.
dogmatic: insist that one is right in one's statements.
Levantine: inhabitant of the Eastern area of the Mediterranean.
acrimonious: bitter in speech and manner.
interminable: seemingly endless.
Kobe: a port in South Japan.
he bulged out of his ready-made clothes: Maugham's Edwardian 'standards' are revealed here. Ready-made suits were the trade mark of the common man, one of the lower orders; the phrase is thus a derogatory one. Maugham went to the 'right' tailor and never departed from his Edwardian standards of dress, even through the Riviera years.
demeanour: conduct, the way one behaves towards others.
60 *vehement and voluble*: emphatic, and speaking fluently at length.
Fifth Avenue: a select and expensive shopping area in New York.
61 *Elmer*: Does Maugham deliberately choose this almost larger-then-life name by way of showing his distaste for (and prejudice against) the American?
deprecating: disapproving.

'Mr Know-All' together with 'The Verger' and 'Sanatorium' – two other Maugham stories – were made into a very successful film titled *Trio*.

Lord Mountdrago

Though a story about politicians, politics were not of interest to Maugham. His only occasional comment was that politicians were all alike.
64 *sententious*: showing too great a care about what he supposed to be right and wrong.
epigram: a witty remark.

psycho-analyst: a doctor who studies the mind in order to treat people with mental and emotional disorders.

65 *jaded*: exhausted.

tranquility: peace and calm.

perturbations: worries and troubles.

phobias: fears of particular things.

faculty: ability.

assuaged: soothed.

66 *quack*: a fake.

Freud and Jung: celebrated thinkers and writers on the human mind and emotions.

hocus-pocus: nonsense or trickery.

incomprehensible, but manifest: not understood but nevertheless apparent.

irreconcilable: various elements that are incapable of being brought together.

67 *industry*: ability to work hard.

repartee: sharp and witty in conversation.

68 *ennobled*: raised to noble or titled rank.

nouveau riche: French for 'newly rich' and usually associated with someone lacking in social graces.

He was coldly insolent . . . . inferiors: it is worth comparing this remark with the narrator's attitude to Mr Kelada in 'Mr Know-All'.

69 *debonair*: refined, or, carefree.

haughtiness: arrogance, excessive pride.

69 *Bourbon*: a European royal line that ruled in France and Spain.

71 *pompous*: self-important.

72 *I was wearing my ribbon and my star*: The ribbon and the star are decorations for distinguished service. (Somerset Maugham himself was made a Companion of Honour in 1953. The Order of Merit, to his dismay, eluded him.)

75 *unprepossessing*: unattractive, not creating a favourable impression.

76 *grotesque*: absurdly distorted.
a dark liquid which I understand is called brown ale: a well-captured touch of a snob who is quite familiar with the subject but feigns ignorance for effect.
77 *bilk*: cheat.
78 *unimpeachable*: beyond reproach or criticism.
79 *at concert pitch*: in full possession of one's faculties, with a sharp mind and clear brain.
incorruptible: wholly honest, incapable of dishonest practice.
lewd: given to sexual desire, obscene.
81 *façade*: outer appearance.
83 *ostentatiously*: in a deliberately showy manner.
altruistic: in the interest of others.
84 *blather*: foolish talk.
intelligentsia: the educated and intelligent people in a society; the word is often used disparagingly, as here.
85 *somnolence*: sleepiness.
89 *empiric doctrine*: based on practical experience rather than scientific proof.
primeval terror: a terror experienced from early Man to the present day; a terror innate to humans.

The Colonel's Lady

92 *'trophies of the chase'*: antlers, stuffed animals and fish, 'chase' being a term used for the act of hunting.
93 *M.C.*: Military Cross.
D.S.O.: Distinguished Service Order. Both these medals were awarded for bravery in wartime action.
propriety: truthfulness.
succour: help in time of trouble.
cottage hospital: small rural hospital.
All he asked . . . candidate: a powerful comment. With characteristic cynicism Maugham encapsulates George Peregrine and his kind of gentleman in one sentence. It

was not that the lower classes were incapable of deciding matters of moment for themselves, but that they should follow his lead unquestioningly in return for his generosity.

affable: amiable, easy to approach.

94 *a chip off the old block*: like father, like son.

95 *highbrow*: scholarly.

Ruin seize thee, ruthless king: Juxtaposed with the words 'Poor Evie' (when it is quoted the second time), this line from a poem has some irony for George Peregrine when the story unfolds.

96 *penny-a-liner*: journalist or hack (mediocre) writer.

Selling like hot cakes: selling in great numbers and very quickly.

97 *vexation*: irritation or annoyance.

98 *get more kicks than halfpence*: receive more criticism than praise.

free verse: unrhymed, without a metrical pattern.

classical metres: standard rhymes and rhyming patterns.

Emily Dickinson: American poet, noted for her short, mostly unrhymed, lyrics.

98 *Landor*: Walter Landor, nineteenth-century English poet.

Heine: Heinrich Heine, nineteenth-century German poet.

Sappho: Greek (sixth century BC) poetess of Lesbos. She was believed to have been a lesbian.

99 *local magnate*: a person of power and rank in the neighbourhood.

100 *Claridge's*: a famous luxury London hotel.

101 *tittered*: sniggered.

102 *desiccated*: lacking in spirit, rather dried up.

The Times Literary Supplement, New Statesman, Spectator: literary journals in which book reviews appear.

103 *The Shropshire Lad*: the most celebrated poem by A. E. Housman, English poet (1859–1936).

malaise: French for 'feeling of unease'.

104 *coherent*: logical and consistent.

tremulous: trembling, anxious.
ecstatic: intense.
languor: feeling of weariness and relaxation.
106 *demure*: reserved, modest.
incomprehensible: beyond understanding.
preserves: restricted place for hunting and shooting.
109 *kicking over the traces*: going out of control, leaving the straight and narrow.
fastidious: very critical, hard to please.
reticent: shy and reserved.
poignant: painful to the feelings.
'It's so rotten . . . . in a lawyer's office': George is again shown to be superficial and a snob. It is purely his pride that has been hurt, and he has no understanding of or any sympathy for Evie at all. The final line of the story further highlights George's feelings towards the woman who is his wife.

Red

114 *Kanaka*: a native Hawaiian.
115 *copra*: dried oil-yielding kernel of the coconut.
Apia: the capital of Western Samoa.
116 *companion*: ladder from the upper deck to the deck below.
117 *They were like a ballet . . . . bygone age*: a characteristic Maugham description, involving the personification of the beautiful coconut trees positioned on the water's edge: a veritable paradise island.
118 *duck trousers*: trousers made of heavy cotton weave.
Pago-Pago: a port in Samoa.
119 *taciturn*: not inclined to conversation
meditative: thinking deeply.
121 *deleterious*: harmful.
123 *Paolo Malatesta*: a character in the writings of the Italian poet Dante.
Romeo: a reference to Shakespeare's famous lover.

repellent: distasteful or repulsive.
plethoric: overabundant.
comely: good-looking.
pre-Raphaelites: a group of painters and writers, including Rossetti and Millais, who founded an association in 1848 to revive the closeness to nature and vivid realistic colours that they considered typical of Italian painting before Raphael (1483–1520).
Apollo: god of light, poetry and music in classical myth.
Praxiteles: a Greek sculptor living in the fourth-century BC.

124 *Delilah took the Nazarite's*: *Judges* 16.4–24; the Bible story in which Samson has his hair shaven by Delilah and thereby loses his strength.

125 *You have never heard . . . . let themselves be loved*: Neilson is referring particularly to his own personal experience and Maugham in his turn, through him, to his own cynical views on love.

126 *ingenuous*: straightforward, innocent.
centaur: in Greek myth, a creature with the head, arms and torso of a man, and the lower body and legs of a horse.

127 *incessantly*: without stopping, constantly.
pandanus: tropical palmlike plant.

128 *premonition*: forewarning.

130 *melancholy*: depression or sadness.
transient: temporary.

131 *ineffable*: great or intense.
Absolute: God, that which is totally pure.

132 *kava*: alcoholic drink prepared from the roots of a local shrub.
Psyche: in Greek myth, a beautiful girl loved by Eros, who became the personification of the soul.

133 *rapture*: great joy.

134 *His love became a prison . . . . open air*: Maugham's imagery of bondage reappears here. Does Maugham realise the

near impossibility of opening that door; indeed, did he ever experience the ties of love?

135 *corpulent*: bulky or fat.

136 *Mother Hubbard*: a full-length unbelted dress.

The Lotus Eater

In Greek mythology the lotus eaters were people encountered by Odysseus in North Africa who lived in indolent forgetfulness, drugged by the fruit of the legendary lotus.

140 *repine*: to be fretful or low-spirited.

141 *Donizetti*: nineteenth-century Italian composer.

142 *espadrilles*: a light shoe with a canvas upper.
attire: clothing.
Hera: in Greek myth, the queen of the Olympian gods, and sister and wife of Zeus.

143 *a fly*: a one-horse carriage.
cicadas: large broad insects which produce a high-pitched drone.
emaciated: very thin.

144 *'Funny old fellow, Tiberius . . . . . about him'*: Tiberius was the homosexual Roman Emperor who retired to Capri in AD 26. Wilson is based on Ellingham Brooks, a homosexual who had fled to Capri after Oscar Wilde's imprisonment and who had been Maugham's first adult lover.
Suetonius: Roman historian and biographer, AD 75–150.
Blue Grotto: a famous cave on the island of Capri.

146 *Paestum*: an ancient Greek colony in southern Italy.

147 *Capri wine my eye*: he had been cheated; it was very cheap wine he had been given.
festa: religious festival and carnival.
acolytes swinging censers: priests' assistants swinging containers for burning incense.

Venus, Aphrodite: in Greek mythology Aphrodite is the goddess of love; Venus is the Roman counterpart.
Faraglioni: a group of rocks.

150 *gratuity*: financial gift, for services rendered.
annuity: a sum of money paid to a person at regular intervals, usually annually.

152 *affronted*: insulted.
felicity: happiness.
Very few people know where to look for happiness; fewer still find it: This is another example of Maugham's cynicism and his repeatedly held belief in his short stories.

153 *It had never occurred to him . . . lose its strength*: It is at least arguable that his character had lost its strength before he left his position in the city or indeed had never developed a strength. He had taken an easy option with suitable excuses masquerading as reasons?
impotent: powerless.
atrophy: waste away.

156 *Perhaps he died of the beauty of that sight*: it is worth comparing the importance of setting and its effects on people in this story and in 'Red'.

So many of Maugham's tales were prompted by his travels. In *The Summing Up* he describes one journey which clearly found its way into 'The Lotus Eater':

> A year later I went to Italy again, travelling as far down as Naples, and discovered Capri. It was the most enchanting spot I had ever seen, and the following summer I spent the whole of my vacation there . . . . I listened with transport to conversations at Morgano's, the wine shop just off the Piazza, when they talked of art and beauty, literature and Roman history.

The reference to Morgano's appears on page 142.

An Official Position

158 *rubicund burghers*: ruddy or red-coloured citizens or successful tradesmen.
159 *perquisites*: incidental benefits or 'perks' of the job.
cavernous: like a vast cave.
neurasthenia: nervous breakdown.
Ile: French for 'island'.
161 *sallow*: an unhealthy yellow colour.
hookworm: blood-sucking parasites which bore through the skin.
162 *precipitated*: moved or thrown.
166 *assuaged*: moderated.
168 *en pension*: (French) in lodgings, with all meals provided.
169 *harridan*: a nagging woman.
171 *dissolute*: debauched, decadent.
172 *exemplary*: a shining example to others, a model of correctness.
fiche: French for 'record' – compare today's 'microfiche' used in libraries.
promiscuity: casual sexual behaviour.
Au nom du peuple français justice est faite: French for 'in the name of the people of France, justice is done'.
173 *avaricious*: greedy.
expiration: end.
Salvation Army: a Christian charity body which helps the poor and needy.
174 *'But if there's nothing ..... happiness*: another snippet of the author's moralising. Compare this view with Wilson's in 'The Lotus Eater'.
175 *Replete*: completely satisfied by food and drink.
176 *malaise*: depression.
176 *disquieting*: creating anxiety.
Suddenly he stumbled against something. He stopped dead .... no good to shout: Maugham's style here is worth analysing

closely; his use of short sentences admirably suits his purpose of creating tension.

178 *He was an honest man and an official of the state*: a lovely line from Maugham to reinforce Remire's delusions of self-importance. At this point in the story he is being toyed with by his attackers and made to suffer a thousand deaths.

180 *Au nom du peuple français justice est faite*: (see note for page 172) a marvellous example of dramatic irony, echoing the use of the same phrase at earlier points in the story.

The Luncheon

182 *But I was flattered . . . . what they say*: an example of Maugham's life-long cynicism towards women. His plays are dotted with similar jibes.

183 *effusive*: gushingly emotional.

185 *palate*: sense of taste.
mortifying: humiliating.
succulent: juicy.

186 *ingratiating*: trying to find favour.
vindictive: spiteful.
complacency: satisfaction, or even smugness.

The Mother

188 *Seville*: a port in South West Spain.
Andalusians: people of this area of Spain.
gallego: porter, a person from Galicia in Northern Spain.
reales: coins of low value.

189 *Carai*: an exclamation.
La Cachirra: the vixen.

190 *oppression*: torment; lying heavily on the mind.
Buena sera: Spanish for 'good night'.

191 *indisposed*: not inclined.
brusquely: bluntly.
homicide: murder.
garrulous: talkative.
gaunt: bony and emaciated.

192 *precocious*: maturing early.
dandy: a man very concerned with the smartness of his clothes. Maugham indicates in this paragraph that it is a national preoccupation to enjoy fine clothes.

193 *repelled*: dismissed or opposed.
conspiring: plotting.

194 *commissions*: jobs to do; shopping.

195 *matador*: bullfighter.
corrida: bullfight.

196 *divined*: to make out or see, as though by a supernatural power. The writer clearly wishes to emphasise the intense love that acts as a bond between mother and son.

198 *embellishments*: extra details to enliven a story; Maugham suggests that exaggerating a story is characteristic of the local people.

199 *impediment*: obstruction or obstacle between the two lovers.
amorous: loving.

200 *jauntily*: cheerfully self-confident.
repressing the convulsive restlessness: holding back the violent emotions which are troubling her soul/spirit.

201 *venomously*: with spite and poison.
palpable: actually felt; La Cachirra reacts as though she had really been hit by Rosalia.

202 *scabbards*: sheaths.

Further reading

Publications

Somerset Maugham was a prolific writer: he wrote more than twenty novels, twenty-five plays, countless essays and reviews, and nearly a hundred short stories. Listed below are some of his more well-known titles and a comprehensive checklist of the publications in which the stories in this volume first appeared.

Liza of Lambeth (1897). Novel.
A Man of Honour (1903). Play.
Lady Frederick (1912). Play.
Of Human Bondage (1915). Novel.
The Moon and Sixpence (1919). Novel.
The Trembling of a Leaf (1921). Short stories; including 'Red'.
The Painted Veil (1925). Novel.
The Constant Wife (1927). Play.
Cakes and Ale (1930). Novel.
For Services Rendered (1932). Play.
The Book Bag (1932). Short story.
Cosmopolitans (1936). Short stories; including 'The Luncheon' and 'Mr Know-All'.
The Summing Up (1938). Essays/autobiography.
The Mixture as Before (1940). Short stories; including 'The Facts of Life', 'Lord Mountdrago', 'The Lotus Eater' and 'An Official Position'.
The Razor's Edge (1944). Novel.
Creatures of Circumstance (1947). Short stories; including 'The Mother', 'The Unconquered' and 'The Colonel's Lady'.

Note: The dates of publication of the above short story collections are not always an accurate guide as to exact dates of composition. In many cases Maugham wrote, and rewrote stories for initial publication in magazines, and only gathered them together in book form at a later period.

Somerset Maugham also wrote seven longer short stories under the title *Ashenden* (1928). In his introduction to this collection he observed:

> I wrote a batch of stories dealing with the adventures of an agent in the Intelligence Department during the First World War. I gave him the name of Ashenden . . . .They are founded on experiences of my own during that war, but I should like to impress upon the reader that they are not what the French call 'reportage', but works of fiction. Fact is a poor story-teller.

Biographical and critical studies of Somerset Maugham

First and foremost is *Somerset Maugham* by Ted Morgan (Jonathan Cape, 1980; paperback: Triad Granada, 1981). This amounts to the only authorised biography of the writer and offers a comprehensive and very readable account of Maugham's long and varied life. Ted Morgan writes in the preface: 'This is the biography of a man whose defects were glaring, but they should not be used to diminish his accomplishments.' Other studies which offer useful background reading include:

William Somerset Maugham – The English Maupassant by D. MacCarthy (1934, now out of print).

Remembering Mr Maugham by G. Kanin (Hamish Hamilton, 1966).

Somerset Maugham and His World by F. Raphael (Thames & Hudson, 1977).

Somerset Maugham by Anthony Curtis (Profile Books, 1977).

Study questions

The Facts of Life

1 What is there in the story to suggest that the author quietly admires the young man's exploits?

2 'Talk of a cat swallowing a canary' (page 21). Do you think Maugham is taking a moral stance when he puts these words into Henry Garnet's mouth?

The Unconquered

3 What parallels can be drawn between the family's behaviour and predicament and the terrible problem and life of the French nation in the period in question?

Mr Know-All

4 'But human beings are incalculable and he is a fool who tells himself that he knows what a man is capable of.' How predictable was Mr Kelada?

Lord Mountdrago

5 Maugham avoided for the most part involvement in party politics, but, as we know, he based many of his characters on real people. Explain with reference to the text why it could be that he had a 'model' in mind in this tale.

The Colonel's Lady

6 Discuss how the make-up of George Peregrine's character and life-style contributed to the unfolding of this story. How does Maugham make the tale poignant and convincing?

Red

7 Discuss the ways in which Maugham creates the setting in this story. What picture of 'true love' emerges?

The Lotus Eater

8 What is your view of the sort of freedom that is portrayed in this story? Bearing in mind that Maugham greatly valued his own freedom, what sort of moral stance does the author take?

An Official Position

9 How is tension developed in this story? Where do your sympathies lie as the story unfolds?

The Luncheon

10 Discuss Maugham's use of humour in this story.

The Mother

11 Discuss the contribution that 'a strong character' makes to this story.

General questions

12 Maugham cast himself as an observer, a non-committed recorder of experience. Consider this view with reference to three or four stories in the collection.

13 'The main thing I've always asked from life is freedom. Outer and inner freedom, both in my way of living and in my way of writing.' Relate this statement to your reading of these stories.

14 Consider the theme of freedom and bondage as it relates to characters in these stories.

15 Maugham's advice to himself about play-writing was: 'His dialogue must be a sort of spoken shorthand. He must cut and cut till he has arrived at the maximum of concentration.' Discuss this advice with reference to Maugham's use of dialogue in these stories.

16 Do you feel that Maugham succeeds in entertaining *and* educating his readers?

17 What moral standpoints does Maugham take up in any of the stories?

18 With close reference to any two or three stories, show how setting affects the actions of the characters.

19 Maupassant claimed that the opening words of a short story were all important. Roald Dahl emphasises how vital it is to have a twist in the tale. What are Maugham's strengths in relation to the openings and endings of his stories?

20 Justice is seen to be done. Discuss with reference to three or four of the stories in this volume.

21 'I write stories about people who have some singularity of character which suggests to me that they may be capable of behaving in such a way as to give me an idea that I can make use of, or about people who by some accident or another, accident of temperament, accident of environment, have been involved in unusual contingencies.' To what extent do the stories in this collection support Maugham's own perceptions of his writing?

22 Maugham is a first-person narrator in three of these stories. What advantages and disadvantages are gained by an author in using the first-person narrator?

23 With reference to three or four stories, discuss the extent to which jealousy motivates characters.

24 From your reading of these stories, what sort of a picture do you form of Somerset Maugham as a person?

25 What do we learn in this collection about Maugham's attitudes towards men and women?

26 'The short story must depict more by implication than by statement, more by what is left out then left in.' Evaluate this comment by H. E. Bates with reference to the stories of Somerset Maugham.

27 From your reading of these stories what would seem to you to be Maugham's recurrent themes. Analyse his treatment of any two themes in detail.

28 With close reference to the text of these stories, show how Maugham is a writer of his period. In what ways, if any, does his work have a contemporary flavour.